Sleuthing at Sweet Springs

A Sleuth Sisters Mystery

by Maggie Pill

Publisher's Note: This is a work of fiction. Names, characters, places, and incidents are a product of the author's imagination. Locales and public names are sometimes used for atmospheric purposes. Any resemblance to actual people, living or dead, or to businesses, companies, events, institutions, or locales is completely coincidental.

Editor: Paige Trisko
Cover Art by Yocladesigns: http://yocladesigns.com

Gwendolyn Press, Michigan, USA

Sleuthing at Sweet Springs/Maggie Pill — 1st ed.
ISBN: 978-1-944502-04-1

Acknowledgements

The Sleuth Sisters and Maggie thank these people for contributing to their success:

*Paul & Debbie for info on raising reindeer

*Dan at State-Wide Real Estate for advice on the business

*Andrew at the DEQ for facts on water bottling/sources

*Kay & Connie for advice/reading as the series progresses

*P.J. for her expertise on medicines and their effects

Any errors in the books are mine, but I could never produce a complete story without input from helpful friends like these.

Maggie

Chapter One

Barb

I lost my sister when she took one step too far.

"Are we finished?" As she spoke, Retta backed up for a wider view and her right foot left the plank platform. Responding to the pull of gravity, her body followed the foot into space. As she waved her arms, fighting to keep her balance, I lunged forward to help. It was too late. One second she was there, her hair aglow in the billboard's floodlight. The next she was gone. There was a soft thud of impact, but no scream of pain.

"Retta!" Fear made my cry louder than was prudent, since our mission was secret and not entirely legal. Dropping to my knees, I crawled to the edge and looked down, searching the darkness for a hopeful sign. Nothing moved. A pale spot below might have been a human face but could as easily have been the kind of limestone outcrop common in Michigan. "Retta!"

Had my campaign for better use of the English language gotten my baby sister hurt or even killed?

A muffled sound came from the ground below, and I turned my good ear toward it. A groan? An appeal for help?

She was giggling. "Lots of nice, soft grass down here," she piped in her version of a whisper. "And the corrections on the sign look good from a distance."

When we'd arrived at the billboard, it had read, BETWEEN YOU AND I, CROLL'S HAS THE FRESHEST FOOD IN ALLPORT. With black paint, Retta and I had changed the word *I* to the objective case *me*. From her present position, it was apparently difficult to tell the change had been made.

Standing, Retta brushed off her black jeans, cupped her mouth, and called softly, “Bring our stuff down. I’ll go get the car.” She added with another giggle, “Use the ladder. My way was faster but the end was a little shocking.”

She was still looking amused after I’d tossed my tools in the back with careless thumps and clunks and got into the car. “You should have seen your face, Barbara.”

My heart was just getting back to a normal rhythm. “I thought you were dead for sure. If you’re going to be part of this, Retta, you have to be more careful.”

“Oh, I’m going to be part of it. That was the deal.” As if I’d never heard them before, she counted the terms of our agreement on her fingers. “I get to do Correction Events with you. I get to be a full partner in the detective agency you and Faye created. In return, I don’t tell anyone you go around fixing errors on roadside signs in the dead of night.”

“You’re part of the agency as long as you don’t order your sisters around,” I said firmly. “You agreed to that, too.”

“I didn’t think that needed to be said,” she countered primly, “because I never tell people what to do.”

Still relieved she hadn’t died in the fall, I left the comment alone. Pushy people seldom admit they’re pushy, and your sister is your sister, even if she is the original Miss Bossy-pants.

CHAPTER TWO

Faye

It was one of Harriet's better days—not that she looked good. Past ninety, her spine had twisted until her ribcage sat cockeyed somewhere over her right hip. Her dentures had been abandoned, since they no longer stayed in place on her shrunken gums. Her lanky gray hair had thinned to reveal large spaces of shiny scalp between wisps. Puny and weakened as she was, my mother-in-law still scared the heck out of almost everyone who had to deal with her.

For her first few years as a resident at the Meadows, Harriet had pretty much run the place, watching over less aware residents (She called it "walking them home" when she escorted dementia patients from the cafeteria to their rooms) and ordering nurses and even doctors to obey her will. After a recent stroke she'd failed, and lately there were times when she'd mistaken Dale for his dad. She often wasn't sure who I was, but if I said, "I'm Faye, Dale's wife," I got a gruff, "Oh, yes. You." Other times a glazed stare told me Harriet didn't recall she had a daughter-in-law named Faye, or any daughter-in-law at all.

When Retta and I arrived on this day, Harriet was almost her old self. As soon as we entered the room she informed us, "The woman across the hall died last night." Tilting her head like an elderly owl she added, "They try to hide it from us, but we know."

As an alarm went off somewhere down the hallway, I said what one is required to say in such situations. "That's too bad."

Harriet licked her scaly bottom lip. "Dying's hard, but I bet you girls don't know why."

Retta had come with me, claiming she'd help me cheer Harriet up. Knowing Retta, I guessed she had a second motive I hadn't heard about yet. My sister isn't a bad person, but she seldom has fewer than three reasons for any help she offers, and two of them will fit her agenda more than they fit anyone else's.

"Why is dying hard, Mrs. Burner?" she asked in her best caring tone.

Harriet grinned, showing her gums. "Because when you get to the end, you start wishing you'd done things different." She gestured at her roommate, whose bed was only a few feet away. "Carrie over there? She let her kids run wild. Now one of them's in jail and the other's in and out of rehab so often they might as well adopt him and call him their mascot. Now Carrie's old and sick, but she's got nobody except the idiots that run this place."

I raised a palm in warning, but Harriet merely chuckled, propelling her wheelchair backward with her foot so she faced Carrie. "She's deaf as a post. Can't hear nothing." She smiled, and poor Carrie smiled back, her expression revealing the truth of what Harriet had said.

I might have reminded my mother-in-law that some of the "idiots" she'd mentioned might be in earshot, but concern for their feelings had never stopped her from speaking her mind before.

It was funny—and not ha-ha funny—that she spoke so casually of her roommate's deafness. I was often embarrassed by Harriet's similar condition, which resulted in loud comments about her dislikes among the staff at the Meadows, her discontent with the meals, and her disgust at having to wear adult diapers. After almost every visit, I promised myself that before I came to the point of living in a care facility, I'd jump in front of a city bus.

As of 2015, Allport didn't have city buses. Unless the city progressed a bit, I'd have to settle for Dial-a-Ride.

Harriet went back to her point about the downside of approaching death. "When you get to be my age," "you look back a lot, and it makes you understand what you should have done different. You could have treated some people nicer. You ought to have taken better care of yourself. Things like that."

I knew my mother-in-law too well to fall into the trap she was setting, but Retta didn't. Leaning toward Harriet sympathetically she asked, "What do you wish you'd done differently, dear?"

The old lady's eyes widened. "Me? I wouldn't change a thing. I was trying to make Faye see she should straighten up and fly right before she gets old and sick like Carrie."

"But Faye isn't—"

"You'll see it someday, Rettie." Harriet smacked her lips in her eagerness to predict my future. "Faye's not going to have anybody when she's old, because those boys of hers are shiftless."

"That's not true." Retta said, but I nudged her and shook my head. Harriet had never warmed to my boys, and I couldn't honestly say they were all that fond of her. Grandmas are supposed to bake cookies and adore their grandchildren. Harriet had once been a gem in the cookie-making department, but she never got the adoring part down.

"Faye just never had the will to stand up to those boys, and look at them now. Every one of them on welfare."

It would do no good to tell their grandmother that none of my three sons was or had ever been supported by the State of Michigan. At times they'd been supported by Dale and me, but that was our business and no one else's.

And "Rettie"? Where had that come from? Usually she called my sisters The Flibbertigibbet (Retta) and The Big Shot (Barb), even when they were within hearing distance.

Suddenly I wanted a cigarette. Due to rising blood pressure and my sisters' disapproval, I'd quit smoking— well, mostly. I knew becoming a non-smoker was best for me, but there were times I regretted giving up the habit. Being around my mother-in-law was when I missed it most, perhaps because in the past I'd have excused myself to go outside and light up, getting that little nicotine high and at the same time escaping Harriet's constant disapproval. I'd never gotten past being the girl who "trapped" her son into marriage, though Dale and I had been happy together for over thirty-five years.

I took a deep breath, reminding myself that Harriet needed me. How hard it must be for her that someone she wanted so much to dislike had become indispensable to her.

The best way forward was to change the subject. "What kind of candy would you like me to bring next time I come?" Any discussion of sweets drove other topics clear out of Harriet's mind, so we proceeded to the relative merits of Dove Promises versus Hershey's Bliss.

CHAPTER THREE

Retta

I went with Faye to the nursing home to cheer up her old prune of a mother-in-law. The visit was as weird as Faye had predicted, with smells no one wants to encounter and Harriet raving about dying and deadbeat relatives and calling me Rettie. I hate it when people misuse my name, but Harriet is really old, so I didn't correct her.

I'd planned that Faye and I would put up posters for the Fall Festival at my church when we were done visiting. I enjoy designing attractive notices on my computer and taking them to the printer, but I've never liked the distribution part. It feels low-class to me to be seen in store entryways and on street corners with thumbtacks and a hammer. I figured I'd drive, and Faye could do the posting. She really doesn't mind.

It took longer than we expected at the Meadows, because one of the medical staff wanted to speak with Faye about Harriet. They went off together, and Harriet promptly fell asleep in her wheelchair, leaving me twiddling my thumbs. I checked my phone and answered a few emails, but Faye didn't return. Finally I took a walk, glancing idly into rooms as I passed. I shouldn't have done that, because it depressed me to see so many gaunt, blank faces staring into the hallway or worse, staring at the walls. When I found a small sitting room with a TV set playing, I went in, hoping to catch a weather report. October is a tricky month in northern Michigan, and it pays to watch for stormy surprises.

In a corner of the room, where she wasn't visible from the doorway sat a petite woman with snow-white hair and extra-thick glasses. I apologized for bothering her, but she waved a hand.

"It's not private property. I just wanted out of my room for a while."

It didn't seem polite to turn around and leave, so I said, "I was visiting a friend, but she's taking a nap."

Her smile was rueful. "That's about all there is to do around here—eat and nap."

"It's a nice facility, though. Very clean and attractive." I probably sounded as fake as I felt.

"That's true," she allowed. "But I'll be glad to get back to my house on Sweet Springs."

"There's nothing like being in your own place, is there?" I said, happy to have a common conversational thread. "My home is on the river out of town. I wouldn't trade it for anything."

She agreed, and there seemed to be no more to say. I was about to leave when an aide came in, her soft soles swishing on the tile floor. "There you are, Clara. It's time for your shower."

The woman's eyes clouded. "Are you going to do it, or is—someone else?"

Irritation flickered across the aide's face, but she answered patiently. "You know Ralph does the showers, Clara. It's a lot safer for you with him in there instead of us girls."

Clara sighed. "I know, but it's embarrassing, having a man—" She didn't finish, but I got the picture. For women of Clara's generation, being seen naked by a male, even a certified nursing assistant, had to be mortifying.

Faye insisted she'd never live in a nursing home; in fact, she was a little loony on the subject. From visiting the Meadows so often, she knew more about life there than I did. Seeing the poor old lady's embarrassment gave me a deeper understanding. No matter how kind the caregivers and how considerate the administrators, giving up control of your destiny had to be hard. Being told when to do everything, having nowhere to go where there weren't other people, and being bathed by Ralph didn't seem attractive to me. I felt sorry for Clara.

A discreet beep came from a device on the CNA's belt, and she sighed. "I've got to get this. I'll be back in a few."

When she was gone, Clara caught my eye and grinned, showing overlarge false teeth. "A last-minute reprieve."

I couldn't help but ask what was on my mind. "Is Ralph okay? I mean, he doesn't—"

"Oh, no, dear. Ralph's as nice as he can be." She shrugged lightly. "That doesn't mean I have to like it."

"But you're going home soon, you said."

Clara smiled at the thought. "Yes. My chickens are no doubt wondering where I am. My niece is feeding them, but they'll be glad to have me home."

I was trying to place Sweet Springs, which I thought was some distance from Allport. "Does your niece live near you?"

"Gail's a city girl, so she lives here in town." Clara shook her head in amusement. "She's scared of any body of water bigger than a bathtub, and she wouldn't recognize Mother Nature if the old sprite walked up and took her by the hand."

"But she's helping out with the chickens while you're in here. That's nice of her."

"Yes." Clara's expression turned thoughtful. "It's kind of a surprise. I hadn't seen much of Gail in years, but for the last two months she's been visiting every weekend."

Since the woman was eighty if she was a day, it made sense to me that her family would want to keep an eye on her. "She's probably worried about you living so far out of town."

"Maybe." She didn't sound convinced.

When I left Clara, the CNA came out of another room, and we walked down the hall together. "That lady seems really nice."

"Clara's great," the girl replied. "Not like some of them that think you've got ten hands and magical powers."

"I'm glad to hear she can go home soon."

The girl looked puzzled. "She's not going anywhere that I know of. Her niece signed her in here because she forgets to eat, wanders around outside—" She tapped her own forehead meaningfully. "That sort of thing."

I glanced back at the TV room. "She seemed okay to me."

"Once we get them in here, they often do better. That doesn't mean they can live on their own."

"Oh." Clara's joyful expression when she spoke of home came to mind. "Will she ever—?"

Anticipating the question, the CNA shook her head. "Her house is way out in the country, and the niece can't get out to see her very often. Doc figures Clara's better off here."

"But she seemed certain she'd be going home."

The CNA smiled ruefully. "Talk to any of them who can still put a sentence together and they'll tell you they're going home. For a lot of them, that dream is the only thing that makes it possible to get through another day."

When I peeped into Harriet's room, she was still asleep and my sister was nowhere in sight. I went back out into the hall and chose another direction, hoping to see where Faye had gone. As I came around a corner there was Clara, sitting on a folding chair near a door with a sign: SHOWER—DO NOT ENTER WHEN DOOR IS CLOSED. Running water sounded from inside. Seeing me, she raised her palms in a helpless gesture. "Hurry up and wait."

Having no good answer, I went with Conversational Old Reliable, the weather. "It's a beautiful day."

"I know," she replied. "One of the girls took me outside this morning. We went all the way around the building so I could see spots where the colors are starting to change. You can feel the crispness in the air." She smiled ruefully. "They wouldn't let me go by myself for fear I'll fall and break a hip or something."

"It's a real problem in nursing homes, I understand."

Her lips pursed briefly. "For some, maybe, but at home I fetch wood, feed the chickens, and putter around the lakeshore every single day. I haven't taken a fall yet."

"Sweet Springs is northwest of town isn't it?" It seemed only right to let her talk about it, since she might never see it again.

"Yes. Do you know it?"

"I've lived here all my life, so I've heard the name, but I don't think I've ever been out there."

"It's a spring-fed lake." She looked away as if picturing it. "Most people don't see it, because it's privately owned."

"You own a whole lake?"

Clara chuckled. "Not by myself. Back in the 1880s, my family came from Canada with three others. They settled around the lake and divided it equally."

"The original families still live on the land?"

Adjusting her glasses, which had slid down her thin nose, she explained. "The Clausens moved to Wyoming in '07 when the economy crashed. The Warners' house burned last month, but they live in Detroit and only visit occasionally. That leaves just two old codgers as full-time residents, my old schoolmate Caleb Marsh on one side of the lake and me on the other."

"And you're here."

"Temporarily," she reminded me.

Avoiding her eyes, I nodded.

Clara sighed. "The niece I mentioned earlier is a real estate agent. She keeps saying she can get me a nice chunk of money for the property." She shook her head as if I'd made an argument for selling. "She'll have to wait till I'm gone to get the commission she wants so much. I can't imagine not being able to look forward to going back home."

***

"The poor woman is sure she'll return to her lake in the near future," I told Faye as we left the Meadows. We'd come in my vehicle, and she readily agreed to help with the posters. "She was sad," I finished. "Her niece wants her to sell it."

Faye pursed her lips. "Sometimes relatives of the elderly can't hide their eagerness to make the shift from family to heirs."

As I pulled up at the curb, she took the first poster, the hammer, and a couple of small nails and got out. As I watched, hearing the tapping of the hammer as she helped me do my errand, I felt a rush of love and sympathy for my sister.

Faye's never had life easy, and it seemed like if one thing got better, a bad thing happened to balance it. Starting our detective agency had been good for Faye, but now her mother-in-law's condition was rapidly deteriorating. The consultation Faye had just attended concerned enrolling Harriet in hospice care.

Years ago Dale, Faye's husband, was disabled in an accident in the woods. Harriet's other children paid almost no attention to the old woman, which wasn't surprising given her abrasive personality. That meant the staff at the Meadows considered Faye the old woman's *de facto* guardian and had approached her about the need for hospice. Faye wasn't looking forward to telling Dale that his mother was on a downhill slide likely to end soon. From what I'd heard around town, Dale's sisters and brother would only take interest when the old woman finally died and it was time to divide her earthly goods.

More to take Faye's mind off her troubles than anything else, I went on with my story after she'd hung the poster. "The CNA said Clara shows signs of dementia, but I didn't see a single thing wrong with her thought process."

We reached the next stop and Faye got out, making that grunt of effort I associate with old people. "Some days are probably better than others," she said before heading off to tack up poster number two. "That's how it goes."

I accepted Faye's assessment, since she was the one with experience. Harriet's days were certainly up and down, and her least favorite daughter-in-law got to deal with all points on the Harriet spectrum.

Chapter Four

Barb

Michigan in autumn is one of my greatest joys. Not one for temperatures over seventy-five, I appreciate fall's cooler days, and no one who has ever seen the change of color can deny its wonders. Maple, elm, and oak trees go from deep green to almost unbelievably bright yellows, reds, and oranges, often beginning at the tips of their branches. Within days the trees are decked out in eye-popping colors.

As fall approached, I suggested a drive through the countryside. My '57 Chevy would soon have to go into storage for the winter, and I wanted to take the old girl out a few more times before I locked her up. Retta suggested the four of us could lunch at a little roadhouse famous for good Polish food. She fussed a little, as always, about her fear that a vehicle as old as mine was likely to break down at any moment. I ignored her. Due to my willingness to pay and the skills of a good mechanic, my Chevy hummed like a favorite tune.

It rained overnight, but the sun had warmed the air nicely by mid-morning. As we drove we pointed out trees that had begun to change. Even some of the roadside shrubs had started turning red. Behind and between the maples and elms, darker green pines and the boles of white birches offered contrast. We were the dullest part of the scene, four middle-aged people passing through miles of natural splendor.

Faye and Dale sat together in the back seat while Retta rode shotgun. A head injury years ago left Dale sensitive to movement, light, and noise, and being too close to Retta made him edgy. She gestured more than most people, and her voice was pitched higher than Faye's or mine. In addition, riding in a car for any distance was hard for Dale, since the scenery rushing by made him dizzy. He generally looked down, so as we traveled, I pulled over periodically at scenic spots so he could snap pictures with the iPhone Faye had recently bought him. With Retta quiet for a change and the calming effect of nature, we were all pretty relaxed.

At one stop we parked along a ridge where the road overlooked hay fields rimmed in the distance with thick woods. We stood along the guard rail, sharing my binoculars as we pointed out spots of color to each other. Thirty feet below us, the hay had been cut and baled, and a tractor chugged along, picking up the huge rolls of hay to take them to storage. Its musty odor brought back memories of our childhood and as usual, the memories were quite different.

"Those huge round bales they make now are a lot better than the little square ones Dad made with that old New Holland," Retta remarked. "Remember how scratched-up we'd get hauling those things around?"

"It took two of us to move one bale," I said, "but Dad tossed them around like they were made of bubble wrap." I paused, picturing him in the haymow, taking the bales off the conveyer belt and stacking them into a neat, crisscross arrangement. "The feeling of accomplishment when all that hay was in the barn was worth a few scratches."

"If you wore pants and long sleeves, they weren't that scratchy," Faye put in. "And we all worked together to get it done. That was a pretty good life lesson."

"Sweating, dirty, bloody, and exhausted, the way every family should be," Retta said with a sniff. "Let's go. I'm getting hungry."

I stopped twice more after that, just to let Retta know she didn't always get what she wanted. We made it to Kowalski's just after noon. The place was crowded and noisy, but a cheerful waitress found us a table. We had a sinfully filling lunch of pierogis, kielbasa, and cabbage with noodles, followed by pie and coffee for Dale and Faye, just coffee for Retta and me.

On the way home I took a different road, one of Rory's favorites. The chief of Allport's police department and my boyfriend (for lack of a better term), Rory loved the spot because the trees grew so close to the road that their branches met overhead, making a tunnel. "This will be gorgeous when the leaves have all turned," Retta said.

"The leaf-peepers will be out in droves by then." Dale referred to tourists who drive north in autumn to see the colors.

The wind came up, sending waves through the foliage around us. A few leaves lost their hold and skipped across the pavement, reminding us that the year was dying. In a week or so the riotous colors would peak, and then the leaves would fall, leaving bare, gray trunks jutting from dull-brown leaf-beds. After that, snow would turn our world to shades of black, white, and gray.

As I slowed for a corner Retta called out, "Stop!"

My tires crunched on the gravel as I obeyed her command. In the rear view mirror, I saw Faye put a reassuring hand on Dale's arm. "What's wrong?"

"The sign back there said SWEET SPRINGS LANE. That's where Clara's house is." I had no idea what she was talking about, but she filled me in, ending with, "I'd like to see it. Do you mind driving in?"

When Retta asks a question like that, it's rhetorical. She expects you to do as she wants. I paused, considering how to say no without sounding crabby and having her pout all the way home.

"Are there signs saying to keep out?" Faye asked. She'd never trespass on someone's privacy, which is one reason I've never told her about my Correction Events.

"Not that I can see," Retta replied. "And there's a real estate sign on that tree. They have to expect people will go in if there's property for sale."

Through a break in the trees I saw a sliver of water that glinted like a sword blade. "It looks like a pretty spot. I guess it won't hurt." Backing up, I turned into the road.

Before I'd gone ten feet Faye pointed out a small sign tacked on a tree. "That says PRIVATE."

"We won't even get out of the car," Retta argued. "I just want to see the house Clara's grandfather built."

Sweet Springs Lane was a dirt road that twisted through a stand of pines, and for perhaps a quarter mile we drove in semi-darkness, the smell of wet needles wafting in through the car's vents. When the road emerged from the trees and turned along the bright lake, it was as if a curtain had been drawn back. Like a turquoise gem, Sweet Springs shone in the October sunlight. The trees on its far side were already tinged with color, ready to burst into full autumn glory.

"You were right. It's a gorgeous spot," Faye murmured.

Despite being a city girl most of my adult life, I appreciate a great view—as long as I don't have to sleep on the ground or sit on a rock to eat my supper. Pulling into a short driveway, past a mailbox with KNIGHT stenciled on it in red letters, I parked the car facing the lake. We all sat for a moment, looking at the beauty that was Sweet Springs.

On our right was a two-story house made of fieldstone, with dormer windows on the upper level and a spacious porch on the side facing the water. The place was tidy except for a large pile of firewood dumped in the yard in preparation for a long winter.

Precisely-aligned tools, a shovel, a rake, and a hoe, lined the garden fence, ready for use.

Though she'd said she wouldn't, Retta slid out of the car and started snooping. Peering through the window in the front door, she turned to us with raised palms to indicate there was no one inside. Reconciled to waiting until her curiosity was satisfied, I got out and walked down to the lake. The water was so clear it looked like the depth at the end of the dock was only a foot or two, but a measuring stick neatly calibrated and attached to the last stanchion indicated it was actually seven feet. A small rowboat attached to a post was painted blue and silver with the stylized lion of Detroit's pro football team stenciled on the bow. The boat was as orderly as the rest of the place, with neatly coiled rope under the front seat and a pair of plastic shoes and a fishing net tucked under the back one. Someone around here took very good care of things.

Steps sounded hollowly on the wood planking, and I turned to see that Faye and Dale had come up behind me. "Is this really a spring?" she asked.

Watching for a few moments, I detected spots where ripples broke the surface and pointed them out. "I'm no expert, but it's definitely bubbling."

"They say it's better for you than other water," Dale said.

"Why?"

"Spring water comes from an underground source, so it's free of contaminants. It's supposed to taste better, too. I bet all the houses out here have wells that tap into the springs."

"A pretty spot and good water, too. Mrs. Knight is lucky." Recalling she was now at the Meadows I added, "Well, she was."

"There's another house over there." Faye pointed to the right, where the corner of a structure peeped out from the trees.

Boot heels tapped behind us, and Retta joined us at the dock, frowning into the harsh light reflected off the water. "And that must be the spot where a house burned recently," she said, pointing straight across. "See the chimney sticking up?"

"I wonder how the other property owners get to their places."

"The road we came in on must continue around the lake that way." Dale circled counterclockwise with his arm. "The bank rises pretty steeply over there, so I doubt there's a way to get back on the main road."

My lawyer's mind leapt to property rights. "The others have to be nice to Mrs. Knight, then, or she could block their access."

"Clara's not that kind of girl." Retta pointed behind us. "There are chickens in a pen back there. They're clumped around an empty water trough."

"Where?" Faye said, her expression concerned.

"Back there."

We followed Retta to the pen, a 20 x 20 space enclosed in—not surprisingly—chicken wire. Inside were a dozen Rhode Island Reds, huddled together to foster group courage. In one corner was a raised coop where the birds could retreat in bad weather and a roost where they could flock together at night.

Neat, hand-sized holes along the back of the fencing had hinged coverings that recalled the chicken coop we'd had on the farm. I'd often been sent to collect eggs for breakfast, and the little doors let me reach them without having to go inside and get my shoes dirtied with manure. I'd learned to be careful when reaching in, however. It's never a good idea to surprise a setting hen, and a chicken's beak on a bare arm feels like a spike driving into the skin.

The water fount—a five-gallon bucket fitted with metal nipples, was dry. Beside it, a trough that should have been scattered with feed was also empty. The chickens' muttered outrage said they weren't happy about it.

Never able to abide suffering animals, Faye turned to the outbuildings along the wood line, intent on finding a bucket. Opening doors, she peered in until she found one and took it to an outdoor spigot. Following her lead, Dale rummaged through the sheds looking for feed.

"I wonder why she didn't get someone to take care of them," Faye said as the bucket echoed with watery splashes. "Maybe the woman does have mental issues."

Retta regarded Faye and Dale with fond amusement. "Clara's niece is taking care of them. She probably hasn't had a chance to come all the way out here yet."

"Then she's not doing her job." Faye hauled the bucket of water to the pen and untied the piece of twine that held the gate closed. Sidestepping piles of manure as best she could, she filled the water feeder. The chickens clustered around, getting in her way so that some ended up with wet feathers. Finished, she stepped back, still disgusted that someone hadn't followed through on a promise and left helpless critters to suffer. "Dale, did you find these ladies something to eat?"

"I did." He stood in the doorway of an elderly plank shed, holding a metal lid. "There's a can full of grain in here." Taking up her bucket, Faye went into the shed and emerged with what she judged the right amount. Returning to the pen, she shook the contents into the trough, tapping the bucket to get the last of the seed out. The chickens swarmed her again, clucking as they jockeyed for position. I might have felt sorry for them, since it had obviously been some time since they'd fed, but I knew from experience that chickens act the same way if it's been five minutes or five days since their last meal.

"I wonder if we should let the poor things go free," Faye said. "They could manage on their own this time of year if they weren't closed in."

"The niece might not be as diligent as she should be," I replied, "but that doesn't give us the right to release domesticated animals to the wild." I gestured at the woods around us. "There are bound to be predators in there eager for a chicken dinner."

"I suppose you're right." Faye was obviously unhappy with the situation. "The pen protects them from foxes and such."

"Tell you what," Retta suggested. "Clara said her niece is a real estate agent. I bet she works for the realty representing the neighbors' property. What if I stop there on my way home and remind her she has a job to do?"

"Let me know what she says," Faye replied. "If she can't do it, somebody has to."

Images of a chicken coop in our back yard sprang into my mind. "You can't take in a flock of hens, Faye."

Tossing the bucket onto the grass, where it clunked to a stop against the pen wall, Faye tied the gate closed. "If the niece doesn't want them and Clara isn't coming back, we have to do something."

"Calm down, both of you," Retta's manner suggested Solomon deciding which mother should get the baby. "I will make sure the birds have a caregiver, so Barbara Ann doesn't smell bird poop when she goes out her back door and Faye Elizabeth doesn't lay awake nights fretting about them."

"Lie," I corrected automatically. "People *lie* awake. They don't *lay* awake."

"Everybody says *lay* except you, Barbara," Retta shot back. "With the lie/lay verbs, that whole present-tense-here-but-past-tense-there thing is just too confusing."

Before I could argue my case Faye broke in, sounding as irritated as Faye ever gets. Retta does that to a person, because she thinks her opinion is superior to everyone else's. "I didn't mean I would take the chickens in myself. The boys could take them on the farm."

"That's true." Faye's two younger sons, Bill and Cramer, had moved to our family farm in early summer. For Cramer, the bunkhouse he'd converted to an apartment and repair shop was a great place to work on his beloved computers. For Bill and his wife Carla, the farm offered a life they'd always wanted: self-reliance in a natural setting, with various herds, flocks, and colonies for company. Though not expert farmers yet, they were happily learning the ropes.

Before we left Sweet Springs, we decided (well, Retta did and nobody objected) to follow the lane to its end-point, circling the lake to get a look at the other properties. The edge of Clara's section was delineated by a rail fence. The second quadrant of the lake shore went with the house we'd seen to the west as we stood on Clara's dock. Similar in structure to hers, its ancient fieldstone gatepost was festooned with an elaborate *C* and a realty sign advertising its availability for purchase.

"People named Clausen used to live here." Retta pointed. "Pull into the driveway, Barbara, so we can get a better look."

The condition of the property was as different from Clara's as possible. Everything was run-down, piles of junk lay at intervals between the house and the lake, and the roof looked like it wouldn't last through another Michigan winter.

Retta's frown indicated disapproval. "Clara said the owners moved away."

"Doesn't look like they're coming back," Dale observed dryly.

Returning to the lane, we drove on. The road became even less of a road, and, hearing mud hit the underside of my car, I resigned myself to the fact that the Chevy would need a carwash when we got back to town. Finally, almost directly across the springs from Clara's house, we came to the ruin we'd seen from her dock. "This place belongs to someone named Warner, or maybe Werner," Retta said. "They live somewhere else, so this was just a vacation home."

"They'd torn down the old place and built a new one." Dale pointed to a pile of rotting logs and clumps of the old mineral wool type of insulation that had been hauled to one side of the yard. In the center of the area was what was left of the newer structure, which had been much larger, judging from the scorched area. Both structures were heaps of rubble, just different kinds.

"The fire crew wouldn't have stood much chance of stopping the blaze," Dale said. "Long trip from downtown Allport."

With not much to see there, we went on. The last property on the lake sat on the sharp rise we'd seen from Clara's dock, almost hidden by trees. The house was small and cramped-looking, and repairs had been made with mismatched materials that gave it an unbalanced look.

"Clara went to school with the guy who lives there," Retta informed us. "He's the only full-time resident left on the lake."

At the top of the rise the road leveled off, running past the house before looping around a clump of maple trees, signaling we'd come to the end. As Dale had predicted, there was no access to the main road down the steep incline, though we could see bits of pavement through the trees.

As I navigated the turnaround, doing the best I could to avoid potholes where the primitive road had washed out, the view before us opened up. Bumping through one last hole, I stopped the car to give everyone a good look.

We sat above the lake about twenty feet, with the Marsh place on our left. The green-blue water rippled gently in the breeze. Green dominated along its perimeter, but streaks of autumn color caught the eye. The three other properties were visible in the distance, like the four corners of the globe laid out in miniature. “Mr. Marsh has the best view of all,” Retta said.

“I hope we don’t scare him,” I said. “He probably doesn’t see strange cars out here very often.”

“I hope he doesn’t keep a shotgun behind the door, in case he does get spooked,” Dale said with a wry grin.

Retta gazed across the empty lake. “I can see why the niece doesn’t want Clara out here. Two eighty-somethings living on opposite sides of a lake isn’t safe for either of them.”

“It sounds like Clara would rather die alone out here than spend the rest of her life with CNA’s and Hoyer lifts at the Meadows,” Faye said. “I know I would.”

“Don’t be silly,” Retta ordered. “Neither you nor Barbara is going to spend one minute in a nursing home. When the time comes, you’ll move in with me, and I’ll take care of you.”

I dared not meet Faye’s eyes in the rear-view mirror, lest one of us let out a snort of laughter. Having Retta “take care” of me would drive me insane within twenty-four hours. At least at the Meadows, a person gets to *think* what she wants to.

“Something odd down there.” Dale pointed at a spot on the shore below us. On the lake side of the house, rough log steps led down to the water. Set into the hillside and leveled with dirt, they made a cheap and effective means of descent. Now, however, there was a splash of bright orange near the bottom step that didn’t belong on the green lawn. Craning my neck to see better, I made out a pair of jeans, gray sneakers, and a shock of white hair.

Retta was out of the car first, hurrying down the slope at an intersecting angle. Her high-heeled boots sank into the soft ground with every step, but she staggered on.

I followed, fumbling for my phone as I ran. When I reached her, Retta was checking the prone man's neck for a pulse.

"Is he—?"

"Dead," she finished. "The poor old guy must have tripped on those steps and broken his neck."

CHAPTER FIVE

Faye

Dale and I were the last to reach Mr. Marsh's body. We went up the driveway, around the house, and came carefully down the steps the owner hadn't been able to navigate. I held Dale's arm, which was necessary though embarrassing for him. He did well enough on even ground, but vertigo kicked in when the way wasn't flat, and he needed me to lean on. Despite being his anchor, I was the one who was huffing and puffing by the time we got there.

Barb had called 9-1-1. Stiffness of the limbs indicated Mr. Marsh had been dead for some time, but Retta stroked the man's wrinkled face as if he could feel it. "I'm sorry," she told the corpse. "It's a terrible way to die."

Shocked as I was, my mind argued the point. In this beautiful setting, at this gorgeous time of year, on his own property, at eighty-whatever, it seemed to me Caleb Marsh's quick death, with perhaps only a moment of realizing his time had come, wasn't a bad way to go.

But then, I'm weird that way.

In just over twenty minutes, we were joined by an ambulance and a sheriff's car. The deputy, one we knew from cases we'd worked on, took our statements and told us they'd be in touch if they needed anything else.

"Bad thing," he said soberly. "The logs on these rustic stairways get mossy, which makes them slippery."

We drove home, shaken as one is by the reminder that death can sneak up on a person. Each of us was probably more appreciative of the beauty of nature—and of each other—as we left Sweet Springs, aware how quickly the wonderful gifts life offers can be snatched away.

CHAPTER SIX

Retta

When we got back to Barb's house—I always think of it that way though it's also where Faye and Dale live *and* the offices of the Smart Detective Agency—I got into my car and started for home. With the tragic end to our outing, I'd almost forgotten about Clara's chickens, but as I passed the So-Rite Real Estate office, my promise to Faye came to mind. I felt a little silly fussing about poultry, but she was sure to call later and ask what I'd found out. Faye's the sweetest person ever, but don't get between her and animals in trouble.

Inside the office, two desks faced each other on opposite sides of the room, a woman at each one. Farther back a private office sat empty, the desk so neat it looked unused. The place smelled of canned, rose-scented potpourri.

One of the women, past thirty years old but trying hard for twenty, was on the phone. The other, my age or a little older, typed at her computer, peering through half-glasses perched at the end of her nose. After glancing at the younger woman with a hint of irritation, she turned to me. "How can I help you?"

"I'm looking for the agent who represents the property on Sweet Springs."

"That's Ms. Sherman." She leaned to one side to look around me, catching her co-worker's eye meaningfully. "Uh, Gail?"

The other agent went about ending her call and stood to greet me. Ms. Sherman was an attractive woman with what I think of as a bad case of Too-Much: too much eyeliner, too much fashion buy-in, too much body hardware. No matter what the designers preach, we girls need to think for ourselves when getting dressed in the morning. Even if yellow is proclaimed this fall's color, that doesn't mean you should put it next to your pasty face in the form of a bulbous, loose-woven infinity scarf.

Of course I would never in a million years say such a thing aloud, so I said, "That's a lovely scarf."

She patted it. "Thanks."

"I like silky ones in muted tones for autumn," I said. "For me, the bulky ones are a little overpowering."

Her smile told me she didn't get the hint, so I got down to business. "I met a lady the other day who lives on Sweet Springs, and I'm wondering if you're her niece."

Gail's nose wrinkled as if she'd caught a whiff of something nasty, but it was gone in an instant. "You met Aunt Clara?"

"I was visiting a friend at the Meadows and ran into her in the TV room." It didn't seem like a great idea to let on we'd snooped on Clara's property. "She wondered how her hens are doing."

She looked blank for a moment. "Oh, the chickens. They're fine. I went out there this morning to check on them."

A sharp movement at the other desk said Gail's office mate didn't believe Gail any more than I did. While I'd seen for myself that the chickens weren't fine, the other woman must have come to her conclusion based on experience.

Gail's blithe assurance was a problem. I couldn't very well call her a liar to her face, and if I didn't, I had to accept her contention she'd done as her aunt asked. That meant coming up with another reason for stopping in. "I understand there's property for sale on Sweet Springs."

Her nails, painted black with little orange pumpkins, tapped on the desk a second too long before she said, "No, there isn't."

Again I couldn't contradict her, but we'd seen the signs: one at the turnoff and one in the driveway to the Clausen house. "I must have misunderstood. Clara said—"

"Clara gets things mixed up," Gail interrupted. "That's why she's in a nursing home."

"Oh. She seemed okay. Told me about the springs and all."

"People with dementia live in the past," she said bluntly. "Clara couldn't stay out there by herself any longer, so I got her into a place where she's taken care of." Her manner became brisk. "I hate to rush, but I have a showing in twenty minutes."

The other woman had stopped typing to listen to our conversation. Noting that two deep lines had appeared between her brows, I thought she was surprised and possibly irritated by what she'd heard. Since nothing I'd said would bother a total stranger, I guessed she was unhappy with Gail.

Barbara sneers at what she calls my "need for intrigue," but something in that office smelled wrong. It wasn't just the odor of stale cigarette smoke emanating from the jacket Gail took from a peg on the wall behind her. She'd lied about the chickens—Okay, maybe she was ashamed to admit she'd neglected her duty to her aunt—but she was lying about the parcel of land as well. Her co-worker bit her lip, as if trying not to say what she was thinking.

Eager to know what that was, I pulled a trick I've used once or twice when I want to speak to someone alone. Casually setting my sunglasses down on the desk where Gail couldn't see them I said, "I'll let you get to your showing. Thanks for your time."

Ten minutes later Gail left the office, lighting a cigarette as she went, and got into a bright red SUV. As soon as she was out of sight, I went back inside. "Did I leave my—? There they are. My husband used to say I'd forget my head—you know." I scooped up the glasses, acting frustrated with myself.

"Mine says stuff like that about me all the time." I looked at the desk-plate to note her name, Norma Ziegler, as she went on. "But when a man loses something, who does he expect to find it? His wife."

"Like the uterus is a homing device." We laughed at my corny man-bashing joke. Glancing at her desk, I noted the pinkish-red can of bargain-store air freshener. Non-smoker versus smoker in the workplace.

"I was hoping that property on Sweet Springs was still available," I said. "It's beautiful out there."

"It is." Norma's fingernails clicked nervously on her desktop for a moment. "I'm surprised the property's gone. Gail didn't mention a sale to me, pending or final."

"It would have been a nice spot for my daughter and her husband for weekends and summer." I let doubt creep into my voice. "Just yesterday someone said the signs are still up."

She sighed. "Gail hasn't been keeping up with stuff the way she used to." She grimaced. "At least you're being nice about it."

"Clients have been upset with her?"

A shrug indicated she shouldn't say more, but she went on. "It's not my business, except sometimes I get to deal with them."

I let my eyes widen with disapproval. "You shouldn't have to explain someone else's mistakes to the customers."

When Norma leaned forward, I knew I'd hit the right note. "This morning I got an email from some people in Ohio interested in the Clausen place. They planned to drive up this weekend to take a look at it." Touching her phone as if in anticipation she finished, "They won't be happy when I tell them not to bother."

"So Ms. Sherman has put you in hot water."

Norma pressed her lips together to keep from further criticizing a fellow agent. "Like I always tell my kids, I've got broad shoulders."

And she did. I could have given her some pointers on minimizing them, but I stuck to my purpose. "Does Gail do stuff like that a lot?"

"She's always been, um, independent." She rearranged some folders at her elbow, and I guessed she was lecturing herself against bad-mouthing a colleague. The lecture must have been successful, because she said, "It's the trouble with her aunt. Since Clara's got nobody else, Gail had to make the decision to move her to a care facility."

"That had to be tough." After a beat I asked, "Will Gail decide what happens to Clara's property if she's judged incompetent?"

Norma shrugged. "I guess so."

"That's a worry for her, but I suppose it's frustrating for you to have a colleague who's so distracted."

She grimaced ruefully. "I try to keep in mind that deciding what's best for someone else is hard."

It is if you care about that person, I thought. We didn't know how much Gail cares about Clara, but we did know she wasn't overly concerned about Clara's chickens.

I left the office with a complimentary chocolate mint that was delicious and a head-full of questions. Why was the property next to Clara's still marked for sale if it had sold? If Gail had made a deal recently, why hadn't she told her fellow agent? There was also the question Faye would ask: Who would take care of the chickens if Gail didn't feel obligated to keep her promise?

When I called my sisters the next morning to report my stop at So-Rite Realty, Barbara said Gail Sherman's failure to take the signs down was probably simple logistics. "Sweet Springs is pretty far out, so it might take a while to get out there and remove the sign. And the fact she didn't tell the other agent was probably an oversight due to the stress of what's been going on in her personal life with the aunt."

Faye argued my statement that Clara was as sharp as a tack. "People in nursing homes often appear capable, Retta, but that doesn't mean they are." Her strongest concern was for Clara's hens, and she was not happy to learn Ms. Sherman had lied about doing her poultry duty.

Chapter Seven

Faye

I was in the kitchen making breakfast when Gabe's head bobbed by the window. Nervous around Barb and terrified of me, Gabe tended to go to the back door, where he was likely to find Dale.

I'd tried to make it clear I no longer held it against the young man that he'd once kidnapped me. The incident occurred before his reformation ("meeting my Lord and Savior Jesus Christ.") He'd paid for his crimes with several months in the county jail, where he met a young social worker who converted him from criminal to good citizen, pagan to Christian, and quite recently, from bachelor to husband. Gabe's life had completely turned around, though he and his new wife Mindy had yet to move out of her mother's house on the north side of Allport.

Once Gabe paid his debt to society, we'd started giving him intermittent work at the agency, hoping to encourage him to stay on the straight and narrow path. Despite that, Gabe looked at the floor 95% of the time when I was in the room and communicated through my husband whenever possible.

At Dale's invitation, Gabe plopped into the chair across from him. It was Barb's usual place, but she's a breakfast skipper. I don't approve, but so far I've only convinced her to come down once a week for the most important meal of the day.

The bacon was already sputtering and bubbling in the pan. Taking a table setting from the cupboard and laying it out before him I said, "You're out and about early, Gabe."

Wincing as if I'd pointed out some fault in his character he replied, "Got up at six to drive Mindy to work."

"Wow." I tried to sound impressed, though Dale and I are usually up by five. Farmer time, Dale calls it.

"We're sharing her car right now 'cause I finally have the money to fix up my truck." His toothy grin appeared. "I got a job."

"That's great." Dale had risen to get our visitor a cup of coffee, and as he set the mug down, he punched Gabe gently on the shoulder. I took the perfectly-fried bacon out, laid it on paper towels to drain, and cracked half a dozen eggs into the pan. Scrawny as an alley cat, Gabe will eat anytime someone offers food. My theory is that kids and animals that grow up hungry seize every chance at a meal. It's instinct.

Though he practically glowed with pride at our approval, Gabe tried to be modest. "The owner at Baxter's Moving and Storage don't mind that I spent time in jail. I start as cleaner and extra staff, but he said if I get training I can maybe get to be their maintenance man when the one they got now retires next year."

"Sounds like a great opportunity."

Gabe cleared his throat as if preparing to give a speech. "I don't want you ladies to think I'm leaving you in the lurch. If you need help on a case, just give me a call. I'll find the time."

I tried to appear grateful. Dale rose and busied himself by refilling his coffee mug, but I saw the smile he hid in the process. Though Gabe saw himself as an integral part of our agency, we needed him about as much as the country needed more people running for President in 2016.

Once we'd eaten, Dale and Gabe went out to Dale's workshop, talking cars as they went. I cleaned the kitchen until my phone chimed. The text was a request that I come out to the Meadows if it was convenient. I don't go every time they have a problem with Harriet, but when they contact me, I know they've already tried everything they can think of to calm her down. With only a tiny sigh, I got my coat, purse, and car keys, leaving a note for Dale that said simply, HARRIET AGAIN.

My mother-in-law insisted someone had broken into her room during the night and robbed her. “I had two peanut butter cups right here in this drawer, and now they’re gone,” she complained as soon as I walked into the room. “I don’t mind sharing, but—” Her voice rose to a bellow.—“I will not tolerate thieves!” She’d already threatened to move out (She couldn’t walk), call the police (We’d taken away her phone months ago), and holler until someone paid attention (That she could do).

Since I never went to the Meadows without a selection of her favorite candy bars in my purse, all it took was a little acting on my part. I opened the top drawer of her night stand, then the second, and finally the third. As I bent over, I dropped candy into the bottom drawer, said, “Found them,” and stepped back so she could see.

“What are they doing in there?” Harriet scowled at the bright wrappers in the open drawer as the aide standing in the doorway shot me a thumbs up. She muffled a giggle, but I didn’t dare show even the shadow of a smile.

“Maybe someone moved them when they put your clean undies away.”

“That’s stupid! I always keep my candy in the top drawer.”

“Well, at least you weren’t robbed,” I said soothingly. “That’s a relief, right?”

“Too bad it takes a detective to find something in this place,” she said. “They said they looked everywhere, and you found them in seconds.” She raised her voice to the hallway. “Idiots!”

As I left Harriet’s room, a spry woman with blue eyes and a cheerful grin waited in the hallway. “Good morning.” I greet each resident I pass, even if they show no sign of awareness. You never know.

"Good morning to you," she responded. "You're Mrs. Burner, Harriet's detective daughter-in-law?"

I made a little curtsey. "Yes, we do investigations."

"She talks about you a lot. She's very proud." Now that surprised me, but the woman went on, "Do you have a few minutes to talk?"

It's hard to know who's capable of holding a reasonable conversation and who's not in a nursing home, but she seemed reasonably competent. Barb would open the office if I was a few minutes late. "Sure."

The rooms at the Meadows are pretty much identical, but the one the woman led me to was nearer the reception desk than Harriet's room. I suspected the staff put my mother-in-law at the far end of the corridor for good reason.

Clara occupied the hallway side of the room. "My roommate is in the common room, playing Bingo." Looking around as if she'd made a social gaffe Clara said, "I don't have a chair for a visitor. I haven't been here long enough to have one."

There was hardly enough room for a chair anyway. Apparently her roommate Alma (whose name was on everything) had lots wrong with her, and all of it required machines for treatment. I smelled alcohol, albuterol, and a mix of other chemicals I couldn't identify.

"It's okay," I told her. "We can sit here." I took the foot of the bed, and she sat down at the head after moving the pillow out of the way. The bed was neatly made, and the few items on the nightstand were arranged in a way that suggested they were exactly where she wanted them. There wasn't much, a comb and brush, a box of tissues, and a stuffed dog with a sign around its neck that said, WELCOME CLARA!

"My name is Clara Knight."

Things clicked in my brain. "Oh. You met my sister Retta."

Clara smiled. "I don't think she told me her name, but she was very sweet."

Everyone says that when they first meet Retta, and it's true. You don't see the strong side until later, when it's too late.

"I'm glad I was able to catch you." With a mischievous smile she confessed, "When I heard Harriet shouting this morning, I figured they'd call you in, so I've been lying in wait." Straightening the blankets between us she said, "If I'd known your sister was a detective, I'd have spoken to her about taking my case."

Retta wasn't originally one of us. Barb and I founded the Smart Detective Agency together, and we'd hoped Retta would stay out of our business. We'd been dreaming, of course. Retta had jumped in with both feet. Oddly enough, in the last few months Barb, once vehemently opposed to Retta as a partner, had begun to actively include her. I was pleased the three of us were cooperating, though it was usually me Retta worked on when she wanted something changed. Barb is much more able to resist persuasion, being pretty much set in her ways.

Clara was waiting politely, so I said, "Your case?"

Her sigh said she wasn't happy about having one. "I don't belong in this place."

Here we go. I opened my mouth to say I had errands to run, but she put up a hand. "Please hear me out. I was living at home, minding my own business. I was—I am—completely capable of taking care of myself. One day in August, my niece Gail stopped by, which she hadn't done for years, and asked if I'd be willing to sell my land and move into town." Clara's lips tightened at the memory. "She had all these arguments about how I'd be safer and have friends to play cards with. Her main push was how much money she could get for it. As if that would make me want to trade away everything my husband and I worked for."

Interested despite myself I asked, "This property's been yours for a long time?"

"My father left it to me, and George and I retired there when we turned sixty. We spent twenty years out there together. The last three years, I've been by myself." Her expression revealed the pain that statement caused, but she didn't dwell on it. "My garden is smaller since George died, but I still have one. I make dill pickles. I keep chickens. I fish a little, though I'm not the fisherman my husband was." See here?" She showed me a scar on her thumb. "Fishhook. I had to drive myself all the way into Allport last summer to get it removed."

"That must have hurt."

"It's worth it if you catch something nice for supper." Leaning over, she touched my arm gently. "I love my home, Mrs. Burner, and I never want to live anywhere else."

"Call me Faye. The woman I think of as Mrs. Burner is in the room down the hall."

That reminded me of my mother-in-law's insistence she too could live on her own if we'd let her. No one wants to admit she's no longer capable of maintaining a home. The niece must have noticed a change, or she wouldn't have suggested moving her aunt and selling the property.

Clara thought otherwise, and she came to the point of our conversation. "Gail manipulated me into this place. I didn't see it coming, and now I have no recourse unless you help."

"Are you telling me your niece—" I hesitated to use the dreaded phrase *put you in a home* "—brought you here because she wants your property?"

"I think she wants the commission." Clara bit her lip before going on. "Every time I try to tell a staff member I shouldn't be here, they pat me on the arm and change the subject."

Having just come from yet another incident where Harriet claimed theft when we all knew she'd eaten her peanut butter cups in the night and forgotten it, arguments flooded my mind. People aren't just assigned to nursing homes. There has to be cause. Elderly people sometimes become paranoid. If the niece wanted Clara to sell her property and move into Allport, it was likely she was concerned for the old lady's safety. Even if she saw a fat commission for herself in the property deal, that didn't mean Clara had been placed at the Meadows without cause.

Clara was watching me closely, as if trying to read my thoughts. "Can you look into it for me?"

"Mrs. Knight, I'm not sure what we'd be able to do."

She leaned forward, and I caught a whiff of talcum powder. "Find out what's happening. Has Gail applied for guardianship? Is my home up for sale? Has anyone been looking into the title? Has it already been sold? It's only been a week or so, and I have no idea how quickly these things can go. Everyone does a 'There, there, Clara' when I try to tell them what's happening." She swallowed. "If I'm declared incompetent—"

Fearing she might be working up to hysterics I said, "You shouldn't worry like this."

Her face took on a hopeless expression, but she tried again. "I have some emergency cash in my purse. I can give you a retainer." Her blue eyes fixed firmly on me. "It won't take more than a few hours of your time. Will you do it? Please?"

"I don't want to take your money."

Suddenly the blue eyes snapped, and the sweet expression hardened to steel. "Young woman. I'm not a charity case, and I'm not stupid. I have a PhD in microbiology, and until we retired up here, I was a member of the science department at Michigan State University." After a pause she said, "Full professor."

"Oh."

Her eyes softened again. “I’m not telling you this to brag. I just want you to know I’m not some crazy old woman.” She put her hands in her lap. “I can afford your services, and I need to know if Gail is working against me.” Tears choked her voice as she said the last words.

“All right,” I said. “I can’t promise anything, but I’ll try.” I glanced out into the hallway, assuring privacy for the moment. “Tell me what you recall about coming here.”

“I got sick,” Clara replied. “I don’t remember much about it, to be honest. Gail had been coming out to visit every weekend. She’d hang around for an hour or so, arguing I should sell and move into town. Last week when she came, I wasn’t making sense. She asked me things like who is the President and what month is it, and I couldn’t answer correctly.” Clara paused. “At least that’s what she told the doctor.”

“You think she lied?”

Clara shrugged delicately. “There was something wrong, I admit that. I felt disoriented and confused. I saw things that weren’t there, even smelled things that weren’t.” She sounded irritated with herself. “Anyway, Gail loaded me into her car and took me to my doctor’s office. By the time he saw me, I guess I was pretty bad off. Next thing I knew, I was stuck in here.” She tried to be calm, but her anger showed. “They’re good to me. I don’t want you to think I’m complaining about the facility, but I should be at home. I’ve got things to do before winter comes.”

“What things?”

“Well, about this time each year I hook up the heat lamps for my girls,” she replied. “Chickens can stand a lot of cold, but just like people, they’d rather be warm than not. Then there’s a man who brings me firewood. He dumps it in the yard and I stack it myself, in a rack close to the house where I can get at it no matter how much snow we get.”

"You stack your own firewood?" Clara weighed ninety-eight pounds, if that.

She smiled. "It takes longer than it used to, but yes. I work for an hour or so at a time until it's all where I want it." Her smile faded. "If I don't move that wood before it snows, it'll be a mess to get at it all winter."

Despite my doubts, ideas were forming. "Any more things you need to get done?"

Clara chuckled. "A dozen at least. It's work running a place all by myself, but I like it. Keeps me young."

That was true. If not for an ankle-bracelet that would sound a warning to the staff if she tried to leave the facility, Clara looked perfectly competent and years younger than her age, which had to be mid-eighties. Promising to return with a decision as to whether we'd take her case, I headed for the exit.

Twenty feet down the hall, I was reconsidering my promise. Had I listened with my heart instead of my head? I tried to imagine how Barb would have reacted to Clara's story. With hard questions, no doubt. "How did your niece manage to convince your doctor you need full-time care, Mrs. Knight?" or "Why didn't you demand a second opinion?" There had to be ways to prove yourself competent, even if a relative claimed otherwise.

Brandy, a CNA I knew well, was at the front desk, filling in a chart. "Hey," I said, "can you tell me why Clara Knight is here?"

It was clearly a violation of HIPAA's privacy regulations, but the girls at the Meadows knew me enough to understand I wouldn't ask if I didn't have good reason. After looking around to be sure no one else was listening, Brandy slid the file into its metal sleeve with a snap and said, "She was quite the wacko when we first got her. Thought there were lizards crawling over everything. On the bed, on the walls, everywhere."

"She seems fine now."

She shrugged. "Twice since she came she's had hallucinations and talked gibberish for a day. The rest of the time, she's as sane as me—if that's sane. Of course she insists she's going home soon, but—" Brandy tapped her pen on the chart. "—wanting to go home isn't exactly rare around here."

I left the building, glad there wasn't a monitor on my ankle to stop me. It wouldn't be a big job for the agency to look into whether Clara's niece was up to something, and in addition, there were a few things I could do for Clara myself.

CHAPTER EIGHT

Retta

Faye called me about Clara Knight's case before she told Barbara anything. That was a first, since she and Barbara Ann are usually the Wonder Twins and I'm just Gleek. Clearly, Faye was looking for support. We all have to agree before we take a case on, and she was afraid Barbara would dismiss a nursing home resident's insistence that her family was plotting against her. Since I'd met Clara, Faye thought I'd be less likely to reject her story out of hand.

"I met the niece," I reminded Faye. "She didn't exactly come across as a criminal mastermind."

"When money's involved, some families aren't warm and fuzzy."

"I did sense Gail isn't emotionally connected to her aunt."

"Then we should look into what she might be up to."

I promised to get to the office by eleven so we could present our argument to Barbara together. It was nine-thirty, so I had plenty of time to do a little online shopping before then. Making another cup of coffee in my Keurig, I settled into a soft chair and sipped pumpkin spice as I shopped.

The next time I looked at the clock it was ten forty-eight. Now, some people can change and be out the door in fifteen minutes, but that's not me. I mean, my nails were a mess and my hair needed attention from the curling iron. Anyway, it was eleven thirty-ish when I pulled up in front of their house, just a few blocks from Lake Huron. I made a little grimace in the mirror, knowing

Barbara Ann would be all grumpy. The woman's never been late for anything in her life.

There was no way I was going to hurry to soothe her feathers, so I sauntered up the walk like I had all the time in the world. I paused to admire Faye's mums, bursting with autumn colors. Some Bourbon roses she was trying to nurture were benefitting from the mild fall weather, filling the air with delicate scent from their round, pink blooms.

The house was attractive, though I'm not a fan of older homes. Painted white with some dignified burgundy gingerbread on the corners, it had a wide front porch that led to a front door with narrow stained-glass side-lights. The door led to the offices, where Faye usually manned the desk in the foyer while Barbara sat in the room behind, prim and unapproachable.

Both my sisters were in Barbara's Ice Palace. While I don't like to criticize someone else's taste, the cream-and-pale-blue room doesn't have a single scrap of fabric to soften it or a splash of brightness to dress it up. For once I got no flak for my lateness, because they were deep in conversation with a nice-looking man.

"Hi," I said, stopping in the doorway. "Sorry to be tardy."

Barb introduced me as Faye pulled up the extra chair. "Retta, meet Rick Chou from Grand Rapids. He's interested in hiring us to do some work."

Mr. Chou stood and turned to shake my hand, and I reassessed my first impression. Not just attractive, he was gorgeous: dark hair with a little gray at the temples. A jaw square enough to cut corners with. And inky-black eyes you could fall right into and swim around in.

"Nice to meet you, Mrs.—"

"Ms. Stilson, but please call me Retta." I caught his scent, expensive and manly. "It's lovely to meet you, Mr. Chou."

"Rick, please." He smiled like he'd just drawn the card he needed to fill an inside straight.

I heard an irritated huff of air before Barb spoke. "Mr. Chou is hoping we can locate his wife."

"Ex-wife," he corrected, still looking at me. "As I told your sisters, Ms. Stilson, my wife left me for greener pastures. At the time, I forget she's listed as co-owner on property we own just south of here on the lakeshore. Now I've decided to sell the place, but she needs to sign off, and I've lost contact with her."

The Lake Huron shoreline south of Allport is dotted with exquisite homes in all styles of architecture from Tudor to ultra-modern. Not only was Mr. Chou movie-star handsome, he was apparently loaded as well.

"Didn't your divorce decree specify who got what?"

He made a comical grimace. "Apparently that means nothing if her name is still on the deed. It's just a matter of a signature, but as I said, I have no idea where she is."

"Will she agree to sign?" Barbara asked.

"The value of the property was taken into consideration in the divorce." Chou raised a crow-black brow. "She hated the house, said log homes belong in the 1800s. She hated the location, too, said it was always cold with the wind off the lake. She'll sign."

A house on Lake Huron was guaranteed a lovely view. The ex-Mrs. Chou sounded like a spoiled brat to me.

"It was an angry parting?" Barbara leaned forward abruptly, causing her chair to make a snapping sound. She examined the poor man as if he were a virus in a laboratory.

"The angriest." He put up a hand to forestall her next question. "You don't have to tell me where she is, since she obviously doesn't want me to know. I just want you to get Candice's signature—at my expense, of course." He smiled disarmingly. "You three can take a weekend in the Bahamas and I won't care, as long as you accomplish that."

Barbara didn't warm to his attempt at humor. "We'll let you know if we think we can help, Mr. Chou. Possibly today, but tomorrow morning at the latest."

When he stood, I noticed he was the perfect height for dancing, just a couple of inches taller than I am. After shaking hands with all of us, he left, flashing me an extra smile as he closed the outside door.

"What do we think?" Barbara asked.

"He's great," I said.

"It's a case, Retta. We're talking about a case."

"Of course. We're going to look up his ex-wife and ask her to sign off on property she already agreed to give up. Shouldn't be a problem once you and Faye hit your computers and track her down." I smiled mischievously. "I'll be glad to report our findings to the client."

"Then we're agreed we'll take Mr. Chou's case." I imagined her rapping a gavel on her desktop to signify the verdict was official.

Faye made a little gesture like she was trying to get the teacher to call on her. "I have a case to consider, too." Briefly she recounted her meeting with Clara, ending with, "I don't think it will be a lot of trouble to look into this. If she's a crazy old lady, we drop it. If the niece—"

"Gail," I supplied.

"If Gail is pushing for Clara to be declared incompetent just so she can sell the property, we need to stop her."

Faye spoke mostly to Barbara. A person might look at the agency and see three equals, but in practice, we deferred to our eldest. Faye, Barbara's biggest cheerleader, never made a move without her approval, and because my full membership in the agency was due to what Barbara Ann called blackmail, I tried to tread lightly.

Though she pondered for some time, I was pretty sure Barbara would say yes. It was obvious Faye wanted to help the old woman out, and Barbara's soft spot is Faye. "All right," she said, pulling open the bottom drawer of her desk with a grind of wood against wood. Taking out her purse, she said, "Faye can start the search for Mrs. Chou. I'll visit Gail Sherman."

"What are you going to do," I asked, "suggest she's trying to cheat her aunt out of her home?"

With that look that says she's got things all figured out Barbara replied, "Would you rather we take the word of a possibly delusional octogenarian?"

"I guess not," I admitted, "but if Ms. Sherman is crooked, she isn't going to tell you the truth."

"That's where being an investigator comes in, Retta. You have to ask the right questions."

Chapter Nine

Barb

The So-Rite Realty office was compact in size and utilitarian in design. As Retta had described, two desks faced each other on opposite sides of the room, but today one was empty. Luckily for me, the occupied chair was Gail Sherman's. She looked up as I entered and flashed a professional smile, probably because I didn't look like someone collecting for the local Fireman's Ball.

Gail wore Power Red, a good color choice with her ash blond hair and green eyes. I cringed at the drawn-on brows, but I try to let other people be who they think they have to be fashion-wise. What irritated me was the assessing look I got, the up-and-down glance that let me know I was being assigned to a shelf in her personal filing system. From the way her eyes went flat, I guessed I was judged a woman of substance but no style.

Nonetheless, she found a hook meant to establish rapport. "I love your coat." She got up, and for a second I thought she was going to come out from behind the desk and feel the fabric. "Did you get it online?"

I had no memory of where the coat came from. It was rain-resistant, had roomy pockets for the tissues I carry at all times due to allergies, and a hood so I didn't have to remember to bring along a hat. Ignoring the question, I put out a hand. "I'm Barbara Evans."

She stood to shake my hand. "Gail Sherman. What can I do for you today?"

"I've been asked to investigate Clara Knight's competence." I purposely didn't say who'd initiated the investigation, and she accepted my statement without question. That told me Clara's mental state had been called into question by formal petition.

"You people work faster than I expected." Further evidence Gail had expected a visit from the authorities. She sounded happy about it.

I didn't correct her assumption that I was from the court. "What can you tell me about your aunt's recent behavior?"

Gail tried for a regretful expression but achieved something more like smugness. "Well, I first noticed it about six weeks ago. I went out to visit, and Aunt Clara was down by the lake. She'd waded in almost to her waist, fully clothed. When I called for her to come back to shore she did, but she insisted one of her chickens was out there drowning. I had a terrible time convincing her the birds were in their pen and perfectly safe."

She paused for a moment, ostensibly to overcome emotion. "She's always been so together, you know? The family was so proud of her and everything she accomplished in life, and now to have her lose it—it's really sad."

"I assume you had her doctor examine her at that time."

Now she looked—or tried to look—ashamed. "Well, no. I thought maybe she was just having a bad day, you know? I took her inside and made her a cup of tea, and we sat and talked for a long time. She seemed okay, especially if I let her go on about when I was a kid. We'd go out to visit sometimes, and Clara loves to tell what a scaredy-cat I was about the lake." Gail shivered. "I can't help it. When I get close to water I feel like it's pulling me in and trying to suck the breath out of me."

Nodding to acknowledge her phobia, I asked, "Was that the only time Clara seemed mentally unstable?"

Brushing some dust off her desktop, she rubbed her hands together. "Oh, no. Every time I went out there, she seemed a little less aware. I started trying to convince her to move into Allport. I told her she could get a little apartment where there'd be people to talk to." Leaning toward me she confided, "She needs to be supervised for her own safety, but I didn't put it like that." Gail's lips tightened. "She insisted she was fine out there."

So far, Ms. Sherman's concerns were the concerns of many who feel responsible for an older relative unwilling to admit she's slipping mentally. At her age, Clara could easily get into a situation she couldn't get herself out of.

I could almost hear Faye's voice in my ear. *And Clara would rather drown in Sweet Springs than live for weeks, months, or years at the Meadows.*

"What will happen to the property if Mrs. Knight remains in the nursing home?"

Gail adjusted the calendar on her desk until it was perfectly aligned with the edges. It took a long time to get it exactly the way she wanted it, and I heard her breathing in the momentary silence. "Since I'm Clara's last living relative, I assume I'll be appointed to look after it. I'll have to assess what's best for her and everyone else involved."

Since "everyone else" was apparently Gail, that was a roundabout way of saying she'd do what pleased her. It wasn't all that nice, but if she became Clara's guardian, it would be perfectly legal.

I asked a question investigators from the court are supposed to ask. "Do you think Clara is happy at the Meadows?"

A big sigh preceded her answer. "I doubt it. She's concerned about who'll watch her chickens, but I'm worried about who'll watch her." She raised her palms as if to end any discussion. "I put her somewhere she's well cared for. What else could I do?"

What else, indeed? My instincts said Gail Sherman was a self-centered woman with no empathy for her elderly aunt, but if

Clara was safer at the Meadows than she was at home, society would not fault Gail's decision.

Chapter Ten

Faye

With the resources we'd developed for our agency on the internet, it wasn't difficult to find an email address for the former Mrs. Richard Chou. Narrowing the search by middle name, age, and an arrest as a juvenile for Minor in Possession (Yes, the internet does haunt your past), I found the Candice Chou we wanted and got an email address. Hoping it was current, I composed a carefully worded message and created a heading I hoped wouldn't come across as spam.

"Can't very well write, YOUR SIGNATURE NEEDED, in the subject line," I told Barb when she returned from her visit to the real estate office.

She chuckled as she hung her coat in the closet under the stairs and closed the door with the thump it took to make it stay that way. "You mean you don't want to sound like the wife of a prominent-but-deceased African banker willing to share millions of dollars with just the right person?"

"Not if I can help it." I sent the email. "Should I keep looking until I find a physical address for her?"

Barb shook her head. "Let's give her a day or two to respond. I don't want to pry into the woman's privacy unless we have to."

"You don't trust Mr. Chou?"

She shrugged. "I don't *mis*trust him, but if Mrs. Chou went to the trouble of hiding her whereabouts from a man she used to be married to, her wishes should be accommodated if possible."

Barb told me about her visit to the real estate office. As she talked I could tell she was half-convinced Gail Sherman, though not a warm person, had done her best for her delusional aunt.

"I asked a friend at the courthouse to see if Gail has filed papers declaring Clara incompetent," I said, hoping to delay a decision I dreaded. "She agreed to look into it but said she's swamped right now. We might not hear from her until Monday."

"Okay." Stowing her purse in the bottom drawer of her desk, Barb sat down in her chair with a sigh. "We'll make a decision about whether to take the case then. Naturally, we won't charge Mrs. Knight if we decide not to continue."

That meant I had the weekend to find something to keep Barb's interest, some hint Clara didn't deserve to be locked up.

Having done what I could for our current clients, I moved on to my plan to help Clara get some of her chores done. With no need for both of us to stay in the office all day, I told Barb I wanted to take my husband and dog for a ride. Already deep in research on guardianship and conservator duties in Michigan, she wished us well.

Dale was out in the little shop he'd created from Barb's too-small-for-a-modern-car garage. Like my sisters and me, he grew up in the country, where neighbors help neighbors as a matter of course. It isn't considered saintly or selfless. It's simply what people do. When we were kids, if a farmer's baler broke down, another farmer loaned him his. When a timberman got hurt on the job, people brought food, collected money for medical bills, and took on his chores until he was able to do them again. With that kind of background, Dale would be my willing helper.

Since the accident my husband had limits, but like any proud person, he didn't like acknowledging them. Stacking Clara's wood was something he could do, so I figured my mission to help Clara would help him too.

As I explained my proposal, Dale replaced the pull-cord on someone's snow-blower. "I don't know if Clara can ever go back home," I finished, "but if she can, it'll be hard for her to catch up on the chores before winter hits. I thought we'd do what we can."

Dale set his wrench in the toolbox with a metallic clunk. "We'll need work gloves, and I'll check the weather in case we get rain."

I often chuckled at Dale's obsession with weather forecasts. I'd told him a hundred times that rain wasn't necessarily a reason to hide in the house, but he insisted on knowing if there was the slightest chance we'd get wet on an outing.

Following him into the house, I put on a light flannel, grabbed my car keys, and called, "Want to ride in the car, Buddy?"

A thump indicated my beloved mongrel had jumped down from our bed. Rapid clicks sounded as his nails hit the wood floor of the hallway, and before I could locate my purse, he was waiting by the door. What dog doesn't know the words *ride* and *car* and respond enthusiastically?

Though he would always be a one-person dog, Buddy and Dale had warmed to each other somewhat over time. Dale had stopped calling him the Hound from Hell, and Buddy had given up trying to keep Dale out of our bedroom. He still didn't like it when he was banished from the front seat, but today he took it with good grace, only growling once at the seating arrangement. As we left the city limits, Bud checked the view from the right, left, and back windows. When he finished he did it all again, making sure he covered all the bases he was allowed.

October's bright-blue weather was exhibited in all its glory. I believe Michigan Octobers are a gift God gives us to compensate for Novembers, which tend to be gray with gray accents. Hunters love the eleventh month, but for me, October weather all the way through to April would be fine.

Since the air had warmed from crispy to pleasant, I rolled down the back window of my Escape for the last mile as a treat for Bud. Experts say it's bad for dogs to stick their heads out a car window, so I didn't do it all the time. Buddy loved it, though, so I gave him a little "air time" when the weather co-operated. It wasn't like the wind would damage my hairdo.

We arrived at Clara's shortly after one. I let Buddy out to investigate the smells of the autumn countryside, and he circled the property, sniffing out critters that had been there before him. Dale and I explored the property, gauging what needed to be done. The woodpile was larger than I remembered, but Dale went right to work, lifting several chunks onto his arm. "Good, seasoned stuff," he said as he hefted it. "At least the wood guy didn't cheat the old lady." Taking another piece he urged, "Check on the chickens. You can help with this afterward."

Buddy followed me to the chicken pen. The rooster eyed me belligerently, but he hadn't been aggressive last time, so I figured he was simply playing his role. Though the water fount was still half full, the birds had eaten all the food I left and were scratching at the hard-packed ground for bugs. The dog growled when he saw them, and the chickens muttered among themselves, their heads bobbing in alarm. I spoke firmly to Buddy, who trotted off to the lakeshore, where some Canada geese were gathered. He worked out his aggression by chasing them off, and the clamor they created seemed to please him.

When I opened the gate of the pen with a bucket of feed in one hand, the birds rushed at me, pushing each other out of the way as if they hadn't eaten in weeks. Though they weren't as starved as they appeared to be, the empty trough told the story. No one had fed them since I'd been there two days earlier. Not only had Gail Sherman lied to Retta about having done as her aunt asked, Retta's visit to the realty hadn't resulted in action on Gail's part to remedy the situation.

Dale paused his work on the woodpile to call, "How are things in Chicken World?"

"Better now that they're fed." Closing the gate I joined him, glancing around as I went. "This place is as neat as a pin."

"I noticed," Dale agreed. "I needed a hatchet to lop off some twigs." He gestured at the nearest shed. "The tools are outlined on a pegboard so they go right back where they came from."

"Clara claimed she does everything herself."

Dale frowned. "You'd think if her mind was going we'd see signs of neglect."

"I know." We looked the place over again, searching for signs the owner was failing mentally or physically. Finding none, I became even more determined to argue for taking Clara's case. Barb was looking at things from her usual, logical point of view, but she hadn't met Clara. I hoped Retta would take my side.

As Dale went back to work on the woodpile, I remembered the heat lamps Clara mentioned. "Should we put heat in the coop so the chickens don't get their combs frostbitten at night?"

Pausing the rhythmic clink of setting wood into place, Dale considered. "We've got no way to turn it on and off, and we wouldn't want to start a fire." He glanced at the bright sky. "I think they'll be okay without it for a while longer. The coop looks tight, and they can huddle together."

Since Dale's the weather expert in the family, I nodded. "Okay. I probably should collect the eggs, though. Looks like no one's done that in a while." Hunting up a basket, I began opening the little trapdoors at the sides of the chicken coop. By feeling around I located one egg, then another, and so on. In the week Clara had been gone, the chickens had been busy, laying large, light brown eggs. The hens didn't seem to mind me taking them but kept up their soft cooing sounds as I filled the first basket. I had to dig up a second one to hold them all, and I proudly showed Dale my treasure trove.

"What are you going to do with them?" he asked, bending to pick up more wood. He'd made quite a dent in the pile, and I set the eggs aside and started doing my part.

"I doubt the nursing home can accept undocumented eggs."

"There's likely to be a rule against it." Dale's tone said what he thought of rules prohibiting people from eating food fresh from the farm.

"I guess we could give them to the niece," I said, raising my voice to be heard over the clunk of wood hitting wood.

He snorted in response. "If she wanted them, she should have come out and helped herself. Looks like she couldn't care less if those birds die of starvation."

I tried to tell myself that Niece Gail might not be as tuned in to the needs of chickens as I was. Still, Clara would have made clear what needed to be done. Did her failure to follow through make Gail guilty of plotting against her aunt, or was she simply a flawed human being who didn't recognize the needs of other species?

I couldn't answer that question, but I did make a decision about the eggs. I'd split them with my sisters and count them toward payment of Clara's bill with the Smart Detectives.

CHAPTER ELEVEN

Barb

On Friday evenings, Rory and I often went for dinner to a little place out of town. Though many of Allport's citizens were aware their chief of police dated a local private detective, it was easier if we left the city limits for our dates. That way no one came to our table to complain about the city commissioners' latest non-decision on the new parking ramp. If he was really fed up, Rory would turn off his cell phone for an hour, trusting that nothing earth-shattering would happen before we finished our meal.

When I spoke of Rory to others, I never knew what to call him. My boyfriend—? lover—? soulmate—? Whatever he was, he looked good when I picked him up at his place. Rory's American Indian blood showed in his shiny-black hair and dark eyes. His Irish mother's genes had contributed an impish smile and a tendency for his hair to curl if he let it grow beyond a half inch long. Climbing into my car, he leaned over to kiss me lightly on the cheek. I caught the scent of Irish Spring as I accepted the greeting before pulling away from the curb.

I knew people—my sisters included—talked about us, wondering when we'd "set a date" or move in together. The truth was that neither Rory not I wanted to give up the independent lives we'd carved out for ourselves. There were no marriage plans. There'd be no common household. We understood each other even if no one else did. Still, it was nice to have someone to spend an evening with, someone who cherished the time we spent together. Maybe that was the correct word: Rory was my Someone.

"Any more snitch reports this week?" I asked, picking up on conversations we'd had over the last month. Mayor Dan Rygwelski had received several emails about Rory, and Janet, the city's secretary, had received several calls about the chief, none of them flattering.

"Yesterday, in fact. Lady Tattletale called to report I took an hour and forty minutes to eat my lunch."

"She's timing your lunches now?"

He huffed in disgust. "Apparently she didn't notice I was taking notes like a college freshman. It was a working lunch with the chief from Clare, discussing how to deal with Halloween pranksters."

"You're plotting against Trick-or-Treaters?"

Rory tapped the dashboard absently. "The City Fathers expect us to prevent the more harmful mayhem that comes with America's current favorite holiday. Chief Jackson and I were comparing methods, so the long lunch was justified."

"Rory, you don't take advantage of your position in any way."

He shifted position on the bench seat. "Someone thinks I do."

"You have no idea who's filing these complaints?"

"None, except it's a woman." I slowed to make the turn into the restaurant as he went on. "Dan just laughs about it. Janet is disgusted because she's been told she can't argue with the caller. So far, it's a joke to them."

I didn't find it funny. "But you work so hard. To not be able to confront your accuser is the worst kind of injustice." Pulling into a parking space and shifting into park, I turned toward him. "Can you trace the calls or track down the source of the emails?"

He shrugged. "The woman knows technology. It would take more resources than we've got in a small city police force."

"Why don't you bring in the state police?"

He spread his hands. "For some loon who makes up stories? It would be embarrassing, not to mention overkill."

"Maybe Lars would look into it." When Lars Johannsen, an FBI agent from New Mexico, helped with a recent case, he and Rory had become friends. Lars and Retta had become…close friends.

"I'd feel silly asking." Rory looked out the window at the darkening woods opposite the lights of the inn. "We'll just hope she gets tired of picking on me and moves on to someone else."

The restaurant was dimly lit and smelled of prime rib. Sounds of clinking silverware were softened by the violins and cellos of classical music. Once we were seated, I ordered from the light menu, as usual, and Rory had the beef with mashed potatoes and gravy. He'd have dessert too, probably tiramisu, while I sipped at a second cup of tea. Such is the metabolism of the over-fifty woman.

As we ate, I described our visit to Sweet Springs and Faye's fondness for Clara Knight. Rory's interest was piqued. "I haven't been out there," he said, "but the fire marshal mentioned it this week."

"The fire marshal?"

"I sat next to him at a county-wide meeting, and he mentioned he's investigating a fire out there. These people had just built a big new house on the lake, and then it burned down. He felt bad about it because the fire was suspicious, which means the owners probably won't collect a cent."

I recalled the property we'd stopped at across the springs from the Knight place. "Insurance won't pay if it's ruled the fire was set?"

"There's an arson clause in their policy—pretty common, I guess." Rory tasted the coleslaw he'd been given and took a second, larger bite. "Ray says the couple had sunk a lot of money into the place."

"So it wouldn't make sense for them to burn it down."

He took a roll from the fragrant basket the waitress had left at the center of the table. I considered having one but decided against it. "If they're telling the truth, nobody benefits from the crime. So Ray's asking himself why someone would torch a newly-built home out in the boondocks."

"A pyromaniac? Teenagers looking for a thrill? Someone who was angry at the owners?"

Rory nodded. "He passed all those theories on to the state police."

Our main dishes arrived and the conversation went on to other things, but the arson on Sweet Springs stuck in my mind. An old lady claimed she'd been forced into a nursing home. A family had lost a structure to a suspicious fire. An old man had fallen to his death. One lake and three property owners in trouble. A series of odd, unfortunate events.

Around midnight, I let myself into the house, using the front door to avoid disturbing Faye and Dale, who occupy the back two-thirds of the ground floor. Slipping off my shoes, I climbed the stairs to my comfortable apartment.

When I entered my bedroom, frenzied scratching sounded at the window screen. Dropping my shoes into a corner, I hurried to the window and slid it open. The cat—*my* cat, I'd begun thinking of her—waited outside, her green eyes wide with anger. Accustomed in the last few months to being fed around eight, she was letting me know that four hours late wasn't acceptable.

"Not to worry," I told her softly. "I know you prefer fresh food, so I brought you some of my dinner."

Sliding the screen aside, I set a piece of chicken on the window sill. The cat lunged for it, her head shaking as she tore off bits and swallowed them. I reached out to scratch her ears, which didn't slow her enjoyment of the meal one bit. Her fur was matted and snarled, but experience had taught me that attempts to detangle it weren't welcome. She wouldn't come inside, and she tolerated only one or two strokes before growling to signal it was enough. No sloppy sentimentality for this feline. Our deal was food in exchange for the honor of a nightly visit.

I'd come to anticipate those visits as if they were gifts.

As girls on the farm, we'd had lots of pets: cats, dogs, cows, pigs, even geese. When I left Michigan to practice law on the West Coast, there had never seemed to be a right time to get a pet. Apartments didn't allow them, and my days were packed with busy-ness. Animals aren't meant to be left alone in an apartment all day long. I convinced myself I wasn't a pet person.

But this cat had arrived in a new chapter of my life. Settled into my Victorian home on a side street in Allport, I was less hurried these days. When we met, the cat had been hungry, wild, and afraid of everything. Over time I'd provided food and, gradually, affection. Beginning with encouraging sounds, I'd moved to light touches on her head as she ate. We'd come to the point where she allowed me to stroke all the way down her back, with a squeeze along her spine that made her twitch with pleasure—at least until she remembered how tough she was. She'd come to trust me a little, and I enjoyed the feeling.

"Sorry I was so late, Brat," I told her softly. I needed to choose a better name for her, but so far nothing better had come to mind. She was a brat, and I liked her that way.

"I owe you a kitty treat, since you had to wait for supper."

To remind me who was in control, the cat left while I went to get the bag.

Chapter Twelve

Retta

Faye felt sorry for Clara Knight. Barbara admitted her case was sad but didn't see anything criminal in Gail Sherman's actions. I was somewhere in between.

The property that was marked for sale but apparently wasn't kept coming to mind. The sign might well have been left up due to an oversight, but the fact that the other realtor in Gail's office was left in the dark was more puzzling to me. Working in the same office, the same room, the two women should have heard each other's calls and discussed each other's prospects. It was hard to imagine Gail not mentioning she had a buyer.

I had a theory. If Gail thought she'd soon get her hands on her aunt's place, she might have bought the property next to it for herself. The owner of half of Sweet Springs might do something with it, like build a resort. The area was quiet, and there was plenty of space for cabins or even condos, along with lots of nearby state land for hunting and the springs for fishing. The practicalities of developing a property that far from Allport were hard for me to imagine, but I'd be the first to admit I knew nothing about real estate.

Faye had pointed out that Clara's place didn't seem like the property of someone with dementia. "Everything is put away," she'd told me in a phone call the night before. "The house looks well-kept."

I'd formed the same impression during our stop, but we'd only seen the outside. The house might be a horror, with butter in the oven and dishtowels in the refrigerator. Clara might be like those people you see on TV who put balls of cat hair in dresser drawers and stack stinky, unwashed milk jugs in the hallway.

Saturday is the day I miss my husband the most. Don seems to linger in the corners of our house and yard. In autumn I can almost see him raking leaves, composting the garden, or cleaning out the garage so two vehicles will fit inside during winter. I can almost feel the cold he used to bring back inside, clinging to his flannel. Because of that, I find it's better if I leave home entirely and find something to keep my mind occupied. Barbara sneers at the number of organizations I join and activities I support, but she's always been alone. I had to find things to do after Don died and the kids left home, or I'd have gone crazy. And as I said, the loneliness is worst on Saturdays, when everyone else is doing things with their families.

Added to my need for distraction is my dog Styx, who loves new places to explore. He's a Newfoundland, so some of his happiest moments come when he finds water he's never taken a dip in before. Therefore, in a blend of curiosity, boredom, loneliness, and doggy indulgence, I drove out to Sweet Springs early Saturday morning—well, early for me. Before we left I spread a couple of old blankets over the back seat of my car so when Styx was done swimming, he could ride back there.

The drive was even more scenic than last time, since the colors were really starting to pop. It had rained overnight, so the road was wet, but the temperature had already risen to the fifties with bright sunshine. There was no wind. The lake was peaceful and still when I pulled into Clara's driveway. The house looked as empty as before. When I opened the car door, Styx just about knocked me down as he rocketed out of the car, ran directly to the lake, and plunged into the water without even putting a toe in first to check the temperature.

While he enjoyed his cold bath, I turned to Clara's house. My thoughts about butter in the oven made me wonder if the inside of the house would reveal the owner's incompetence. Climbing the steps to the front door, I peered in. Everything looked the same as it had the first time I was there. I checked the back door and all the windows I could reach. Locked. Ignoring the little voice in my head that said I shouldn't, I began looking for where she'd have stashed the spare key. Everyone has one, and it's just a matter of thinking as they think. Would Clara put a key where it was most convenient for her or where it was least likely to be found? I figured somewhere in the middle—not too hard to get to, but not in plain sight either.

I didn't find it on the porch. My spare key hangs in my garage, but Clara didn't have one of those. That meant it was probably in one of the sheds. Getting a flashlight out of my car, I went through them, searching three of the four before I saw it. Along the outside of the doorframe was a nail, and on the nail was a key. Not easy to find in the dark space, but low enough for Clara—and for me—to reach without stretching.

The key fit the front door, and, with a slightly guilty glance around to be sure I wasn't being observed, I entered Clara's house. I was *not* snooping, though I could almost hear Barbara Ann sniffing in disapproval. Clara had asked for our help, and I was trying to get an understanding of exactly what her situation was. In the end, what I was doing would help everyone.

The place smelled musty, as old homes do after being closed up for any time at all. The entryway had pegs on the wall for outerwear, and I noted an assortment of old coats on one end, probably for working outside, and better ones on the other, no doubt for going into town.

Beyond that, the living room opened to the whole width of the house. Only one corner seemed occupied: a comfortable chair, a table stacked with books and magazines, a television set into a cabinet so it could be hidden from view, and a laptop leaned against the table leg. Noticing the chair had distressed patches, I concluded there'd once been a cat. Since Clara hadn't mentioned it, I assumed it had crossed the Rainbow Bridge.

Husband and cat both gone. Poor Clara. No one can replace your spouse, your other half, but the love of an animal helps. I pictured her seated in that rocker, holding her cat each night until it, too, died. No wonder she'd turned her affections to her "girls," the chickens.

Pulling myself out of that particular pit, I went on to the kitchen, which was more modern than I expected. Twin ovens hinted at a love of cooking, and the large refrigerator held more than two people could eat, much less one little old lady. The plants I'd expected were located there, where they got lots of light. I couldn't name most of them, but I guessed that Clara, being a scientist, had interests beyond raising geraniums and spider plants. The soil in the pots felt dry, so I watered each of them generously, hoping that would sustain them until a decision was made about Clara's future.

I took a quick look at the rest of the house, which was cute in the same old-fashioned way my parents' home was. The most heart-wrenching part was Clara's bedroom. Half of the space in the walk-in closet was dedicated to what I guessed had been George's favorite outfit: a plaid flannel shirt, a pair of bib overalls, and some beat-up brown boots. I understood completely. I kept some things of Don's, too. There's comfort in seeing them, touching them, smelling them from time to time.

When I finished looking through Clara's house, I locked the door and put the key back where I'd found it. Nothing I'd seen indicated the owner was failing mentally. The dishes were neatly stacked in the cupboard. The laundry had been kept up. Even the film of dust I found on the furniture was minimal, easily the collection of the week or so she'd been gone. Clara had not neglected her housework or her outside chores. A point in her favor—and Faye's.

Dusting off my hands, I called to Styx, who was still swimming after the ducks and biting at the water. He didn't obey, even after several commands, so I finally got a treat from the bag I keep in the glove compartment of the Acadia. That brought him to shore. Once he swallowed his treat, Styx shook himself off (I stayed well back). Then I dried him off with one blanket and opened the back door so he could lie (or *lay*, since Barbara wasn't around) on the other, which I'd spread on the seat. He stayed there all of twenty seconds before joining me in the front. Styx's size made squeezing between the seats quite an adventure, but he was determined.

"You smell like a wet dog," I told him in mock disgust as he settled his big butt on the passenger seat. Completely getting the joke, he grinned at me and leaned against my shoulder, dampening my shirt.

Leaving Clara's property, I turned to the left, heading for the Clausen place. "If we're exploring, we might as well do the whole lake," I told Styx, who seemed completely agreeable to the idea.

The FOR SALE sign was gone. I made a mental note to ask Faye to find out who'd bought the property. The place was as junky as I remembered, but I decided to look around, thinking there might be attractions that weren't obvious at a glance.

When I opened the car door, I wasn't quick enough. Seeing the lake ahead, Styx pushed his way out and bounded toward it before I could stop him. Huffing joyously, he plunged into the water again. Sighing deeply, I told myself it wouldn't take *that* long to dry him off a second time. In the meantime, I turned to satisfying the curiosity that had brought me there.

The house was in bad shape. Peering through the windows, I saw nothing of interest inside, no antique woodwork or salvageable items. A few battered pieces of furniture stood abandoned along the walls. Years of visits from squirrels and bugs had rendered them useless. The piles of junk around the exterior were just that—junk. As I circled the yard I saw more piles in the woods: tin cans and bottles, rusty appliances, and even a tractor with no tires or steering wheel. If someone planned to make a resort out here, he—or she—had a lot of cleanup to do before starting construction.

Finishing my circuit of the yard, I went down to the lake, where Styx was emerging from the water. I stepped back for a second, letting him do the shake thing once and then again. He ran toward me, still dripping, and I spoke firmly. "Styx. Do *not* jump. No!"

He jumped, of course, knocking me backward a few steps, then set his front paws on my shoulders, his way of letting me know how much he loved me for bringing him out there. "I know, Baby. It's a really nice lake, isn't it?"

Unable to answer verbally, Styx gave me a wet kiss and waited for me to scratch his ears. When I'd done that, he slid his feet down my front, muddying my shirt and jeans all the way, and wagged at me. Notice I didn't say he wagged his tail. Styx wags his whole body.

Heading back to my vehicle, I made repairs on my clothing as best I could, using the damp blanket. I really didn't mind. Dogs need to have fun, just like people do, and I'd brought along a jacket I could put on to cover the worst of it.

As I worked, a noise made me turn, and I saw two cars pass the drive. Headed toward the main road, they had to have come from either the Marsh place or the site where the Warner house had burned. Marsh was more likely, since there was nothing left at the other spot. I craned my neck. Seeing one car on a private lake with no permanent residents was one thing. Two was more surprising. Though I crouched and peered through the trees, all I got was a glimpse. Both vehicles were large. The first was white, the second darker. When they were gone, I chuckled at myself for gawking. Since I didn't know anyone from either the Warner or the Marsh family, what good would it have done if I had gotten a good look?

Calling to Styx, I rubbed him down with the blanket and remade his bed in the back seat. Very firmly, I told him to lie down and stay. Then I got into the front.

Following the road and my curiosity, I turned left and started around the lake to the Marsh place. I wasn't even out the Clausens' driveway when Styx jumped into the front, rubbing his wet body on me again before settling into his rightful place on the passenger seat with a satisfied huff.

There was no sign of anyone at Fred Marsh's former home, and no car tracks that would indicate someone had been there since the rain. Parking next to a battered Jeep Cherokee that looked like it hadn't moved in weeks, I got out, this time managing to do so without Styx joining me. As far as I could tell, nothing had changed since the day of Mr. Marsh's death.

"Well," I told Styx as I got back in, "I don't think those cars came from here."

The Warner place yielded a different result. I hadn't paid much attention as we passed the driveway earlier, but on the way back I slowed down to look. There were tire tracks, so the vehicles I'd seen had come from there. Had it been utilities workers sent to take care of some detail?

On Saturday?

The Warners lived somewhere near Detroit. Perhaps a relative was watching the place.

Watching what—an empty lot?

I had no answers, but I promised myself that come Monday, Faye and I would find out who'd bought the Clausen property and who might want to own more of Sweet Springs.

As long as I was there, I took a walk around the ruined Warner house, again managing to leave Styx in the car. He cried mournfully, but no way did I need a wet dog in my car who'd also rolled in ashes. Hopping from one grassy spot to the next to protect my shoes, I did a quick trip around the clearing, which smelled of burnt things. Charred and melted remnants of appliances, furniture, carpeting, and even sculpture lay scattered about. The place had been finished, or nearly so. Now it was worth nothing.

As I walked I saw little markers outlining the house, one every ten feet or so. They must have been placed there by investigators, but I didn't know what they signified.

Leaving the Warner property, I drove back around the lake, stopping again at Clara's. I'd forgotten to check on the chickens, and Faye was sure to ask about them when I told her I'd been here. In order to leave Styx trapped in the car again, I tossed a doggie treat into the back and got out while he rooted for it. He was just starting to dry, and I didn't want to go through the taking-a-dip thing again.

The chickens had food and water and looked to be content. The firewood was now neatly stacked in a rick close to the house. I should have known Faye would look after Clara, just like she looks after everyone else.

Styx had whined when I left him in the car, but his voice suddenly turned to a threatening bark. He's not usually aggressive, but he was in a strange place, and I'd gone out of his range of sight. "Calm down, Sweetie," I called. "I'm right here."

The growls didn't stop, so I hurried back. "Styx! Be quiet." He kept on, interspersing short barks with growls. His nails screeched against the glass as he pushed on it angrily, eager to get out.

"Okay, we'll go home right now." He stopped clawing at the window but let out a few more sounds to let me know he was unhappy with the place.

As I started to get in, I noticed a footprint near the rear of my vehicle. It was bigger than mine, and the tread design wasn't even close to the shoes I wore.

Had Styx barked to let me know someone was creeping around my car? I scanned the area but saw no sign of anyone. The print might have been Dale's, made when he and Faye came out yesterday.

But the rain overnight should have erased it.

As I stood puzzling over the print, Styx went ballistic, throwing himself at the window. I turned to see a man coming across the yard. He was slightly built, wearing jeans, boots, and a corduroy jacket. His face was hidden by a ski mask, his head by the coat's deep hood, but his posture was threatening. In his gloved hands he held a hoe, gripping it as if it were a quarterstaff.

Instinct warned his intentions toward me weren't good. Pulling open the car door, I threw myself inside and locked the doors. The man stopped, shoving the hoe forward in a gesture that said, "Go!"

Styx was making so much noise I could hardly think, but I was perfectly willing to do as the man indicated. Starting the car, I jammed it into reverse, sending dirt flying as I backed out of the driveway and took off toward the main road.

I was shaking on the drive back to Allport, but I tried to rationalize what had happened. In the end I decided it was one of two things. One possibility was that a relative of one of the property owners had been out there for reasons of his own and concluded I was trespassing, (which technically I was). He'd decided to scare me off and been a little too aggressive about it.

The other possibility was that a stranger had happened by and wondered if there was anything worth stealing in my vehicle. If that was the case, my macho dog had scared him off.

"Good boy, Styx," I told him. I always felt safer when my baby was with me, and in this case, he'd come through like a champion.

Chapter Thirteen

Faye

For several months, my weekends had been spent at the farm. Sometimes Dale went along, but other times, like when he was deep into the entrails of the neighbor's snow-blower, he begged off. Around ten on Saturday morning, wearing what Cramer, my youngest son, called my mom jeans, I took Buddy and drove out to the place where Barb, Retta, and I grew up. Cramer lived in the old bunkhouse, which he'd renovated into a home more tech-ish than I could understand or appreciate. Since he tended to stay up nights, he wasn't usually seen until lunchtime. Bill and Carla lived in the farmhouse, along with three girls they'd taken on as foster children after the girls' parents died.

When I came down the long driveway and parked on the grass, it felt like I was sixteen again. My mind knew Mom and Dad wouldn't come out of the house to greet me, but in my heart it still felt like they might. I got out of the car, loving the feel of the place, the sights I'd known for fifty-plus years, even the smells of manure and silage.

The youngest foster girl, six-year-old Daisy, ran toward me, her arms out in welcome. Glad as she might be to see me, her real enthusiasm was for Buddy, who greeted her as if they'd been separated for months. My one-person dog made an exception when Daisy was around. He even tolerated the mutt she'd adopted from the Humane Society, a one-eyed Lab Daisy named Brenda. It should have been Brendan, but since he'd been neutered, no one objected. Brenda limped along behind Daisy, waiting patiently for her to finish hugging Buddy before sniffing at him.

"Bill and Carla are in the garden," Daisy announced. "Digging 'taters."

As I passed the barnyard, six reindeer galloped forward to greet me until the high fence stopped them. Sure that I'd have treats for them (which I did and would provide after I greeted the humans), they followed on their side until I turned toward the garden. Daisy and the dogs stayed behind, chasing each other in some game only they understood.

My son, his wife Carla, and Iris, the oldest of the three sisters, were at the far end of the garden, harvesting potatoes. The odor of turned soil rose, and darker clumps of damp earth lay piled atop the drier topsoil. Bill was doing the digging with a pitchfork while Carla bent to pull the tubers away from the plant and toss them gently onto the ground. Iris followed, collecting them in a burlap sack. Three full ones leaning against the garden fence indicated a plentiful crop, and they were only half-way through the patch.

"Need some help?" I asked as I approached. Bill wouldn't let me do the digging, since it's hard work, but I would have enjoyed it, at least for a while. Lifting a potato plant and turning up those big, starchy goodies is a little like finding buried treasure.

Bill straightened, bending backward to ease strained muscles. "Pansy wants you to look at one of the cows."

"Okay." At the barnyard gate, I let myself in, a tricky task with several reindeer noses searching my pockets and sniffing my hands for treats. I'd cut a couple of apples into slices before leaving home, and I took them out of the zipper bag and distributed them, making sure everyone got his or her share. Then, pushing the deer gently out of my way, I entered the barn in search of Pansy.

If Iris was the Earth-goddess type and Daisy was the budding socialite, Pansy, the middle sister, was the animal whisperer. She was currying Agnetha, smoothing her coat with the curved metal gadget. I greeted the girl and patted the horse that was technically mine but practically Pansy's.

"We rode up to the top of the hill to look for color this morning," she said without stopping her task. "It was really pretty when the sun came up behind the trees."

"I'll bet it was. What's wrong with the cow?"

"She got her leg caught in some barbed wire. The cut's little, so Bill doesn't want to call the vet—"

Money was always an issue for Bill—in fact, for all three of my sons. While they weren't as hopeless as their grandmother pronounced them, they probably would never be financially comfortable. It was because they cared about living beings more than they cared about money, and I had no problem with that.

Pansy's concern showed on her serious face. "You're worried about the cut," I said. "Let's take a look."

I'm certainly not a veterinarian, but a lifetime of being surrounded by animals has given me some skill with minor illnesses and accidents among our animal friends. I checked the cow's leg as the girl watched anxiously. The wound was small and almost certain to heal by itself, but I could see that Pansy didn't want to leave it to chance. "We've got some bag balm somewhere, right?"

"Sure, but that's for udders, not legs."

"I think it's just what we need for this."

Once she located the jar, I patted the cow's neck and talked to her while Pansy smeared the lanolin-based cream over the cut. She seemed relieved to have done something, and the cow meandered off, unconcerned with the doings of mere humans.

Pansy went back to currying Agnetha, so I picked up a brush and went to work on Dolly, who had once been a cart horse on

Mackinac Island. When my sons moved to the farm, we'd let the handlers up there know we were willing to adopt horses too old or sick to pull anymore. We gave the animals a comfortable place to live out their lives, and the handlers avoided the stigma of selling them for dog food. Dolly's lung problems had made it difficult for her to draw carts up the hills on the island, but she was better since coming to the farm, where life made no demands on her. Bill had already been contacted by a handler who'd be sending us another retiree from the Island's stock of horses when the tourist season ended in a few weeks.

As we worked, I told Pansy about the hens at Clara's house. "How could she leave them out there?" she asked in disbelief. Pansy almost single-handedly cared for the flock of peafowl on the farm, since the birds didn't tolerate just anyone. "Somebody should turn her in to the cops."

"I made sure they're okay, and I'll go back every few days," I assured her. "I just feel bad that Clara can't see to them herself."

"Can't she tell the people at the Meadows she's going home whether they like it or not?"

"The doctor apparently thinks she's in danger out there. She's old, and she has some mental issues."

"She's crazy?"

"Not crazy, in fact she seems perfectly sane to me. They say she has spells of delirium, though, so she could easily get hurt."

"I guess she does need somebody to look after her, then."

My answer was more an argument inside my head than a reply to Pansy. "Except if her mental state is declining, you'd expect to see signs of it. Retta says the house is as neat as the yard." I didn't want to think about how Retta knew that, but she'd texted me that morning, promising details when we got together.

Giving Agnetha's rump a final pat, Pansy moved on to Anni-Frid, our third horse. I continued to work on Dolly, a much larger area to cover. While it's considered a chore by many, grooming a horse is soothing for me, like petting a cat or scratching a dog's ears. Dolly's hide fluttered every once in a while as the brush passed over it, relaxing the muscles and removing dirt and loose hair. Lulled into saying more than I should have, I told Pansy about Clara's contention that her niece wanted her property.

"Clara seemed okay to me," I finished. "It's hard to think she might lose her home and her freedom because a relative wants to make a commission from selling her property."

We worked for a few minutes more before Pansy said, "This lady lives on a lake?"

"Sweet Springs is what's called a spring-fed lake. The water comes from an underground aquifer, so it's clear and clean."

"Mr. Getzmeyer talked in class last week about bottling water. He says it's usually bad for the environment, but companies make people think it's good."

Pansy's fifth-grade science teacher was a confirmed environmentalist, and his views on natural living and wise stewardship of our planet had made him her current idol.

I thought of Retta's refrigerator, the top shelf stacked with plastic bottles of water. "I guess some people feel that way."

"What if somebody wants to fill water bottles out of that lady's lake? What if they want her in that nursing home so she doesn't see them doing it?"

"I think there's more to the process than filling bottles and selling them. There are laws and rules about it."

"Oh."

We went on with our tasks, but as I breathed in Dolly's pungent, horsey smell, I was thinking. In Pansy's childish mind, Gail Sherman was hauling empty plastic bottles out to Sweet

Springs to sell to the bottled water drinkers of the world. Though her mental image was wrong, her basic idea might not be.

CHAPTER FOURTEEN

Retta

By the time I made it back to Allport, it was a few minutes before twelve, which is when my bank closes on Saturdays. On the way I'd decided not to tell my sisters about the man at Clara's house. Barbara would only sniff and say something about my snooping, and Faye would worry. Nothing bad had come of it, so it would be a secret between Styx and me.

Styx remained in the car, reeking in that wet-dog way, while I went inside. I had quite a few transactions to complete, so the drive-through wasn't an option. The teller's manner grew sulky as the clock ticked to almost ten after by the time we got everything done, but the job requires working with customers, even those who show up near closing time. As I left I pretended not to notice the nasty look I got from the manager, who stood at the door, waiting to lock up behind me.

Coming out of the bank, I ran into Rick Chou—literally. I'd stopped for a moment to put my paperwork into my purse, and I stepped forward again without looking. At the same time, Rick rounded the corner, head bent to protect his eyes from dirt the wind had lifted from the sidewalk. When we collided, he put out a hand to steady me.

"Ms. Stilson! I'm so sorry."

I was glad I'd buttoned my coat all the way to hide the mud Styx had smeared on me, but still, I was a mess from my trip to Sweet Springs. Only a pressing need to visit the bank had made me chance the trip in my state, and of course I ran into the most attractive man I'd seen in weeks.

The best I could do was smile coquettishly. “Totally my fault. I wasn’t watching where I was going.”

Taking my arm, Rick escorted me to a sheltered corner of the bank building. “Your sister called to say you’ve decided to take me on as a client. I appreciate that.”

I was appreciating the way one lock of his dark hair swept over his forehead. “She’s probably on the hunt for your ex-wife as we speak. If travel becomes necessary, that will be my part.”

“Your sisters don’t travel?”

“Barb says she’s seen enough of the world, and for Faye, Allport’s pretty much all there is.”

“But you have a different outlook.” His tone hinted I was the wise one.

“I’ve been a few places,” I said modestly.

“I’d like to hear about that sometime.”

It was the most obvious of hints, and I hesitated for a moment. I’d been seeing Lars Johannsen for several months, but Lars lived in New Mexico. He’d visited a couple of times over the summer, but when he left the last time, I’d been irritated with him. He and Rory Neuencamp had gone out to Rory’s cabin and spent three full days putting a new roof on it. Of course they’d come in to take Barbara and me to dinner each evening, but I still felt neglected. Out of seventy-two hours in Michigan, Lars had spent twenty-four of them with Rory.

Barbara was her usual brusque self when I mentioned it. “Good grief, Retta. The man’s enjoying himself, and the cabin certainly could do with some modernizing.”

That was fine for her to say, since she and Rory could see each other as often as they wanted to. If Lars really cared, wouldn’t he want to spend every minute of his time in Michigan with me?

Rick was waiting for an answer. "I'd like that very much," I told him, setting a hand on the sleeve of his smooth leather jacket. When we parted, we had a dinner date for Monday evening. Actually, it could have been that very night, but a girl never wants to let a man think she's got nothing else to do.

CHAPTER FIFTEEN

Barb

I had lunch by myself on Saturday, since Faye was at the farm and Rory had gone bow hunting. Though I considered that a strange pastime, I knew enough not to say so in northern Michigan, where many depend on such pastimes for food, sport, and the trade hunters bring to the area.

It was a nice change to choose a restaurant without considering someone else's opinion. Though Rory didn't refuse to eat Thai food, I was aware he wasn't a fan. It's a common problem with couples, and as Henry Higgins complains in *My Fair Lady*, in order to take each other's wishes into account, a twosome often ends up doing something neither of them really wants to do. Loving the smell of ginger and the delicate ambiance of our local Thai restaurant, I often ate there when Rory wasn't around. In similar fashion I suspected he chose Don's Dogs when lunching by himself.

After a half portion of Drunken Noodles, I put the remainder in a take-out carton and left the restaurant. A pickup truck was passing and the driver, seeing me, pulled over to the curb. "Hey, Aunt Barb."

"Cramer!" I walked over and leaned in the passenger side window. "How are things?"

"Good." He gestured at the restaurant. "Did you have lunch there?"

"Yes. I love their jasmine tea."

"Me too. Wish I'd come along when you were going in instead of coming out."

An idea had formed in my head at the sight of him. “Are you really busy with work right now, Cramer?”

He leaned his elbow on the steering wheel. “Everybody wants their computer fixed day before yesterday, but I keep up.”

“Great. I need a little work done.”

“Sure thing. I can come to the office—”

“Um, no.” Opening the door, I got into the truck, which smelled faintly of French fries. “This is something we’re going to keep between us.” I grimaced. “Say no if you want to, because it’s not totally legal.”

Cramer regarded me sideways, a slight smile playing at his lips. “You need a hacker.”

“Yes.”

“What makes you think I’d do something like that—I mean—”

“It’s my understanding that anybody who *can* hack will, if it’s important to them.”

After a moment Cramer chuckled. “I forget you spent a long time as an Assistant D.A.”

“Met a few hackers in my day, and you, my dear, if you aren’t one already, are a hacker waiting to happen.”

The smile turned to a full grin. “I’m white-hat all the way, Aunt Barb. I’ve done a little, but just a few times, and just for fun.” He scratched at the beard he’d started growing, which made him look like a kid dressed as Noah for a church-school play. “I bet you’re going to entice me farther down the path.”

“It’s a very good cause.” I told him about Lady Tattletale, ending with, “She hasn’t succeeded in putting Rory’s job in jeopardy yet, but she needs to be stopped.”

“And she has the skills to hide her identity?”

"Apparently. Rory doesn't want to treat it like a big deal, but I can tell it bothers him."

Cramer's hand left the beard and scrubbed through his shoulder-length hair. "I'll see what I can do, but you'll have to give me all the information you can get your hands on."

Getting out of the truck I promised, "I'll talk to Janet at the city office and ask her to help."

Cramer shifted into gear. "Phone calls I can't do much with, but if she'll forward me the emails, I can find out where they came from."

"Good." Did I feel guilty asking my nephew to use his skills to sniff out Rory's pest? A little. But Rory was too noble to help himself, and I suspected Lady Tattletale didn't intend to stop until she'd destroyed Allport's chief of police.

CHAPTER SIXTEEN

Faye

Iris, Pansy, and Daisy were raised in the church, though the one they'd attended was, to put it in Barb's terms, "slightly medieval." Bill and Carla weren't churchgoers, but they didn't want to dismiss out of hand what the girls' now-deceased parents had taught them. The compromise we worked out was that Iris, Pansy, and Daisy came into town with me on most Saturdays when I left the farm, spent the night in my guest room, and went to church Sunday with either Retta or me. Dale, who always made the tired joke about the church roof caving in if he ever entered, generally made himself scarce on Sunday mornings.

Daisy enjoyed getting dressed up, which was the custom at Retta's church, so she usually went there, her hair curled, her nails polished, and her fragrance upscale. Pansy preferred my church, where things were less formal and they sang "good" songs. Always the diplomat, Iris alternated between the two.

Since we had a guest youth choir at my church that week, all three girls chose to attend with me on Sunday morning. They made a pretty picture, as Barb, Retta, and I must have long ago, similar in looks and like stair steps in height. I won't say the girls were always perfectly behaved—Daisy giggled at inopportune times and Pansy had a tendency to snort when the Scripture reading included words like *breast* and *ass*. Still, they were willing to attend, which was more than my boys had been. I enjoyed the worship hour even more than usual with them beside me.

After the service we went to my house, where we changed clothes and got Buddy before heading back to the farm. Cramer had done the morning chores and then gone somewhere with friends for the day. Bill and Carla had taken the opportunity provided by the girls' absence to drive to Traverse City for a fall festival. I had the girls and the farm to myself until five.

Carla was a vegetarian, and though she didn't insist the rest of the family follow her choices, there was seldom anything in their refrigerator I considered edible. Knowing this, I brought along a cooler of real food I'd prepared for Sunday dinner: fried chicken, shrimp salad, green beans fried in bacon fat with almonds and bacon bits, and a chocolate dessert I invented: brownies covered with cream-cheese-mixed-with-whipped-topping covered with more whipped topping. Everything looked yummy, and there was plenty for us to eat and still have leftovers for the girls' lunches at school the next day.

My daughter-in-law didn't mind me treating her girls to comfort foods on my visits. They hadn't known much indulgence in their short lives, and Carla had once commented to me that a few extra calories were a small price to pay if the girls felt a little spoiled when I treated them to my full array of cooking skills.

After the meal we went for a walk, or as Pansy quipped, "a waddle, since we're so full." Autumn makes Michiganders aware of the dwindling number of days left when walking is unhindered by boots, icy winds, and snow drifts. The colors were still brightening, and we followed the path up the hill, past the barn, and into the woods. Buddy and Brenda explored holes and sniffed at trees. Pansy and Daisy ran ahead, finding leaves they liked and putting them into bags for craft-making. Iris, conscious of her dignity, stayed beside me and made polite conversation. "Pansy says you're working on a case, Aunt Faye?"

We'd become "Aunts," an easy term for those who are like family but not actually related.

"Two of them," I told her. "There's an older woman we're trying to help, and a man who needs us to locate someone."

"I'll bet people are happy when you find out things for them."

Our work didn't always lead to happiness. In her case, we'd found that her mother was dead. To steer the conversation away from that, I went back in time to our first investigation.

"In one case we had just about everyone in town mad at us."

"Everybody?"

"Well, one man in particular was our nemesis. Do you know that word?"

Iris was the reader of the trio. "Your worst enemy."

"Right. He wasn't happy, even though we found the truth."

"Did he say he was sorry when you were right in the end?"

I shook my head. "Stan Wozniak isn't the type who apologizes."

"He sounds like a real stinker."

I chuckled. "That's a good word for him."

"I'll bet Aunt Barb told him off." Pansy, who'd been eavesdropping, joined us, making the old, dead leaves rustle by dragging her feet. "She isn't afraid of anybody."

"Certainly not Mr. Wozniak," I agreed. "I'm pretty sure he knows by now not to get in her way."

***

Though I made most of the day-to-day decisions concerning Harriet, Dale visited his mother every Sunday evening. Going to the Meadows was hard for him, both because he hated seeing her so frail and because the buzzing alarms and cries of incoherent patients made him jumpy while he was there and depressed afterward. I provided moral support, keeping up a bright line of chatter both during and after the visits. When Carla and Bill returned that afternoon I went home, changed my clothes again, and drove Dale to the nursing home.

Harriet sat slumped in her wheelchair, a tray of food on a rolling cart before her. Gently pulling her into a more upright position, I looked at the tray and shook my head. The food didn't look bad, and when I touched a plate, it felt warm, but she'd eaten almost nothing. While I understood the efficiency of feeding almost everyone the same things, Harriet wouldn't touch the green beans, would only taste the coleslaw, and would cut and chew no more than one or two bites of the meat, since it took effort on her part. Pudding was the one thing on the tray she'd finish. If Harriet had a tooth left, it was her sweet tooth.

"Chicken looks good, Mom," Dale said as we sat on her bed.

She surveyed the tray with distaste. "You can have it."

"No, thanks. We already ate." It was a lie he told every week, since his presence seemed to awaken some maternal need in Harriet to feed him. Taking up her fork, Dale speared a small bite and held it before her. "Try it."

Harriet obeyed, which always surprised me. As combative and contrary as she was to everyone else, she complied without argument to any command Dale gave.

When she'd eaten the first bite, he cut another and fed it to her. "How is it, Mom?"

"Good," she mumbled.

My throat closed at the scene, both pleased and saddened at seeing how our roles reverse as we age. I remembered feeding my own children bite by bite, encouraging and coaxing, as Harriet had no doubt done decades ago for her youngest son.

"That's good, Mom. Here comes another one, so open up."

Suddenly I was fighting tears—sorrow for Harriet, so unlike herself, and longing for the past, when both she and Dale functioned with complete, almost fierce independence. "I'm going to look in on Clara," I said softly. Harriet wouldn't miss me as long as she had her boy there, and it was good for Dale to do something for her on his own.

Clara was in bed, and her vague greeting revealed she wasn't sure who I was.

"It's Faye Burner, Mrs. Knight. You asked if I'd look into—some things for you?" I didn't specify the things, since Clara's roommate was awake and listening with interest.

"That's nice of you, dear." Though she was polite, I could see Clara didn't have a clue what I was talking about.

"I went out and made sure your chickens are okay."

That she responded to. "My chickens, yes. Make sure you scoop out of the brown bag, Gail. They don't like the other kind." She smiled weakly and gripped my arm to emphasize her words. "Only the feed in the brown bag."

As I left the room, the aide I'd spoken to before was pushing a wheelchair containing a semi-conscious patient down the corridor. Stopping her I said, "Clara Knight isn't doing well today."

Her dark brows met over her eyes. "I know. She started in again last night, imagining all sorts of things. Today she's been kind of out of it, sleepy and nauseated."

"She was fine on Wednesday."

She nodded. "Isn't that what I told you? She's in her right mind one day and out to lunch the next."

As we drove home, doubt nagged at me. Had I put the agency in a sticky situation? The niece wouldn't be happy to learn private investigators had responded to her crazy aunt's complaints. How long before she called and demanded we keep our noses out of her family business?

CHAPTER SEVENTEEN

Retta

Anyone who saw Barbara prepare for one of her Correction Events would split a side laughing. She takes it all so very seriously—Barbara Ann Evans, Avenger of Grammar Crimes. At first when I'd joined her crusade to fix spelling errors and such around Allport, she hadn't been thrilled. After a while, though, she'd begun to enjoy my company. We laughed a lot, which was good. Barbara needs to laugh more. In addition, I was pleased to be her partner, with Faye for once the sister with no idea what the other two were up to.

After I fell off the platform, Barbara turned cautious. "What if it happens again?" she asked. "What if there isn't a convenient clump of bushes to break your fall?"

I'd promised to be ex*treme*ly careful as we went on another quest. When Barbara proposed changes to a sign in front of a local restaurant, I noted it required no ladders or climbing. The sign was at ground level, made with those plastic letters that fit into a track, so all we had to do was move things around.

We pulled up just after midnight, parking in the alley and skirting the street light. Along with the smell of old grease, I immediately recognized the problem as we approached the sign. In the list of specials for the week one line read: TUESDAY-TACOES. Once we removed the unnecessary *E,* we'd be on our way. I did that, but Barbara frowned at the Thursday line, which said, POTATOES, HAM & SQUASH. Taking a pair of scissors and a square of black poster board from her knapsack, she made a comma. When she was finished, the Thursday line said, POTATOES, HAM, & SQUASH.

"Why the extra comma?"

"It's not extra." She pointed, as if a glance would convince me. "It's required."

Frowning, I considered the phrase. "I don't see what difference it makes."

"It specifies there are three separate items. Otherwise one might think the ham and squash are mixed together."

"What if they are? I don't see the need for an extra comma."

"It's not extra," she repeated. "It's called an Oxford comma, and its purpose is clarification."

Barbara was the Grammar Ninja—some might say Grammar Nazi—and I was just along for the fun of it. I didn't mind helping her clean up the all-too-common mistakes in local usage. For many in Allport, knowing better than to say, "I seen that movie," is the height of grammatical correctness. Still, the Oxford comma thing seemed fussy to me.

But then, that's Barbara to a *T*.

"If you ask me, it looks dumb," I said. "Four words—no, three words and an ampersand, and you put in two commas?"

"Nobody asked you." She was crouched, picking up bits of black poster board she'd trimmed away, but she looked up at me with her "Barbara disapproves" expression.

Reaching up, I took the home-made comma down. "Look at that. It's perfectly clear without it. If you order Thursday's special, you get three things."

Snatching the piece from my hand, she put it back in place. "Now the reader is *sure* she'll get three things. Without the comma, it might only be two."

Knowing I couldn't win, and aware we shouldn't stand there all night arguing about it, I let out a big sigh. "Whatever, Barbara

Ann. Let's go before you find something else that doesn't suit your Oxford sensibilities."

CHAPTER EIGHTEEN

Barb

At the Allport Public Safety Facility, I was led to a ten-by-ten office stacked with so many books, pamphlets, and papers about fire, fire prevention, and fire investigation that it seemed itself a fire hazard. Fire Marshal Ray Socolovitch, also deputy chief, was a fortyish man with a receding hairline and a Sam Elliot mustache. The fire crew, though hired and paid by the city, was contracted to cover the entire county. Since Ray was investigating the incident at Sweet Springs, Rory had asked him to tell me what he could about it.

"Place burned right to the ground," he told me after the preliminaries had been completed. "An old lady on the other side of the lake called it in—"

"Clara Knight?"

He nodded. "That's her. The smell of smoke woke her up, but by the time we got a crew out there, there wasn't much to do but save the chimney." He grinned at the old fire-fighters' joke.

"And you suspect arson?"

"I can't comment on that, since the case is ongoing." He smiled to excuse the refusal.

I smiled too. "The fact that it's ongoing over a month after it happened indicates you're not comfortable calling it accidental."

Socolovitch shrugged noncommittally, and I realized the interview could go no further if I asked direct questions. I decided to do some guessing instead, in hopes he'd give up some clues if I wandered onto the right track.

"Let me tell you about my case," I began. "Mrs. Knight is now at the Meadows. Apparently she's not mentally competent."

He frowned. "Really? I didn't get that impression."

"Could you explain the impression you did get?"

"I remember thinking she was really with it for an old gal." Socolovitch folded his arms across his wide chest. "When she smelled smoke, she went out to her dock with binoculars and located the fire. She called it in, giving specific directions about how the road circles the lake. She knew we'd see the fire from the main road and might not realize we had to go past her place to get to it." As another memory rose, he chuckled. "At first light when we were cleaning up, she came putting across the lake in a Detroit Lions boat with coffee and fresh-made cookies."

"That doesn't sound like someone who's slipping mentally."

He adjusted some files on his desk. "Later I interviewed her about the fire, and again, she seemed sharp to me. The owners of the house had worked on it all weekend—this happened the Tuesday after Labor Day. Mrs. Knight went over to see what they'd got done before they headed back south. She said they were real proud of it and they'd never have burned it down."

"But that's where your investigation is leading?"

He cleared his throat. "Nadine and Earl Warner were back in Auburn Hills twenty hours before the house caught fire."

"They might have left something on, like a space heater."

Again he looked as if he'd like to say more. "We didn't find that to be the case."

I paused, trying to figure out what he couldn't tell me. "You found clear indications of arson." When he merely quirked an eyebrow I said, "But the fire was set after they left?"

Socolovitch sighed. "Let's just say there are unanswered questions."

He couldn't share his theory of what the answers might be, so I shared my own unanswered questions. "Clara thinks her niece, who's a real estate agent, wants her out of the way so she can sell her property." Drawing a circle on his desk with my finger, I pointed as I explained. "One quarter of the Sweet Springs property has been on the market for some time. According to what we're told, it sold quite recently. Another of the property owners died last week, so it's possible that piece might go up for sale soon. Clara's property makes a third section that could end up on the market. It seems odd to me that the fourth and final property has experienced a suspicious fire."

Socolovitch was intrigued. "You think someone wants to own the whole lake?"

"We're considering the possibility."

"Why?"

I shrugged. "No clue."

He rubbed at his neck. "That fits my case."

"What do you mean?"

"Just that the Warners planned to retire up here. That house was their dream, so—"

"—They wouldn't burn it down for the insurance."

Rubbing at his jaw, he chuckled. "After ten years in this job I'd never say what someone might do, but it doesn't feel like owner arson to me." Unaware he'd passed the point of confidentiality he added, "It wasn't an accident, though. Someone made sure there wouldn't be anything left for us to save."

I thought of the markers Retta had described and guessed they indicated points where fuel had been applied. "The arsonist didn't try to hide that the place was burned on purpose."

His curt nod indicated I was correct.

Having learned what he could legally tell me and a little more, I rose to go. "I appreciate the help. We'll keep what you told us private, and we'd appreciate the same consideration."

He rose to shake my hand. "From what Rory tells me, you won't even tell him what we talked about."

"It always pays to keep professional matters separate from personal."

The look I got was quizzical, and I realized I sounded cold and a little pompous. *Oh, well*, I told myself as I left the building, *I might sound that way because it's the way I am.*

***

Back at the office, I went to my computer and started a search. We had the Warners' first names and their city of residence, so without much trouble I found the specific address, along with a phone number. Setting my glasses down a little on my nose to help with focus, I entered the digits into my phone, listening for a little beep with each one to make sure I got it right. A woman answered.

"Is this Nadine Warner?"

"Yes."

I explained who I was. "I'm a private detective working for Clara Knight. Do you know her?"

"Of course," she replied. "Clara and George have lived on Sweet Springs since I knew the place existed."

"Which is how long?"

She took a moment. "We've been married eleven years, and I started going up there with Earl a year or two before that. We drove up for the funeral when George died a few years back."

"Have you noticed odd behavior from Clara lately?"

"What do you mean?"

When I explained that she was in a nursing home due to possible dementia, Mrs. Warner gasped. "That's ridiculous! We invited Clara to our campfire Labor Day Weekend. She came over in her little boat with home-made chips and salsa, and we sat around until ten, telling stories and laughing."

"You believed she was mentally competent at that point?"

"More than competent." Nadine gave a little giggle. "I watch what I say around Clara, because she knows something about everything. I'm always afraid she'll think I'm a dummy."

"That's very helpful." It was and it wasn't. It helped to know that two objective people thought Clara was sane, but it didn't solve the question. Faye had admitted at breakfast that Clara mistook her for Gail when she stopped in the night before.

Had Clara's doctors checked for physical causes of her spells of confusion? Brain tumors, chemical imbalances, even a urinary tract infection could have odd effects in older people.

Picking up a cow-shaped stress ball from my desk, I squeezed it a few times, trying to decide what to say next. Since Nadine didn't sound like a criminal I said, "I'm sorry your house burned."

"Thanks." Her voice turned sad. "We put so much work into it, and now it's gone."

"Will you rebuild?"

"No money. We borrowed quite a bit to build the new place."

"I'm sorry." I avoided the insurance problem. No sense rubbing salt in the wound. "What will you do?"

"We might have to sell the property to pay off the loan. It's that or pay for years on a dead horse."

That rang an alarm bell. "Have you been contacted by a real estate agent, by chance?"

"Well, not formally, but the weekend after the fire, we drove north to see the damage. While we were up there we ran into someone Earl knows, and she said if we did consider selling, she hoped we'd let her represent us. At the time we said no, because we were sure we'd rebuild. We didn't know then it was arson." Her voice shook a little. "The insurance company can refuse to pay, even if they can't prove we set fire to our own place."

"The agent who wants to represent you, who is that?"

"I don't remember her name."

"Oh." I set the stress ball down and watched it return to its original shape.

"I can ask Earl when he gets home. Or you could ask Clara. He told me she and the real estate agent are related somehow."

CHAPTER NINETEEN

Barb

Because it might pertain to our investigation, I told Faye about the fire marshal's suspicions. I also reported my conversation with Nadine Warner and the fact she and her husband were forced to consider selling their lake property.

"I shouldn't say a case of arson comes as a relief," Faye said, typing information into our case files as she spoke, "but it makes Clara's story more believable, which makes me feel better about us taking her case."

I wasn't aware an official decision had been made, but I figured we could do some further work for Mrs. Knight. "While you were gone yesterday, I went online and looked up Sweet Springs in the plat book." I handed her a sheet with property owners' names: Clara Knight, Mark Clausen, Nadine and Earl Warner, and Caleb Marsh. "That last one will change, of course." Taking up a pen, I scratched its point on my notepad until I got ink then made a note to find out who Marsh's heirs were.

As Faye considered the list, I summed up what we knew. "Absentee owner Mark Clausen has apparently sold his parcel, but no change has been made in the official records."

"Knowing how overworked the county clerk's staff is, that isn't surprising," Faye commented.

"Of course a deed doesn't have to be recorded right away, or even recorded at all," I said. "If Gail bought the land herself, she might keep it quiet to gain time to buy up the other parcels."

"Things seem to be working out in her favor."

"True. Mrs. Warner said the fire might force them to sell the property to pay off the loan they took out on the new house. And Caleb Marsh's heirs might part with a small, cramped house at the end of a road going nowhere." Looking at the map of the area hanging on our office wall, I touched the blue, almost perfect circle that was Sweet Springs. "If Gail becomes Clara's guardian, she could control the whole lake within a few months."

Faye frowned. "For properties that have been owned by the same families for more than a century, that's odd."

"The question becomes what does she have in mind? She's no entrepreneur with deep pockets who might fund a resort. A hunting club is possible, I suppose, but we've already got several of those in the area, so I doubt that would be a money-maker."

Faye's eyes turned upward, the classic sign of memory retrieval. "Pansy suggested Gail might plan to sell the spring water." She smiled. "She pictures Gail on her hands and knees, filling plastic bottles. I know it's more complicated than that, but might Gail have something like that in mind?"

"I don't know much about the subject, but let's see what we can find out." Turning to my computer, I typed in "bottling water" and after a few misfires, found a decent site and read a few lines. "Property owners have the right to what the state calls 'reasonable use' of water resting on their land. Several farmers have been sued by their neighbors for taking lake water to irrigate crops." I was silent for a few seconds more as I read. "The ruling was that as long as it didn't drastically lower lake or stream levels—and there are specifics about how much can be taken and how often—the landowner is entitled to fair use."

Taking off my glasses, I rubbed my eyes, which stung most of the time in autumn from ragweed and mold. "I know spring water is considered ideal for bottling, but building a plant has to be pricey. Where would Gail get the money for that, even if she did own the whole lake?"

"Maybe she's offered it to an established bottler," Faye replied. "They'd either build a plant or pipe the water to where they want it."

"That's it. Gail's putting a deal together to either sell or lease Sweet Springs water to someone with the financial resources to develop it. They probably plan to market it as a specialty water brand so they can charge more."

That brought a question to Faye's mind. "Where will Gail get the money to buy two more parcels of lake property?"

"Typically in this type of financial deal, Gail will get financing from a bank because she has a deal in place. The bottler has agreed in principle, believing she'll soon own the property." I rolled my eyes. "From what we know about Gail, I'd guess she assured everyone involved that the other landowners were eager to sell and emphasized the fact she's already got half the lake under her control."

"That explains why she kept her officemate out of the loop. Competition could have raised the price on the Clausen property."

I nodded agreement. "She offered them low dollar and said it was the best they'd get."

"They're nowhere near Michigan, so how would they know the real estate market here is rebounding?" Faye's mouth twisted. "If she gets the rights to Clara's land, she'll only have to pay market price for the other two."

It wasn't a bad plan, as long as Gail worked quickly, before anyone knew what she was up to. "Do you think Gail came up with this idea on her own?"

Faye frowned. "You've met her. What do you think?"

I shrugged. "She isn't the brightest daffodil in the garden, and she's got no background for it. The woman grew up in Allport and peddles real estate on a very small scale. She shaves off her eyebrows and draws them on with a pencil two shades too dark."

"Which has nothing to do with being a criminal."

"I'll admit she radiates greed, but I can't see her making a long-range plan to obtain a string of properties, lining up a deal on said properties, and making the legal arrangements to transfer them without letting anyone in town know what she's up to."

Before Faye could argue, I switched sides. "On the other hand, she's been trading real estate for years. She might have picked up a thing or two and recognized a chance to make real money." I huffed a sigh. "Then again, we might be going in the wrong direction entirely. We need several important pieces of information, like who bought the Clausen place. We just don't know enough to decide if Gail's a big crook or a little one."

Rising from her chair with a grunt of effort, Faye said, "Let's have lunch and let ideas percolate through our brains. We might come up with something brilliant."

Pushing myself away from the computer, I followed her to the kitchen, rubbing a spot on my elbow that hurt whenever I spent too much time pecking away at a keyboard. The ulnar nerve was to blame—or maybe I was. I knew I should take frequent breaks but tended to get caught up in research and forget.

A few times each week, Faye cooked for me in an attempt to see that I got what she called "decent food." Left to my own designs, I could eat twice a day, every day, in restaurants. I'd done that for most of the twenty-plus years I lived in Tacoma. Faye did her best to counteract that sacrilege with home-cooked meals, delicious but calorie-laden.

As we ate creamy potato soup (with bacon, of course) along with French bread Faye had made that morning somewhere between 5:00 and 7:00 a.m., we continued discussing the possibility that Gail wanted to own the whole of Sweet Springs.

"Bottlers are always looking for suitable springs," Faye said. "Several places in the state fought to keep plants out, but they lost or at best got a reduction in withdrawal amounts."

"Homeowners don't have the financial resources to fight corporations and win." Taking my last spoonful of soup I mused, "I wonder what the first step would be in getting a corporation interested in a place like Sweet Springs."

"Let's find out." Faye took my empty bowl and plate from in front of me, and I was left with two bites of bread in my hand. I finished it as we made our way to the front of the house again and sat down at our respective computers.

A half hour later we knew that in order to see if a bottling plant was feasible, a person or entity first had to get the water tested. If the quality was acceptable, the state would be asked to assess the site's suitability for such an operation. Once a favorable result was obtained, the permission for water use was transferable, meaning the landowner could sell water to a bottler without further application to the state. The amount of water taken could not deplete the source, harm existing wildlife, or inconvenience other property owners on the shore.

"It would be an advantage to own all the land around the lake," Faye said. "There's nobody to object."

"Gail has probably already tested the water's purity, since that's just a matter of taking a sample. I wonder if she applied for a water use permit."

Faye leaned toward the computer, squinting a little. Rubbing at a smear on the screen, she brightened. "I don't know about that, but here's an email from my friend at the courthouse. Gail did apply to become her aunt's guardian."

"Will she be successful?"

"Clara's doctor signed her into the Meadows for her safety. The staff will testify that her sanity comes and goes. How long will a judge consider the question of whether an octogenarian can return to her home on a lake miles from anyone?"

"Someone from the court has to interview Clara and ask if she wants a guardian."

"Then we have to hope the interviewer shows up on one of her good days," Faye said. "Anyone who saw her the way I did last time will conclude she's unable to answer for herself."

"Guardianship would allow Gail to sell or lease the property, as long as she's acting in her aunt's best interests."

"She'll say Clara needs money to pay for her care at the Meadows."

"Which might be true." Despite Faye's concern for Clara, I wasn't convinced we should take on this fight. "Do we want to interfere with a relative's perfectly legal decision?"

"I wish we could speak to a doctor about her," Faye mused. "When Harriet has a urinary tract infection, she gets really goofy. What if Clara's problem is something simple like that?"

I gave her a look. "You don't think people at a nursing facility would check for that sort of thing?"

"The staff at the Meadows is good, and Doctor Allen is competent, but the workers run from one patient to the next, resolving situations and preventing meltdowns. The doctor comes in once a week and sees dozens of patients in the few hours he's there."

I shuddered. "Imagine what that's like: an endless line of people dealing with pain, confusion, and debilitating illness."

Faye counted on her fingers. "So what does the court have? Gail says Clara's losing her marbles. Medical people see her mental state waver from fine to pretty much out of it. They learn that Clara lives alone, far from a hospital and possible help." Raising her palms, she asked, "Who's going to ask for an in-depth study to find out the cause of her odd behavior? A relative might, but if Gail wants Clara to remain at the Meadows, she isn't about to."

Conceding the point I said, "I suppose it's not good when the person who's trying to get control of one's land is the person who deals with her doctor."

"Clara's perfectly lucid at times," Faye insisted. "There might be a physical cause for her spells of confusion that no one's looking for because Gail keeps saying she's loony. If they could find out the cause and clear it up, Clara might get out of there."

"And go back to the springs to live on her own? Is that wise?"

She met my gaze. "It's how I'd want it if I were in her shoes."

Knowing Faye's dread of being dependent on anyone, I changed the subject. "Clara's problem aside, do we really think Gail is eliminating possible objections to her plan by buying up the other properties on the lake?"

"I certainly do. And things are falling into place for her."

"What about the convenience of a fire on one property and a death at the other? Are you thinking Gail caused either or both of those things to happen?"

Faye hesitated. That was going farther than she wanted to—at least at this point in time.

"Yoo-hoo!" Retta stuck her head into my office. "What are you two looking so serious about?"

Faye explained our theory that Sweet Springs might be the target of water developers, ending with, "I wish we knew someone who could explain all this to us in layman's terms."

Retta had taken a hairbrush out of her purse and was repairing the wind damage the trip over had caused. I considered telling her how many skin cells she was scattering over my office, but it would have been a waste of breath. Instead I said, "We need to find out how easy it is to get permission to do large water withdrawals from a place like Sweet Springs."

"I know someone you could ask, but you aren't going to like it." Retta's hair, reddish-gold this week and now in proper order, bounced as she waggled her head at me.

"And whom do you know who's a water expert?"

She snickered. "Whom, Barbara? Who even uses that word anymore? It's almost as silly as your Oxford comma thing."

I shot her a look, but she turned to Faye. "The other day Barbara and I were discussing the Oxford comma. She's a fan; I'm not."

"It provides clarity." My lips felt stiff. "If you say, 'I invited my parents—comma—Wonder Woman and Superman,' it isn't clear if the invitation included two people or four."

"And who can't figure out that Wonder Woman and Superman never had children together?" Retta shot back. "I stopped reading comics a while ago, but I'm pretty sure they didn't have any children at all. The sentence is perfectly fine with one comma."

Faye sighed. Though it was the first time she'd heard this particular argument, it wasn't the first time she'd served as sister referee. "Retta, you said you know an expert on water rights?"

"I haven't met the guy." She sat on the edge of my desk. "But some engineer moved to Allport a few months ago from Florida, where he worked at a bottling plant. Nowadays he's employed by our old buddy Stan Wozniak at WOZ Industries."

CHAPTER TWENTY

Retta

When I left the office, Barbara was preparing to drive out to the local base for WOZ Industries. The fire in her eyes told me nobody out there had better refuse her request to interview the new guy, even if Stan Wozniak had once barred her from entering the building. That was during her investigation into the death of Stan's daughter, and I thought for a while back then that either Stanley or Barbara was going to murder the other. It was simply a question of who lost control first.

Faye walked me out to my car, and I knew she was fretting over Clara's future. I'd told her I visited Clara's house and merely peeked in the windows. I did *not* tell her about the scary man who'd chased me away, because Faye worries about stuff like that, even after it's over. She'd have felt guilty about letting me go out there alone, though there was no way she could have known and she couldn't have stopped me anyway.

Faye was sure Gail Sherman was dishonest in her motives for becoming Clara's guardian. Since I'd met Clara, I was sympathetic. She seemed competent to me, and while I wasn't sure she should be living out at the springs alone, that didn't mean she needed full-time care and an ankle monitor.

When Faye mentioned the possibility of a physical cause for Clara's confusion, I asked what that might be. She listed some problems she'd seen because of Harriet's years in the nursing home. "It would be nice to talk to Doctor Allen about Clara, but HIPAA laws will prevent him from telling us anything."

"I've met Doctor Allen a few times, and I think he might tell me what we want to know."

"Really?"

I gave her arm a pat. "Let me see what I can do. Since I volunteered with the hospital auxiliary, I knew when and where the good doctor ate his lunch."

Our hospital cafeteria was the old-fashioned kind, meaning it served cardboard sandwiches, glutinous casseroles, and overly-sweet desserts. It smelled like tuna most days, with overtones of burnt coffee. Usually I avoided the place like the plague, but Dr. William Allen either enjoyed the bland food or was used to it after decades in Allport. When his rounds were finished he went there for an hour, always alone, always at the same table, and shoveled in the day's special while doing one crossword puzzle after another from those books sold in drug stores.

It took almost bumping into him to get him to notice me. When he looked up, his eyes narrowed as he tried to refocus. Flashing a big smile I said, "Dr. Allen, isn't it? You took care of my son when he broke his ankle skate-boarding."

It was obvious he didn't recall, and I hadn't expected him to. Most doctors see the problem, not the person. Still, he nodded, his expression betraying interest in me if not in the long-ago injury. "Dangerous things, those skateboards."

"May I join you?" I'd arrived with a tray, and I glanced at the almost-full cafeteria. "Everybody seems to be eating late today." It wasn't true, but he was looking at me, not at the room.

Belatedly remembering his manners, he stood. "Please, sit."

After the niceties had been observed, I steered the conversation in the direction I wanted it to go. "What keeps you busy these days, Dr. Allen?"

"Bill, please. Dr. Allen makes me feel like I'm on duty."

"We can't have that."

After we chuckled together, I waited for him to answer the question. He rambled a little about cutting back on his practice so he could spend more time with his grandchildren. That led to mention of the Meadows, where he was staff physician, a job I guessed consisted mostly of showing up and listening to the same complaints he'd heard the week before. I seized on it, though, since it was what I'd been hoping for. "Isn't that a coincidence? I was just up there." I went on to tell him about the interesting woman I'd met, "Clara Something. She tried to tell me she didn't belong in a nursing home."

He took on the injured air some medical people get that hints they know best, though the rest of us don't get it. "She's quite insistent on that point, but her personal physician signed the papers."

"Is it possible he overlooked something?"

At first his laugh was harsh, but he tried to moderate it, perhaps to appear less cynical and therefore more attractive. (Did I mention Dr. Allen is divorced?) "They all think they can go home, Ms. Stilson."

"Retta," I corrected.

"Retta, you aren't eating your lunch."

Looking at the sad square of lasagna on my tray, I tried not to flinch. I took a bite and chewed, taking a large drink of water to wash it down. Smiling, I got back to the real reason for my presence. "I'm sure someone as thorough as you looked at her physical condition to make sure she doesn't have something that's easily curable."

"Oh, yes." Because he said it too quickly, I concluded he hadn't been all that thorough. "She'd been failing for several months, and her family recounted several incidents where she might have been hurt or even died at home." He adjusted his glasses. "I was told she lives—lived—some distance from the hospital, and the—er—reporting family member could no longer take responsibility for her safety."

I had to tread carefully so as not to seem too interested in Clara. Taking a second bite of my cold, greasy main dish, I said, "I had an aunt once whose behavior got weirder and weirder until they finally realized she had a brain tumor. I hope Mrs. Knight doesn't have one of those."

He made a gesture of dismissal. "Of course we ruled out the obvious possibilities. There's no brain tumor."

"I understand some drugs can make people act funny."

"Clara didn't take any—" He stopped himself. "Her personal physician made the decision. We make thorough evaluations of each patient, both when they arrive and periodically afterward. No patient at the Meadows is neglected."

His voice had taken on an aggrieved tone, so I hastened to change the subject. At the same time, I began planning my getaway as soon as I could manage it. *Bat your eyes and smile*, I told myself. *Then remember suddenly that you have a meeting across town in twenty minutes.*

CHAPTER TWENTY-ONE

Barb

I probably could have found out the new WOZ employee's name some other way, but part of me still resented the high-handed treatment we'd once been subjected to from the company's owner and CEO. As a result, instead of calling or asking discreet questions around Allport, I went directly to the local office, determined to let the people there know their boss didn't intimidate me one bit.

WOZ had started as a stone quarry, but the Wozniak family had diversified over the years. Nowadays Stan was into computer parts, automotive accessories, and a dozen other profitable enterprises. The Allport location wasn't headquarters anymore, but it was still the most impressive edifice in the county. Located near the original quarry, WOZ Allport was three stories of glass and brick. It was a '70s-type building, with suspended fluorescent lighting and dark-paneled walls. It wasn't well sound-proofed, and inside the lobby I could hear the beep-beeps of backup alarms from the heavy equipment down in the pit.

When I asked at the front desk, the Barbie-like receptionist said I must be looking for Enright Landon, head of operations. I asked if I might speak to Mr. Landon.

"Let me see if he's in his office." Picking up the phone with exaggerated care so as not to damage her extra-long nails, the woman glanced up and stopped, a wary expression on her face.

"Miz Evans, isn't it?" The voice came from behind me, but I didn't have to look to know who it was.

I turned, hoping my neck didn't flush as it does sometimes when I'm nervous or angry. "Mr. Wozniak. I heard you'd left Allport to live in Detroit."

"I drive up from time to time to see to things," he said. "This time of year, the drive itself is a reward."

Making a sound of agreement, I waited, wondering what came next. Would we discuss the fall colors at length? Would he order me off his property? I had no idea.

"You're here to see Landon?"

"Um, yes. We have a case that involves water rights, and we were told he's the person to speak to."

Wozniak nodded. "Landon knows more about water than anyone I've ever met." What happened next made me recoil in disgust. Stan Wozniak actually put his hand on my shoulder. "I'll take you up. His office is on the second floor."

Confused by his benevolent attitude and feeling weird about being touched by Wozniak without invitation, I let myself be led down the corridor. The only other time I'd been there, he had watched from his second floor office as I was escorted out of the building. It seemed we were going to let bygones be bygones.

As Wozniak led me to the elevator, chatting about Mr. Landon's vast knowledge of land and water usage law, I reminded myself that people like him often simply forget incidents in their past when they've behaved badly. If they stayed angry after every fit they threw, they'd soon have no one to talk to. I guessed his victims seldom brought up past unpleasantness. Who wants to relive the horrors of being screamed at?

When we stepped off the elevator, Wozniak touched my arm lightly to steer me onto the carpeted strip that led to Landon's office. It took everything I had not to shiver. He seemed unaware but stopped in the doorway of an office where a man sat at a cluttered desk. About forty, with a full head of hair balanced by a full, dark beard, he wore a khaki shirt with two pockets. One held pencils and pens, the other bulged with something tubular, possibly a bottle. Half-glasses sat near the tip of his nose.

"Enright, are you busy?"

His voice was assertive, and I guessed no one in his employ would ever say, "Yes, I am, Mr. Wozniak. Come back later."

Slipping the glasses off and laying them on the desk pad, Landon looked up, his manner deferential. "Just doing some forms for the state."

"No end to those." His tone hinted there should be. "This is Ms. Evans of the Smart Detective Agency. She'd like advice on water usage laws."

"Oh." Landon glanced briefly at me then looked away. "Sure."

I hesitated, hoping Wozniak would leave, but he didn't. Behind us came a woman with a cart containing coffee with all the trimmings. I was offered decaf, regular, or amaretto. Though it smelled wonderful, I refused, eager to get down to business. Wozniak waved the woman off, and she backed away with a smile. He stayed.

I considered asking for privacy but didn't have a good reason to do so. Having seen Wozniak angry, I wasn't interested in experiencing his temper again. My questions for Landon would have to be hypothetical.

"Mr. Landon, I'm looking into a case where an individual seems to be attempting to buy all of the property around a lake. My sisters and I theorize this person might be thinking of getting into water bottling. What can you tell me about the process?"

Landon gathered himself as if I'd asked him to interpret the laws listed in Leviticus. He looked at me only occasionally as he spoke, and for the briefest moment. "It depends upon the body of water, of course. Lakes in Zone A locations are excellent sources for bottled water. The state would do an assessment of the possible repercussions of water withdrawal. If it's determined the lake can sustain itself, and if no neighbors object, the permit would in most cases be granted."

"Then it would be an advantage to have only one landowner on the lakeshore."

"Well, yes." He used a fist to make light taps on his desktop, apparently a nervous gesture. "One seldom gets legal objections from deer and raccoons."

Wozniak, whose brain was meant for business, caught on immediately. "Would it make more sense to build your own plant or simply buy up the land and sell it to an established bottler?"

"Most people don't have the capital to get a plant started on their own," Landon replied. "Bottlers are always looking for new sites, though, so it's potentially profitable if a landowner offers a viable property with no objections from local sources."

Wozniak's left hand rose to rub lightly at his chin. "No lengthy court battles holding up the plans."

"Exactly. One Florida bottler I'm aware of encountered difficulty when local citizens objected to the closing of a local swimming hole. There was another case where people tried to stop the transport of piped water over delicate habitats. In the end landowners were allowed to do as they wanted with their property, but the controversy caused a good deal of delay."

I asked a few more questions, and Landon explained the basics of bottling water. His manner was precise but emotionless, and it felt like I'd asked Siri for information, not a human.

Wozniak picked up on the possible pitfalls of the premise with an ease that surprised me. Like him or not, the man had a quick grasp of business, even a business he'd never been involved in.

"I think I understand the process better now." I said when my questions had been answered. "Might we call on you again if we need more information?" In reply Landon wrote his cell number on a sheet of note paper and handed it to me. He looked up for a millisecond before lowering his gaze to the desktop again.

As we returned to the elevator, Wozniak said, "So your agency is thriving, Ms. Evans?"

"It is." *No thanks to you,* I thought, but I wasn't going to be the one to reignite old fires.

He seemed to want to say more, but the silence grew long as we waited for the car to return to our floor. When the ding indicated it had, Wozniak stepped back. "I'll let you get back to it then." He watched me as the doors closed, his brow furrowed. He was probably concerned I'd disrupt operations at WOZ with my investigation. He could frown all he wanted. I didn't really care what old Stanley found to worry about.

CHAPTER TWENTY-TWO

Faye

I tiptoed into Clara's room, since her roommate was napping. The room smelled of orange cleaner, and the floor was shiny. Clara sat on the bed, reading a mystery novel, but she set it down with no apparent regret when she saw me.

"How are you today, Mrs. Knight?"

"Better, thank you for asking." She inclined her head toward the visitor's lounge. "Shall we relocate?"

"Of course." I followed her down the hall and into the visitors' lounge. There was no one there, but a jigsaw puzzle was laid out on a side table, the pieces turned up and the frame almost complete. A dice game, decks of cards, and a few board games sat on a low shelf. The ever-present TV flickered in the corner, set on a game show but muted. The lounge was mostly window-dressing since overall, residents were beyond games and such.

Once we were seated in two institutionally bland upholstered chairs, Clara addressed the situation directly. "I was out of my right mind for a while there."

"Yes." There was no sense denying it.

She shook her head. "I don't understand it. I'm clear as a bell and then suddenly things get all mixed up in my head."

Wanting to offer comfort but aware there might not be any, I asked, "How long have these spells been bothering you?"

"The first one I remember was when Gail found me wandering outside on September 15th. She says it wasn't the first time, but I don't recall the others."

"And since you've been here, there have been more."

She seemed about to cry, and her voice was low. "Yes."

"And you've never had anything like this until recently?"

"No—" She hesitated. "Well, once. When George died, I became depressed, and the doctor I had at the time prescribed one of the tricyclics. It caused me all sorts of trouble, from dry mouth to delirium." Her jaw worked as she recalled the feeling. "Once I realized it was the medicine, I quit taking it."

"Did your niece know about this?"

Her eyes met mine as understanding dawned. "Caleb Marsh called her when he became concerned about me. She didn't come out right away, and by the time she did, I'd figured out what was going on and got myself back to normal."

"But you told her what you'd taken and how it affected you."

Clara nodded. "Come to think of it, what I've been experiencing lately is very much like what I felt back then."

CHAPTER TWENTY-THREE

Retta

Monday turned into a long day. Faye called to update me as soon as she found out about the anti-depression drug Clara had once taken. "If Gail knows that drug makes her aunt loopy," she concluded, "she might be slipping it to her on the down-low."

"I wish I'd known that before I had that long, boring lunch with Doc Allen yesterday. I could have asked about the side effects."

"What she experienced when she initially took the drug is very similar to what's been happening lately."

"You think Gail gave Clara this tri-whatever then took her to the doctor with stories of repeated episodes." As we talked, I applied mascara, blotting the excess away with a tissue. "That and her odd behavior convinced him to put her in the Meadows."

"And every time Gail visits, she gives her aunt another pill."

"The resulting confusion, along with Gail's 'eyewitness reports,' convinces everyone the old woman has dementia."

"Even Clara thinks there's something wrong with her."

"How would Gail get her to take the drug without knowing it?"

"Put it in something, her tea, probably."

Faye considered for a few seconds. "What do we do with this information?"

"It would be best if we had the actual pills."

"And how are we going to get them?"

My lack of an answer made Faye suspicious, and she sputtered, “Do *not* break into Gail’s house, Retta. In the first place it’s illegal, and in the second place, Barb would have a fit.”

“How can you even think I’d do that, Faye? We’ll just have to put our thinking caps on and figure out some other way.”

My thinking cap in this case was a cute champagne and burgundy beret I’d bought from Lord & Taylor, which added the perfect touch to my tan North Face jacket. Reassuring my obviously doubting sister as I ended the call, I adjusted the beret to the best angle and took my car keys from the coat pocket. As I closed the door behind me, I imagined Faye shaking her head at what she guessed I was about to do. I made her a silent promise, *Don’t worry, Sis. I won’t get caught.*

First I drove by So-Rite Realty to make sure Gail Sherman’s car was there. Then I proceeded to her house on a pleasant side street on the south side of town. It had only taken one phone call to a mutual acquaintance and an apparently innocent question to locate Gail’s address.

In small towns many people don’t lock their doors, and even fewer have security systems. The only reason I had one at home was that Don, my now-deceased husband, was a cop who’d seen too many crimes of opportunity. Even so, I don’t use the thing like I should. It’s a hassle that doesn’t seem worth the effort most of the time.

In addition, nobody thinks twice about telling you stuff about their neighbors. When I knocked on Gail’s door, a man raking leaves in the next yard told me she was at the realty office, seldom returned for lunch, and often didn’t get home until dusk. We stood in a cloud of dead-leaf odor as we talked, and he was so willing to share information that I hardly even had to prod.

Thanking him, I got into my car and drove around to the other side of the block. Parking in a driveway where there was a for sale sign, I pretended to be looking the place over, as a potential buyer might. When the leaf-raker went into his garage, I hurried up to Gail's back door and tried the lock.

Okay, so not everybody in a small town leaves their doors unlocked.

Hearing a leaf-blower start, I moved to the far side of Gail's house. The place next door seemed deserted, which was good, because Gail's garage window, a horizontal slider, was unlatched. It was a little high for a petite girl, but I managed to reach it by stepping on the gas meter and boosting myself up. I said a little prayer that the people who lived across the street were away at work as I slid the window open and half-climbed, half-fell inside. My plan was that if I got caught, I'd say Gail had borrowed my lawnmower and I'd come to get it back.

I landed on a shelf cluttered with car stuff, and the noise I made as window scrapers and travel mugs relocated brought another concern to mind. Was there a dog?

Probably not, I decided. A real estate agent is gone night and day. If Gail had a pet, it would be either a cat, which was no cause for concern, or a dog that traveled with her. I hadn't seen any sign of a dog at the office, and Gail seemed like a cat person to me. While I have nothing against cats, dogs are superior in every way, especially for keeping their owners safe.

There was a cat, a Siamese. I shooed it away from the door as I let myself into the house. The look I got said it was moving because it wanted to, not due to the demands of a mere human.

Gail's house smelled like the cat, another reason I prefer dogs. The place was furnished for comfort: a huge TV, lots of electronics, and countless examples of shabby chic. I went directly to the bedroom and checked the nightstand drawer. If I had pills that weren't mine, that's where I'd keep them.

They weren't there, so I began a search, going through each cupboard in the kitchen, the cabinets in both baths, and the hall closet. Nothing.

Standing in the center of the house, I tried to think. Where would they be? I doubted she had them with her. The safest thing would be to take a pill or two to the nursing home at a time, not carry around a medicine bottle with Clara's name on it.

The glove box of her car? That would be tough for me, since I had no way of getting in there to see.

I was about to give up when something occurred to me. Could Gail's hiding place be as trite as her underwear drawer? I felt my nose curl at the idea of sifting through some other woman's undies, but it seemed right.

And it was. As my fingers ruffled through the contents of the back left corner of the third drawer, I first touched a sachet bag—lilac—and then something plastic and round. Pulling it out, I read the name of the prescription recipient on the label: CLARA KNIGHT. Taking out my phone, I took several pictures: the pill bottle lying where I'd found it in the drawer, the dresser with the drawer open, and the whole room from the doorway.

It didn't prove a thing—a lawyer would say I'd put the bottle there myself not to mention the whole breaking-and-entering thing—but I was convinced Gail took the medicine from Clara's house. Of course a lawyer could say she was taking the pills herself, but Barbara, Faye, and I knew that wasn't true. We'd do something about it somehow,. At the least we could warn Clara not to take food or drink her niece brought her from now on.

I might have driven a little over the speed limit to get home. Rick Chou and I were meeting for dinner, and I'd told him I'd drive myself. There's nothing worse than being stuck for a whole first date with a man who turns out to be a dud—not that I expected Rick to be one of those.

The restaurant was far enough out of town that I didn't think we'd see anyone who might ask about Lars or mention seeing me to my sisters. It was also far enough away that I'd need extra time to get there, which meant I had to get ready in a hurry. I hate that—it's much more fun to take my time, try on different outfits, and make sure I look exactly the way I want to. Since I hadn't planned on an unlawful entry that afternoon, I felt rushed and not quite put together.

Whenever I drive too fast, I say a little prayer that if I get caught, it will be an officer who knew my Don. They'd never give me a ticket because of what I'd done to make cops safer. After my husband's death I toured the state for two years, pressing for better body armor for officers. I even wrote (well, co-wrote) a book about the tragedy that left me a widow with two teenagers and split the profits 50-50 with the Michigan State Police. The book sold like crazy for a year or two, and while it was a hot item, the state and I both made good money.

I made it home without police notice. When I got out of the car, I could already hear Styx barking to welcome me home. He liked to play this game where he didn't let me into the house. Standing on the other side of the door, he bumped it closed each time I tried to open it. The game could go on for some time, and I usually enjoyed it, but now I said firmly, "Styx, let me in. I've got a date." Because he was a really smart dog, Styx only closed the door in my face a few more times before he finally backed away so I could come inside.

After a shower with lavender aroma-therapy beads and a little primping, I noticed a message on my phone that read: THE HIGHLIGHTS OF HIS GLOBAL TOUR INCLUDE ENCOUNTERS WITH NELSON MANDELA, AN 800-YEAR-OLD DEMIGOD AND A GARBAGE COLLECTOR.

Barbara Anne. I was supposed to see the horrible consequence of leaving out the Oxford comma: making Nelson Mandela into an ancient half-god and trash man. My return message was succinct. IF YOU PUT AN OXFORD COMMA IN THERE, MANDELA DOESN'T RIDE A GARBAGE TRUCK, BUT HE COULD STILL BE AN ELDERLY TITAN.

I joined Rick at the restaurant only twenty minutes late. I'd texted I was on my way (waiting until the road was clear of traffic, of course), and he insisted I needn't apologize. "It was worth the wait." His appreciative gaze said he meant it.

The restaurant had a pianist most nights, and I heard "Misty" as Rich ordered a bottle of wine. When it arrived, he poured two glasses and offered a toast. "To the future. To us."

"To the future."

Just then I saw something over Rick's shoulder that made me swallow hard. Rory had entered the dining room with Barbara on his arm.

"What is it?" Rick asked.

"My sister."

"Oh." He turned to look. "The business-like one."

When Barbara saw us, her smile turned frosty. She said something to Rory, who also frowned. My sister no doubt disapproved of my dating a client. Rory disliked what he saw as me cheating on his friend Lars.

"Should we invite them to join us?" Rick asked softly.

I gave him a look. "Are you crazy?"

His expression turned knowing. "You're right. We don't need company while we're getting to know each other."

"Just smile, say hello, and let them sit somewhere else." I spoke out of the side of my mouth as I rose and opened my arms to hug Rory. "Lovely to see you both," I told them. "It's too bad we didn't know you were coming, or we'd have waited to order."

CHAPTER TWENTY-FOUR

Barb

"I could not believe it," I told Faye the next morning. We'd had our breakfast—pancakes and sausage—and Dale had gone outside. I was rinsing the dishes under warm water, something I insisted on, since she was determined to cook for me. "She's dating a client. And what about Lars?"

Faye wasn't nearly as shocked as I was. "In the first place, we don't have a rule against that." She grinned. "As far as I know, our only rule is that Retta can't mention changing our name to The Sleuth Sisters ever again. In the second place, I don't think she and Lars made promises of exclusivity. And third, look at it from her point of view. How many attractive men our age are there in Allport?"

Though she was correct, I wasn't ready to look at anything from Retta's point of view. I liked Lars Johannsen. I thought Retta should be able to figure out she shouldn't date clients without a rule spelling it out. And Chou struck me as a bit too smooth—not criminal, necessarily, but definitely not brother-in-law material.

Chou was handsome, but I doubted he planned to hang around Allport once his property sold. Retta was angry with Lars for spending what she considered too much time with Rory on his trips to Michigan. Even as the old maid in the family, I knew enough about men to know they need time with male friends once in a while. I hated to see Retta throw away what she had with Lars, which I thought was good, for a man who'd be gone from Allport soon, probably forever.

Retta often claims she doesn't tell people what they should do, but of course she does. I really don't tell others what to do, but I confess I sometimes have strong opinions.

The least likely of us to judge another's actions, Faye dropped the subject of Retta's date. "I haven't had time to catch you up, but Clara told me yesterday she once experienced delirium while taking an anti-depressant. Retta and I think Gail might have used that same medicine to cause her aunt's 'spells' and convince people her mental competence is deteriorating."

"Where would she get the same drug Clara took?"

"The easiest way would have been to steal it. People often don't dispose of medications they've stopped taking. Prescriptions can sit on a shelf in their bathroom for years."

Remembering my own medicine cabinet, where there were at least two prescription bottles half full of allergy pills I'd probably never take because they made me sleepy, I nodded. "How do we deal with that?"

"I called the pharmacist at Baskins' and asked about the effects of tricyclics. She said they can be dangerous, especially for older people. They can easily overdose and die."

A thump sounded as a door closed somewhere at the back of the house. "At least Clara's aware of it now. If Gail brings her something to eat or drink, she'll refuse it."

"And if that leads to no more episodes of confusion, it will be a big step forward for Clara. She might get to go home after all."

I doubted that. Since Caleb Marsh was dead, Clara had no neighbors. It was doubtful her doctor would release her from the Meadows unless she agreed to get a place in town, possibly in the senior center. I decided I'd suggest that to Faye so she could pass it on to Clara if things got to the point that her competence was re-established.

My computer had booted, and I checked our email. "Mrs. Chou has replied." Quickly scanning the note I reported, "The email account we contacted her on is mostly unused these days, but she checks it occasionally. She'd forgotten all about her name being on the deed to the house."

"Sounds like she might be co-operative."

"She's cautious, though. So her ex won't find out where she is, she doesn't want to reveal her present location."

"It won't be hard to find her now that we know we've got the right Candice Chou."

"I don't want you to do that." When Faye looked up in surprise I went on, "Do you have any idea how many women I met as an attorney who were terrified of their husbands, ex-husbands, or ex-boyfriends? Candice Chou put a lot of effort into getting away from that man. I don't want her to get the impression we're on his side."

Faye nodded. "I see what you mean."

She did, but only as much as a person who hasn't dealt with years of battered, terrorized, and murdered women can. As a prosecutor I'd had more than my share of such cases, and I'd never gotten over the horror of it. If Candice Chou felt the need to keep her whereabouts from her ex, I was willing to do whatever she asked, even if it meant giving up the case. The problem was that if we refused to help Chou, he'd simply hire some other agency to track Candice down, one that might not be as tuned in to keeping the secrets she wanted kept.

Pulling the keyboard shelf out, I said, "I'll tell her we'll make every effort to make signing the documents completely secure."

My typing was interrupted by the sound of Buddy's frustration, and I guessed he'd shut himself in the back entryway again. The dog insists on closing the door while he eats, but once he's finished his meal, he becomes furious when he can't get back into the kitchen.

"I thought you were going to fix it so he can't close the door," I said, trying to keep the irritation out of my voice.

"We thought about it, but Buddy thinks he should be able to eat in private." Pushing herself away from her desk with a scrape of plastic wheels, Faye stood.

He's a dog, I wanted to say. *He hardly thinks at all!*

Knowing better than to verbalize that, I took advantage of her absence to place a phone call I'd been considering since last night.

"Federal Bureau of Investigation, Albuquerque. How may I direct your call?"

"Agent Lars Johannsen, please."

"One moment."

As I waited, I wondered what I'd say. *You'd better come to Michigan before you lose your girlfriend? I hate to tattle, but my sister's flirting with a killer-handsome Asian guy?* Anything I said might create trouble, but saying nothing was equally unpalatable.

"Johannsen."

"Lars, it's Barb Evans."

It took him a beat, which wasn't surprising. A call from me was probably the last thing on his mind. "Hey, Barb, what's up?"

There it was. *What's up indeed?* "Um, I wondered if you're planning on flying north anytime soon."

"Why, is there something going on?"

Yeah, but—"Not really. I just thought we might—take the Agawa Canyon tour." I had no idea where that came from. "It's a train in Canada that tours the countryside, and it's particularly beautiful in autumn." I sounded stilted and false but hoped Lars didn't know me well enough to discern it.

"I've got nothing pressing right now, so I could take a few days. Is Retta okay with it?" From the tentative note in his tone, I guessed he was aware she wasn't completely happy with him.

"I thought we'd surprise her. I'll set everything up and tell her it's just the three of us girls. When we get to the depot, you and Dale and Rory can be waiting."

"Sounds nice. When are you thinking?"

"As soon as possible." That sounded desperate, so I added, "The colors fade rapidly once they hit peak."

"Yeah." There was a pause and the sound of pages flipping, and I guessed he was checking a calendar of some kind. "I could come Friday night if you can arrange it for Saturday. I'll fly back early Monday for some things I've got going on Tuesday."

"All right, I'll get tickets for Saturday. Give me a number I can reach you that isn't the Bureau."

He complied, and we said goodbye. Lars went back to Bureau business, I presumed, and I went about figuring out how to get Retta to agree to the Agawa Canyon tour for no apparent reason other than my supposed desire for a train ride.

Chapter Twenty-five

Faye

Out at Clara's place that afternoon, I could have sworn the chickens recognized me. Except for the rooster, who kept his distance, they seemed downright affectionate. When I crouched in the center of the flock, one young hen let me pet her smooth feathers as she nestled under my arm like a kitten.

Refastening the gate of the pen, I heard a vehicle pull into the driveway. I went around the house to see who was there, and a man in a snazzy blue pickup truck rolled down the window and called, "Hello."

He was in his thirties, wearing a tattered sweatshirt and a battered cap that said, Proud Member of the NRA. The tone of the greeting and his curious look told me he wondered what I was doing on Clara's property. Walking over to his truck so we could speak without shouting, I explained about meeting her at the Meadows and learning of her needy chickens.

"I bet that was supposed to be Gail's job," he said when I finished. "The girl isn't known for expending effort that doesn't benefit her directly." He put out a hand. "I'm Fred Marsh."

As we shook hands, I got the connection. "Related to Caleb Marsh, I assume. Sorry for your loss."

His lips tightened. "He was my grand-dad."

"My sisters and I were the ones who found him."

He sighed. "I guess that's good, or he might have been there for days. I came out on Sundays and did the heavier chores for him." Glancing across the lake he added, "Today I'm going to start cleaning the house out."

"You plan to sell the property?"

He nodded. "I've got my own place. My brother lives in Lansing, and no one else in the family has any interest in living this far out of town."

"It is pretty remote."

"Actually, we already have an offer."

It didn't take a shrewd guesser. "From Gail Sherman?"

He nodded. "She says it would be a shame if strangers bought up the lake we played in as kids." Chuckling lightly he added, "That's a switch, because I don't recall Gail liking the water much." He glanced at the wood, now neatly stacked in the rick. "She hopes to get her aunt to move into town, at least during the winter months."

I paused, trying to form a question in a neutral way. "You said you're not surprised Gail neglected the chickens. What did you mean by that?"

He became apologetic. "Not that she's a bad person or anything. As a kid she was—" He couldn't find a word he was willing to put there, so he switched to something less negative. "People grow up, you know, and they're not like they were in school." His fingers drummed on the steering wheel, revealing uncertainty about his own words.

I wasn't sure how many unreliable young people I'd known who turned into model citizens as adults. Maybe it could happen, but I still doubted the character of a woman who could leave a flock of animals penned and unable to fend for themselves.

"Gail's been real nice about Grand-dad's house," Fred was saying. "She offered to buy it as is, and it's not exactly a palace." He gestured at the neat yard behind me. "Clara keeps her place up, but Grandpa had arthritis. I did what I could, but to be honest, a buyer would be better off to blow that house up and start over."

"The view from his place is wonderful, though."

"That's true, but the last few years Grandpa had to pay somebody to plow all the way around the lake in the winter. And in spring the road is like the surface of some weird planet—all rocks and holes. Clara has the best spot, if you ask me."

"Did you know she's been placed in a nursing home?"

His brown eyes bored into mine. "Did she fall or something?"

"It appears she has some mental issues."

"Huh." He glanced at the lake. "I usually stop and talk to her if she's outside when I come by, and she seemed okay to me. In fact she kind of watched over Gramps since he got crippled up. I guess it can happen fast at that age, though. They just lose it."

Unwilling to share that Gail Sherman might be plotting against her aunt, I made a noncommittal murmur.

Fred gestured toward the Marsh property. "We're all sorry to give the place up, but we figure it's good to have one of the original Sweet Springs families take over. Gail will keep things natural, she says."

I doubted that but didn't say so. "It's got to be hard to have to make that decision when you lost your grandfather so suddenly."

"Yeah." He looked across the peaceful, sparkling lake. "I keep wondering why he tried to go down those steps. We'd talked about how dangerous they are when they're wet, and I'd already put away the boat and everything else down there." His voice softened as he went on. "I reminded him all the time how slippery the logs get on frosty mornings. I said he should stay off them." Fred shook his head. "He said he would. He promised."

***

The more I thought about the conversation with Fred Marsh, the more convinced I was that Gail Sherman's plotting was more criminal than we'd thought. I ran it by Barb that evening, ending with, "You say the fire marshal suspects the fire was set. Clara says she was forced into the nursing home. Mr. Marsh fell down his steps and died. One of those things by itself is sad but not suspicious. Taken together, they're kind of scary."

Barb rose and started pacing, her heels clicking on the wood floor. "You think Gail wants that lake property so much she isn't willing to wait for it to become available?"

I shrugged. "I'm saying it's possible. The people out there have known her all their lives. While they might understand that she's self-absorbed, we all tend to believe people we know won't cheat us. The neighbors call on the Realtor they know when there's land to be sold."

"The devil you know rather than one you don't."

"Yes. Gail was probably aware that arson voids an insurance policy, which would put the Warners in a difficult financial position if the fire inspector ruled their place was burned on purpose. While they were still trying to figure things out, she offered to buy it. That could be opportunism, but I think we have to consider she might have created the opportunity herself."

"She went out there and burned the house down, leaving evidence that could only lead to a finding of arson." Barb's tone was disbelieving.

"Look at it the way Gail might," I argued. "There was no one there, so the risk was minimal. No one got hurt in the fire. She probably told herself it wasn't all that evil."

"What about Marsh? Do you think Gail murdered him?"

I sighed. "That's harder to imagine, but it might have been a spur-of-the-moment thing. Gail goes out to talk him into selling. They're standing in the back yard, near the steps. She presses too hard for the sale, Mr. Marsh gets upset and orders her off his property. It's over before she realizes what she's done."

Barb dabbed delicately at her nose with a tissue. "If you're right, she's getting desperate. Setting fire to an empty house and arranging to have Clara institutionalized are non-violent, though nasty, things to do. But if she's so determined to have her way that she pushed that old man to his death…" She tossed the tissue into the wastebasket. "We have to stop her."

I reached for my phone. "I told Retta to ask around and find out what she can about what kind of person Gail is."

"If she isn't too busy playing footsie with Rick Chou."

"Barbara!" She looked faintly regretful about the nasty crack, so I went ahead with the call. "Retta? Are you busy? Oh." Barb was watching me, and I saw the smile start. "Well, I don't want to interrupt your plans, but we—I was wondering if you've had time to ask your friends about Gail Sherman." After listening for a while, I thanked her and ended the call, skipping over the fact that Retta had been baking a "treat" for Mr. Chou.

"Not many people like Ms. Sherman," I reported. "Apparently she'll steal your man if you don't hang onto him with both hands. However, she couldn't have burned down the house on Sweet Springs. Retta's friend at the travel office says Gail was in New Orleans that whole week for a conference."

"I guess that dampens our theory."

"Not entirely," I replied. By now I was picturing Gail with horns and a pitchfork. "It just means she's not working alone. What if she has a financial backer, or someone who helped her connect with the water bottling company? The other person could be just as willing to commit crimes as Gail is."

"Faye, are you saying Gail is perpetrating a criminal conspiracy with another person?"

"It's possible." I warmed to the idea. "If someone's working behind the scenes, Gail would simply do as that person told her to. He uses her greed and lets her set things up while he stays out of the limelight. Doesn't that make sense?"

"We'll see."

When Barb says that, she sounds exactly like our mother. The unspoken message is *You're wrong, but I'll let you find out for yourself.*

Her next statement came out of the blue, and I had to take a second to adjust. "I thought maybe we'd ride that train up in Canada this weekend, the three of us."

"The train?"

"You always say you want to do it, every year, and we never do. I thought maybe this was the year."

"Oh." I wasn't sure where this was going.

"I mean, we should do more things together, and I know you like scenery, and so do I. Retta, too."

Barb was babbling, something she seldom does, and I saw a telltale flush on her neck, just like I get when I tell a lie.

"I suppose we could look into it," I said. "I can go online and see what the tickets cost."

"Oh, I already did that. It wasn't that expensive for six tickets, and it will be my treat. We could drive up early Saturday morning and be back home by your bedtime."

"Six tickets?"

"What?"

"You said you bought six tickets, but you mentioned the three of us going."

Her face revealed irritation with herself. "Yes."

"What are you up to, Barb?"

After a heavy sigh, she fessed up. "I invited Lars to come up for the weekend. I thought if he were here, Retta wouldn't be so tempted by that sleazy Rick Chou." She must have realized how she sounded. "I know. It's her business, but—"

"Remember how mad you got at her for telling Rory you were attracted to him when he first came to town?"

"This isn't like that. Retta's already attracted to Lars. It's just that Lars isn't around very often." She touched her lips before continuing. "I was hoping you'd convince her to come along. The guys can be there waiting for us."

"Rory and Dale are in on this?"

"Not yet, but they will be."

I shook my head. "This is a very Retta-like thing you're doing, *Barbara Ann.*"

She huffed disgustedly. "We wouldn't have to go to these lengths if she weren't such a-a-flibbertigibbet." I tried not to smile as Barb fell back on one of Harriet's favorite put-downs. In a calmer tone she went on, "We both know Retta doesn't want to lose a man like Lars."

"I'm not sure we know that," I said, "but I suppose it won't hurt for her to be reminded that he's a good man."

CHAPTER TWENTY-SIX

Retta

My sisters and I had a phone conference Wednesday morning, to make sure we all knew what was going on with our two cases. Meeting that way was an advantage for me, since I was in my bathrobe, sipping Spicy Eggnog coffee.

Barbara made no comment about my dinner with Rick Chou, though I was sure she and Faye had discussed it. Despite the snide things I knew she was thinking, I don't just jump into bed with any good-looking man who comes along. In the first place it's pathetic, and in the second place, a man likes to think he's worked to gain a woman's affection, even if the woman decides from Day One exactly how things are going to go. So far we'd shared only a few exploratory kisses. Rick was pretty good at that, so things were moving along well.

Barbara kept the call professional, and the only time it was uncomfortable was when she reported the former Mrs. Chou's caution about meeting us. "She refused any sort of mailing or FAX that could be traced to her workplace or home, so we're making special arrangements for her to sign off on the deed."

"What's her problem?" I asked. "She must know Faye can find her with very little effort."

"Her *problem*," Barbara said in her lecturing tone, "is her ex-husband." Her voice became louder and softer as she paced the office. "If she doesn't want us to know where she is, I trust she has her reasons."

"She's a nut case. Rick didn't know she had mental problems till after they were married."

"*He* says." Now Barbara's tone was sarcastic.

"It's not our job to figure out how much truth one or the other has on his—or her—side," Faye broke in. "We can handle her concerns by meeting in a neutral spot."

"Right," Barbara said. "I've asked her to name a place that makes her comfortable, perhaps an airport in a big city. Retta can go there and get the necessary signatures. Chou did say he'd pay travel expenses." She sounded eager to make Rick pay, but the plan suited me. I was interested in meeting Candice Chou to see just what kind of loon she was.

We moved on to the Knight case. Faye had formed the theory that Gail Sherman either had a partner or had hired someone to commit arson in order to hurry the sales at Sweet Springs along. I was doubtful about the second part. "You haven't met her, Faye. She's spoiled, but I can't see her finding shady men in bars and handing over envelopes of cash so they'll commit crimes for her. And Gail certainly didn't kill Mr. Marsh."

"Why do you say that?"

"I'm not sure, but she's—I don't know—too prissy."

"Murderers can't be prissy?" Faye's tone was uncharacteristically impatient.

I took a sip of coffee while I tried to come up with the right words. "Gail is a person I can see flirting with another woman's husband or stretching the truth about a piece of property, but not someone I can imagine shoving an old man she'd known her whole life down a flight of steps to his death." It was only a feeling, but I appealed to Barbara, who operates only on logic. "You've met Gail, Barbara. Do you disagree?"

"Actually, no." She thought about it for a second. "Maybe Faye should meet her. She has a good sense of people."

Though she didn't say it, I thought Barbara was looking for a way to get Faye back on track. I guessed in her eagerness to protect Clara Knight, Faye had turned into a real Gail-hater…or disapprover, since Faye doesn't have much capacity for hatred.

Barbara's idea was a good one in another sense. Faye often sees past clothes and looks and community standing to get a sense of an individual's motives. "That's a good idea," I said.

"I don't want to—"

"How else are we going to assess Gail's possible guilt, Faye?" She didn't offer an argument, so I went on before she could think of one. "Now about the water thing. Barbara, did you ask that guy at WOZ Industries if the water in Sweet Springs is suitable for bottling?"

"His name is Enright Landon, and no. Stan Wozniak never left the two of us alone, so I didn't mention the specific site. I didn't think it was any of his business."

"Stanley was there?"

"Yes, and he was actually kind of nice to me. It was creepy."

"Stanley's never nice unless he wants something," I said. "I can't imagine he's forgiven you for standing up to him."

"My thought exactly."

I couldn't think of a way Stanley connected with Gail Sherman, but I filed the information away. "Someone should ask this Landon if Sweet Springs is a good possibility for bottling. Shall I do that?"

"I don't know if you're the right one for the job," Barbara said. "Landon isn't the type you can practice your arts on."

Barbara doesn't like my interview style, because schmoozing is totally foreign to her. Where she's direct, I'm conversational. Where she demands, I encourage. My way works better—at least for me. She'd never get answers just by lowering her eyelashes.

In addition to her disapproval of my interrogation technique, I suspected Barbara was a little peeved at me, since I was winning the Comma War. I'd found three articles claiming the Oxford comma is fading from usage. Newspapers gave it up long ago, admittedly because they're concerned about space. Language luminaries such as James Thurber and H.L. Mencken disapproved of it, and the *New York Times Style Guide* (from 1937, but old doesn't mean it's wrong) discouraged its use, saying too many commas slow a reader's progress.

I'd sent Barbara links to each article. Her reply had been a terse text message: YOU CAN HAVE MY OXFORD COMMA WHEN YOU PRY IT OUT OF MY COLD, DEAD HANDS. The girl is nothing if not serious.

"I'll play dumb and say I don't understand the process," I told my sisters. "Mr. Landon will never guess we suspect him of being in collusion with Gail."

"We don't," Faye objected before adding, "Do we?"

"Gail didn't think of this scheme by herself. This Landon guy comes to Allport and all of a sudden there's interest in a lake that's been ignored for centuries. I'd say they met somewhere, got to talking about water for some reason we'll never understand, and ended up hatching a plot to sell Sweet Springs to the highest bidder. He has the contacts; she's got the skills to talk the residents into selling their land."

"Give me a second," Faye said, and I heard a keyboard clicking.

As she worked I went on, "If someone is murdering people, it's much more likely to be a man. Women are much less violent overall, don't you think?"

A derisive snort told me Barbara didn't necessarily agree. "Maybe I should be the one to contact Landon," she said. "We've met, so there's a basis for further conversation."

"What are you going to say? 'We met at WOZ the other day but now I need to talk with you again because I suspect you of arson, abusing old ladies, and murder'?"

Faye broke in. "Gail Sherman was the agent who sold Enright Landon a home last spring in the Huron Delight Subdivision, 821 Sand Lane."

"Great. I'll go out there this evening."

"Retta, maybe—"

"Barbara Ann, it isn't like I need to understand the intricacies of English punctuation to talk to this man." I let my tone hint at underlying meaning. "You two need to think up a reason for Faye to meet Ms. Sherman. Maybe she can say she's interested in buying Mr. Marsh's house. If Gail is willing to help her do that, we're going in the wrong direction and have to rethink our theory. If she puts road-blocks in your way, she's probably trying to save the property for her bottling scheme."

"Fine." Barbara's tone betrayed irritation that I was getting my way, but she couldn't argue with my logic. "I'll handle the arrangements with Mrs. Chou. Let's meet here at ten tomorrow morning and see what we've found out."

To prove to myself I didn't care what Barbara thought, I called Rick and arranged to see him later that evening. I made it a casual offer, mentioning I'd be in town on business and could meet him for a drink. His quick reply told me he was more than willing, and I began looking forward to furthering our relationship. I went to make my bed, thinking as I worked that Rick might get lucky and join me there tomorrow, after I met Enright Landon and decided if he was a likely partner in Gail Sherman's plot.

Chapter Twenty-seven

Faye

When I went into the kitchen to make lunch, Gabe's truck was parked beside the house. I guessed he was in the workshop with Dale and, noting the time, also guessed we'd have a guest for lunch. Accordingly, I made three grilled-cheese sandwiches, set out a jar of pickles, and filled a large bowl with potato chips.

Dale and Gabe came in right on time, and I asked if Gabe would like to share our meal. He graciously agreed.

For a while the conversation was all about his repaired truck and his new job. I affirmed that the truck looked like it was brand new and listened as Gabe recounted his tasks at the moving company. "I work afternoons. First I wash the trucks and get them ready for the next day. After the staff leaves, I get the office squared away. Mr. Bobier likes everything in the right place."

Gabe was learning the requirements of moving and storage, and we got a brief lecture on the steps involved. "You don't just throw things in," he said. "You have to plan, so when you want something it ain't behind three other things."

I didn't have to contribute much, because Dale was actually interested. He seemed fascinated to hear how movers loaded a truck and planned their route to minimize problems like low bridges and narrow streets. I'd never realized it took so much effort, but then, I had no reason to care. Watching Dale and Gabe, I was pleased my husband had a friend to sit and chat with, even if that friend was the last person I'd have imagined.

When we'd finished eating I started clearing the table, but something Gabe said piqued my interest. "—they let me ride along so I could see what they do. It was just out to WOZ Industries, but still."

"You were at WOZ yesterday?" I asked.

"Yeah. They were putting stuff into storage and Cal—he's the driver—let me carry some of the smaller things out. I set them on the ground beside the truck, and Jerry—that's the other guy—he decides how it should go in so the load is balanced and all."

"What were they moving?"

Gabe shrugged. "Furniture and boxes full of papers and some old office machines, like a printer and some computers. I guess they got a new guy out there, some genius type, and Mr. Wozniak let him redo his office and buy all new furniture for it."

Dale nodded. "They say if Stan likes you, you're golden." With a grin he added, "And if he doesn't like you, you're gone."

Something funny came to Gabe's mind. "There was this woman there that wanted to give us advice on how to do our jobs. Jerry knew her, I guess, because he told her to go back to making up stories about property values."

"What does that mean?"

Gabe shrugged. "I guess she sells real estate, but Jerry didn't think much of her. He told us later that she lied to his cousins about this house they bought."

"Lied?" Dale frowned. "Can real estate agents do that?"

"Not supposed to. Jerry said she mentioned a little problem with the septic system, but it turned out they had to redo the whole thing."

"That's not right."

"I know. She had a place in all those papers they have you sign that mentioned it, but the cousin missed it." He shook his head. "He should have taken her to court."

I hadn't had much to do with real estate in general, but in any profession there are those who play fast and loose with the rules. "Did Jerry mention the woman's name?"

Gabe took a slurp of his Coke before answering. "He never said her last name, but I'm pretty sure he called her Gail."

***

Going undercover, as Retta calls it, isn't my favorite thing. I don't like pretending to be someone I'm not, and I hate deceiving others. Still, I was the one Gail Sherman hadn't yet met, so it would be me who sounded her out about selling land on Sweet Springs. When I called, I learned she was due in the office at three. As I finished cleaning the kitchen, Retta called to ask what I planned to wear. She rejected the first three outfits I described.

"Wear the black and tan jacket I bought you for Christmas last year," she ordered. "Put black slacks with it—you do have black slacks, right?"

"Yes." I tried to quell the *Duh*! in my voice, but aside from my jeans, black pants are all I own.

"Okay. We'll have to hope the blacks match up."

I was confused. "Black isn't just black?"

"Of course not, silly! Anyway, put a bright top under the jacket and add some jewelry that didn't come from Wal-Mart—Barbara will have something you can borrow."

I tried not to be resentful. She wanted to help, and if Barb's report was correct, Gail Sherman was the type who would judge me by my clothes and jewelry.

"Have you got a little hat?"

"A hat?" I had a couple of toques that kept my ears warm when I had to be outside for any length of time in winter, all of them slightly ratty. She was thinking of my graying, blunt-cut hair, which I sliced off with scissors whenever I got tired of dealing with it, and trying to figure out how I might hide it. "No."

She thought about that. "Okay, fluff your hair with your hands before you go in, and don't comb it afterward. With luck she'll think it's one of those made-to-look-messy styles."

"Anything else?" I was still trying not to sound sarcastic.

"Put on a little blush. You're kind of pale. I don't suppose you have a stylish fall coat."

"I have a hoodie for not-too-cold and a corduroy for getting-kinda-cold."

She groaned softly. "Wear Barb's navy one. It's a little outdated, but it's good quality."

I ended the call, shaking my head at her concerns. Do people really worry that much about how they present themselves to the world each day?

An hour later I showed up at So-Rite Realty, dressed according to Retta's commands. Barb's coat was unbuttoned, since there was no way it would close across my chest.

Both agents were present, but I approached Gail's desk after tossing the other woman a smile I hoped indicated the choice was nothing personal. Once we'd done introductions, Gail asked me to sit down. When the other agent excused herself to meet a client, I got down to business.

"I just drove up from West Branch," I told her. "A friend called to tell me I should look at some property before word gets out that it's going up for sale."

"Nice to have friends that keep you informed." Gail glanced at the map on the wall behind her. "Where are you looking?"

"Sweet Springs. She says the heirs of an elderly man who died out there will probably sell his place."

Something went on behind her eyes. "Who told you that?"

Tilting my head as if to excuse the refusal I replied, "Private source. Do you know anything about it?"

She tried to make her expression rueful, but it looked smug to me. "I'm afraid you were misinformed. They're going to keep the property in the family."

I frowned. "My friend was pretty sure they'd sell."

"They did consider it, but in the end they couldn't see it go to strangers." Setting her fingers on her keyboard Gail said, "I can show you some similar properties on other lakes in the area."

"No, thanks. I really like Sweet Springs."

Her fake eyebrows descended. "There was a woman in here the other day asking about land out there. Do you know her?"

"No." *Keep it simple. Don't explain.*

"You look alike. She's a lot younger than you but still."

"No," I repeated.

"Another woman came in wearing a coat a lot like the one you have on. She let me think she was from the court, but I found out later she wasn't. She looked like you, too. Same eyes, same smile." Gail sat back in her chair and glared. "Do you want to tell me what's going on?"

The heat of embarrassment rose up my neck. "I used to stay with a friend out there when I was a kid," I said, but my voice sounded weak. "I thought it would be nice to retire there."

"What friend?"

"Excuse me?"

"Who was the friend you stayed with? I know everyone who ever lived on Sweet Springs."

"It was years ago. You're too young to remember her."

"Liar!" Gail's voice rose to a shout, and I flinched. "Something's going on here, and I don't like it. You people are up to something, and I *will* find out what it is. When I do, things will happen. It might be a lawsuit. It might be a PPO to stay away from my aunt. It might be charges filed with the Allport police. Somehow I'll make you take your noses out of my business."

"Ms. Sherman—"

"Don't bother to lie anymore. You aren't even any good at it."

Marshalling my dignity, I rose. "If you can't help me with the property, I'll let you get back to your work."

Gail didn't bother to answer, but her glower followed as I left the office. I kept my face averted, since it was burning. I had told my lies badly, resulting in Gail connecting me with Barb and with Retta. Now we were all on her radar. Still, I'd accomplished one thing. We knew now that Gail wasn't going to let anyone buy property on Sweet Springs if she could help it.

***

I stopped at the Meadows before returning home in hopes Clara would be well enough to answer some questions. As I entered two aides stood chatting at the front desk. One whistled and the other said, "You look nice, Mrs. Burner. Been to a funeral?"

"Nope, just a normal day."

Going on I saw Glenda at the meds cart. "Hey, Faye." She patted the sleeve of Barb's coat. "Is there a funeral today?"

My lips went stiff. Can't a woman wear nice clothes without people assuming she's headed for church? "None I'm aware of."

Clara was working on a Sudoku puzzle, and to my relief, her face brightened when she saw me.

"Faye, it's good of you to stop by." Gesturing at the puzzle she said, "Keeps my mind occupied."

"I don't have much to report, but we're working on your case," I said, sitting on the opposite end of the bed. We'd agreed to wait for more complete information before sharing with our client. "And I have a question."

She set the book aside. "Go for it."

I'd begun to consider the practicalities of setting up the scheme we suspected. If Gail was indeed trying to interest a water developer in Clara's property, she might well have shown it to him at some point. "Did your niece ever bring anyone with her when she visited your place?"

Clara gave the question some thought. "Not to the house." My hopes took a dive, but a moment later they rose again. "Someone came with her once, but Gail came inside alone."

"Did she say who was out there?"

"A friend. They had plans to do something later." Clara bit her bottom lip. "When she came to see me, Gail seldom stayed long. We'd have a cup of tea, she'd tell me about her work, and then she'd say she had to go."

"She didn't invite her friend in for tea?"

"No. I wouldn't have known anyone was out there except I happened to glance out and saw someone on the dock. When I mentioned it, Gail said her friend was probably taking pictures."

"Was it a man or a woman?"

Clara patted her lips with her index finger as she thought. "I only saw the person from the back and from a distance. I remember blue jeans and one of those sweatshirts with a hood. It was pulled up and tied, so I didn't see hair length or color." She frowned, trying to remember more. "Brown shoes."

"Tall?"

"For a woman, perhaps, not for a man." Clara rubbed her forehead as if trying to stimulate her memory. "I said she should have brought the person in, but Gail said, 'My friend doesn't like meeting new people.' The next time I looked out, he or she was gone, back in the car, I suppose."

CHAPTER TWENTY-EIGHT

Retta

Huron Delight was indeed delightful, if you didn't mind your house sitting fifteen yards from your neighbor's. The development contained a half-dozen architectural styles, individualized by use of color, trim, and placement. Sometimes the garage was on the left; other times it was on the right. Some had a small portico out front; others had a long porch with evenly-spaced columns.

I hadn't called ahead to announce my visit, not wanting to give Mr. Landon a chance to think about why a second person from the Smart Detective Agency was seeking him out. (I hadn't won my sisters over to the idea of changing the name of our business to the Sleuth Sisters yet, but they were coming around. I could sense it.)

The air was fresh with the tang of Lake Huron, half a football field away. Ringing the bell, I stepped back and waited. When I glimpsed movement behind the sidelight, I stood up straighter and smiled. Good posture is essential, and a smile makes you look ten years younger.

A woman opened the door, which was unexpected. From Barbara's description of Landon, I'd pictured a bachelor, married to his work and suspicious, even fearful, of women. There a lady of the house, though, and she was the type the word *alluring* was coined for. Though not classically beautiful, she had the kind of tall form that makes any clothing style look attractive. I guessed her to be in her late twenties. Long, dark hair hung perfectly straight to her shoulders, at which point it curled inward just enough to frame her face. Her eyes were large, and artful makeup made them seem like the dark pools romance novels love to mention. Her best feature, high cheekbones, was accentuated with the lightest touch of blush. A woman after my own heart, she'd made the effort to look attractive despite the fact that she wasn't expecting company.

"I'm Retta Stilson, from the Smart Detective Agency." I offered a business card. "Is Mr. Landon here?"

"My husband isn't home from work yet." Her head tilted slightly as she looked me over. "What's this about?"

"We're hoping to draw on his expertise about water rights."

A tiny frown came and went on her high forehead. "En said someone asked him about that the other day at work."

"My sister. At the time we were seeking general information. Now we have more specific questions."

"I see." She thought for a moment then glanced at the clock. "He called half an hour ago to see what I wanted him to bring home for dinner. He should be along any minute." Stepping aside, she opened the door wider. "I'm Diane Landon. You're welcome to come in and wait."

"Thank you."

Leading the way to a living room with a cathedral ceiling and lots of brass, Mrs. Landon indicated I should sit down. I chose a cream-colored settee in a smooth microfiber fabric, and she took the chair closest to it, adjusting the gray tunic dress she wore over pumpkin-colored leggings.

"I'm sorry to have come at your dinner hour."

She waved away my apology. "Our dinners are late because En has been working every night until at least six. This is the first chance Mr. Wozniak has had to come north since En signed on, so they've spent a lot of time together." She raised perfectly groomed brows. "I guess there's lots to discuss about WOZ Industries and water quality in Lake Huron."

"I'm sure the new job is demanding," I said, adding with a smile, "I know Stanley pretty well."

She murmured something non-committal, and I went on. "May I ask how you came to Michigan from—Florida, wasn't it?"

"Zephyrhills."

"Right. Where the bottled water comes from."

She smiled. "Yeah, water certainly put that town on the map."

"Your husband worked at a bottling plant there?"

"We both did. It's how we met." She smiled. "Of course I was on the line, and he was up in the management stratosphere."

A picture came to mind: Enright Landon in an office overlooking the factory floor, glancing down and spotting the lovely Diane below. If she'd given him her Mona Lisa smile, it was no surprise he'd somehow closed the distance between them. It looked like things had worked out for both of them.

"It must be quite a change for your husband to go from water quality oversight to working for a stone quarry."

"I suppose." She shrugged off the idea of interest in WOZ and her husband's place there. "En wanted to try something new, and we heard Michigan has a nice climate."

Would she still believe that after a year in Allport? Though I loved snow and winter sports, our winters are long. Until we got involved in criminal investigation, I'd spent a couple of months each winter at my second home in Florida.

Sounds of entry came from somewhere out of sight and a second later a man spoke. "Wait a second!" I guessed his comment was to a dog, since I heard the click of claws on the tile floor. A man appeared and set his briefcase, coat, and a large

Applebee's bag on a side table. A Bassett hound bounded into the room and greeted Diane enthusiastically.

"Jolie!" she said joyfully. "Daddy brought you home to Mommy!"

"The vet's office texted to say she was ready, and I thought I'd pick her up on the way to save you a trip." Seeing me in his living room, Landon froze, unsure how to react. Since Diane and the dog were busy, I rose and introduced myself.

"Margaretta Stilson, Mr. Landon. Most people call me Retta."

"Pleased to meet you." Barbara's description of Landon as the stereotypical scientist was spot on. He'd taken off the glasses she mentioned, but I could still see the two red marks where they'd rested on either side of his nose. He seemed unable to look directly at me, and his eyes darted around the room as if seeking some talisman to provide courage.

The smell of food wafted toward me, something spicy, I thought. After a brief, embarrassed pause Diane asked, "Would you like to have supper with us?"

"I've already eaten," I lied, "but I don't want to keep you from your meal."

"I'll set things out while you ask En your questions," Diane volunteered, taking up the food bag. The dog followed eagerly, its oversized ears dragging against the surface of the rug. "Come on, Jolie, Mommy will find a treat for you."

Her departure made her husband even more nervous. Perched on the edge of the one hard chair in the room, he looked like a kid brought to the principal's office. "What is it you want to know, Ms. Stilson?"

"My sister says you were kind enough to explain how a lake becomes a source for bottled water. Now we're wondering if a specific lake called Sweet Springs might be suitable for such a project."

Landon studied the wall behind my left shoulder. "I don't know the place."

I gave him the general location and told him what Faye and Barbara had discovered about its qualities. Slightly more comfortable with a subject within his expertise, he listened carefully, even glancing at me once or twice. "We've learned it's a Zone A source," I finished, "and we think someone might be planning to exploit it."

Something flickered in Landon's face. "*Exploit* is the word."

Surprised, I asked, "You don't approve?"

"To be honest, Ms. Stilson, the work I was doing in Florida made me sick. Putting a pure natural resource into plastic bottles and selling it to clueless, spoiled consumers is the worst sort of waste." Landon no longer seemed shy, and it was clear he wasn't objective on the subject.

I resolved right then to cut down on buying bottled water, at least a little.

"You've never been out to Sweet Springs, Mr. Landon?"

He frowned like a robot who'd had been asked if it liked daisies. "To tell you the truth, since we moved here I haven't seen much except the quarry and my office."

"Has anyone at WOZ mentioned Sweet Springs to you?"

"Not that I recall." He smoothed his beard absently. "I'm not very good at socializing." He smiled ever so slightly. "Diane says my head is always somewhere else."

If he was telling the truth, Enright Landon wasn't likely to be Gail Sherman's confederate. But looking at his blank expression, I couldn't help but wonder if anyone was as stereotypically nerdish as this. I tried to see past the beard and judge if he was playing a role, but it was difficult, since he looked mostly at the floor.

"You believe bottled water is a bad idea?"

His manner turned pedantic. "Of course there are legitimate uses for it, such as in disaster areas. But for everyday purposes? The bottles clog landfills, and energy is wasted in processing something that comes out of most people's taps." He shook his head in anger. "I couldn't be part of it anymore."

"So you moved to Michigan."

He glanced at me for half a second. "The job here came along at precisely the right time."

"With WOZ." I shifted my feet. "How's that working out?"

"Mr. Wozniak has an excellent grasp of business, but he needs someone like me to handle the ever-expanding governmental regulations and environmental concerns at the quarry." That sounded like it had come directly from the job description.

"And you and Stanley get along all right?"

"Mr. Wozniak says I'm the perfect employee." Landon sounded proud. "I guess I don't have much of an ego."

"I keep telling Enright he's too nice." Stepping into the doorway with a bit of chicken in her hand, Diane spoke to the dog. "Jump, baby! Jump!"

Jolie obeyed, but Diane held the meat just out of her reach. Ears flapping, the dog tried again, causing a musical, three-tone laugh from Diane. "Jump, baby!"

When she'd had enough entertainment, Diane let the dog have the meat. "She likes it when we play with her."

"They do love attention," I replied. "My Newf loves to play."

"A Newfoundland! How big?"

I rattled off Styx's height and weight, and Diane oohed with appreciation. "I'll bet walking a dog that size is a workout."

"True. Sometimes he walks me and other times he runs me."

"Where do you take him?" she asked. "I don't like walking in the development where it's all concrete and cars. The lakeshore is nice, but I'd like to find places with trees where Jolie can explore a little."

"I know lots of places like that."

Diane asked shyly, "Could you show us sometime? I don't know anyone here, and En's always at work. I'm alone a lot."

Loving a dog is always a sign of a kind heart. Diane had experienced life outside Allport, Michigan, which would be refreshing. And she obviously needed a friend.

"I'd be glad to pick you and Jolie up tomorrow around ten, if you're free. I can show you a couple of good places to walk, and then we can let Jolie explore my favorite nature path with Styx."

"That would be great."

I rose. "Now I'll get out of here so you two can have your dinner. Thanks for your help, Enright, and Diane, I'll see you tomorrow."

***

Rick was waiting when I got to the Southside Club. He rose to take my coat, telling me I looked beautiful and audibly sniffing my perfume as he leaned over to push in my chair. I ordered a glass of wine, while he asked for a refill on his gin and tonic. I also ordered deep-fried mushrooms to serve as my supper. Someone nearby had some, and the nutty, oily smell reminded me I was hungry.

"Did all go well at your business meeting?" Rick asked.

"I think so." I knew better than to tell who I'd met with, so I left it at that.

"Is your detective agency pretty active?"

I shrugged. "We stay busy."

"Lots of little old ladies who've lost their cats?"

Uncomfortable, I lowered my eyes to the tabletop. "We've solved a couple of murders, found a person who was missing for years, stopped drug dealers from killing an innocent man, and prevented a terrorist attack on Mackinac Island."

"Really." Now his tone irritated me. "The police didn't have anything to do with it?"

"I didn't say that. We work with the police, and I think they respect our skills as much as we respect theirs."

"That's cool." Rick had picked up on something in my tone, and he switched topics. "What do people do around here in the wintertime, when all the tourists go home?"

"I like to snowmobile," I replied.

He made a mock shiver. "Don't you get cold?"

"Not if you dress for it, and it's really beautiful out in the woods." An image of Lars piloting my spare sled came to mind. Despite the fact that he'd lived in a warm climate most of his life, he'd taken to snow and riding the trails like he was born to it. When we weren't being shot at, Lars and I had a great time on the trails together.

The ice in Rick's drink clinked as he took a sip. "I'll have to come back in January and let you introduce me to the sport."

"I'd be glad to," I responded, "but what if your house sells? You won't have a place to stay."

"Maybe I'll have a friend I can bunk with by then." The message was clear, and I lowered my eyes demurely. This thing—if it was going to become a thing—would proceed on my timetable, not Rick's.

Once again aware that a shift was required, he asked, "So what's with your sister and the local cop?"

"Rory? They're enough alike that they make a good pair."

"Meaning he's not very warm and fuzzy either?"

He had Barbara Ann pegged. "That about sums it up."

"I suppose they trade information on crimes and stuff."

"When it's appropriate." I had to giggle. "Barbara Ann never does anything that isn't appropriate."

That was when the fight broke out. I didn't see it coming, but we learned later what led up to it. Colin Belknap is a regular at the Southside. He usually doesn't bother anyone, just drinks himself into a stupor every night. Since he lost his driver's license and his wife long ago, he stumbles the few blocks back to his home several nights a week after midnight, no threat to anyone but himself. Clem Hiller, also a big drinker, sat next to Colin at the bar that night. Clem's name is actually Ronald, but he resembles a character created by Red Skelton decades ago, Clem Kadiddlehopper, so hardly anyone calls him Ron.

The argument had to do with stock car racing and a new rule put into place to protect drivers. Their disagreement led to a shove and then to punches. A well-placed blow from Colin sent Clem stumbling backward, where he smacked into our table, skidded across it like he was on an ice rink, and landed with a grunt of surprise on the floor on the other side. In passing, his steel-toed boot caught Rick on the chin, splitting it open like a squeezed grape.

"Oh, my god!" Rick shouted as blood dripped onto the table. "Oh, my god!"

The barmaid bellowed like an angry elk at the two brawlers, and the fight, such as it was, was over. Picking himself up from the floor, Clem leaned toward Rick, peering through the haze in his head. "That looks bad, man. You better put pressure on it."

Colin came over and stood beside Clem. "Here, buddy." He offered a dingy handkerchief, but I had already grabbed some napkins from the bar.

"Are you all right, Rick?"

"No, I'm not all right. I'm bleeding." His tone was nasty, but I knew he wasn't mad at me. Nobody expects to be sweet-talking one minute and dripping hemoglobin the next.

Needless to say, our romantic evening was over. After accompanying Rick to the ER and waiting while he got three stitches, I drove him home. The officers who responded to the bartender's call had recognized me, and they couldn't have been nicer. After they put Colin in the cruiser and sent Clem home with a sober friend, they offered to drop Rick's car off at his house. When we got there the keys were in the mailbox, as promised.

I saw Rick inside and created an ice pack out of a zipper bag and some freezer-burnt green beans I found in the fridge. Once that was done, I left him sprawled on his couch. He hardly noticed when I closed the door. All the romance had gone out of him, and Rick was just a guy with a big old boo-boo.

I drove back toward town, but the to-do at the bar, the police siren, and the whole emergency room experience had left my ears ringing and my eyes seeing spots. I doubted I'd be able to get to sleep when I got home, so I drove around for a while to relax a littel. Passing the development where the Landons lived, I turned in on a whim. Night made everything look different, and it was fun to speculate on why the lights were on in one house but not in another.

The sidewalks were empty, which made sense on a cool night in a place like Huron Delight. People had already walked their dogs, put out the trash, and done the yard work. The hours after ten were for being inside, watching TV or surfing the net.

I didn't intentionally turned down the Landons' street—or maybe I did and didn't recognize my own curiosity. I slowed when I came to their house, noting a single light in an upstairs room, a flickering blue that was probably a TV.

As I passed, I noticed there was someone out, a young man with what appeared to be a scraggly beard. It was hard to tell, because his face was buried in the deep hood of his jacket. His outfit was pretty much black with black, jeans, jacket, shoes, the works. He was walking in a hurried, hunched manner, and when he saw me he stopped. After a second he dug in his pockets and came up with cigarettes and a lighter. I'd come almost to a stop, but I realized I couldn't just sit there staring. As I passed, he turned away, apparently to block the wind as he lit his cigarette. I got the impression of youth, some homeowner's teenaged son, perhaps, who'd sneaked out at night to smoke. I went around the block and came back to try to get a better look, but he was gone.

CHAPTER TWENTY-NINE

Barb

When I first retired to Allport, my walks had been solitary and always early in the day. Though I still liked a brisk walk in the cool (sometimes cold) of morning, Rory and I had begun meeting after his shift ended on Wednesdays and Fridays at a small park just north of town, where we walked the lakeshore together. We'd fallen into a pattern of pushing it on the way out to get our metabolism up then taking it easy on the way back so we could talk. Afterward we sometimes spent the evening together; other times we returned to our separate homes.

I told Rory Faye's theory about the events on Sweet Springs. "It's troubling," I told him as we traced the water's edge, "I hate to upset the Marsh family, but if there's a possibility that old man didn't die by accident, I want to know about it."

One of the most lovable things about Rory was that he trusted my judgment, possibly because of my years of experience as an assistant District Attorney. If I said something needed looking into, he took it seriously. "I'll ask Doc Cortman about it," he offered.

"Thank you."

He put an arm around my shoulders. "Anything for a friend."

***

The next day Rory called to report his findings. "The medical examiner can only say for sure that Mr. Marsh died from the fall."

I sighed. "I was afraid of that."

"However," Rory sounded pleased with himself, "the sheriff's men found evidence that someone was at Marsh's place that morning, after the rain but before your arrival."

"Evidence?"

"There was a muddy footprint on the bottom step of the front porch. According to your statements, none of you went to the door, and the print is smaller than Marsh's."

"That means someone might have been with him—"

"*Might* is the operative term. Someone might also have come to the door, knocked, and when there was no answer, left."

"Marsh could already have been dead at that point."

"What you've told me suggests another possibility." I heard Rory's chair squeak as he went on. "Someone could have knocked and gotten the old man to go outside with him."

"Telling Marsh there's something he should see on the lake."

"Maybe. When they get to the back of the house, he pushes Marsh down the steps. Once he makes sure Marsh is dead, he erases his footprints, at least most of them, and leaves."

Realizing we had nothing to prove any of that, we sat silent for a few seconds. "Pure speculation," I finally said.

"And the M.E. ruled the death was accidental."

"An elderly man, slippery steps. Simple answer."

"Unless you look at what's happening on the other properties out there." I heard Rory sigh. "Do I talk to the sheriff, or do you?"

"He'll listen to you sooner than he will to me." When he made a sound of objection, I said, "It's a fact of life, Rory. You're a fellow cop and you're male. Right now it only matters that he pays attention to what we have to say."

Chapter Thirty

Retta

Diane and Jolie were waiting in the driveway when I arrived Thursday morning. The day was overcast but not cold, and Diane looked darling in black leggings, a long, burgundy tunic-type sweater, and a matching hat and scarf in pink. Most of the time I don't mind being petite, but when I see a woman with legs that long, I get a little envious. Tunics make me look like one of the seven dwarves.

I got out of the car and made doggie introductions. Styx was a perfect gentleman. He sniffed, of course—dogs do that—but otherwise he was as sweet as he could be. Jolie responded well, making little hound-sounds of joy and excitement.

I showed our new friends several spots that had walking paths, explaining the advantages of each. "This one's usually deserted in the daytime," I said at the county park, and at the sports pavilion, "This one's plowed all winter, at least by noon."

The last place I took them was the trail along the river. "There are three loops," I told Diane. "The first one follows the bank for a while then turns into a stand of pine trees so big you'll feel like you're lost in a forest. The two longer ones cross a bridge to a small island. One circles the edge and returns; the other crosses to the opposite side then follows the bank to the bridge where we turned off the highway. Those trails take a while, at least two hours for one and closer to three for the other."

We took the short trail. Enough leaves had fallen that our passage was noisy with the swish-swish of our feet pushing through. The dogs found plenty of interest in the squirrels that scooted along the path or scampered up nearby trees. We kept them on their leashes, since it was new territory for Jolie. Styx understood, though he shot me a mournful look when a squirrel darted across his path and he couldn't chase after it.

Diane and I chatted amiably about Allport, finding decent stores (We agreed there wasn't much worthwhile shopping), locating a decent dentist (I recommended mine), and getting a Michigan driver's license. She wasn't very political; in fact, she had no idea who most of the candidates were. Her biggest interest seemed to be celebrities—who was having whose baby. Now I keep up, so that was okay with me, but I couldn't help but think what Barbara would say about the lack of depth exhibited by the wife of a man as brilliant and educated as Landon.

Diane did have some interesting things to say about Stanley Wozniak. As we talked about their decision to relocate Diane said, "Mr. Wozniak was determined to get Enright up here. It would have been hard to turn down his very generous offer."

"Stanley has to pay well, because he's a little hard to work for," I said. "It's good that your husband has an even temperament and doesn't mind working a lot of hours."

"That part's a pain," she agreed, "but we like it here so far." Digging in her jacket pocket, Diane took out a pack of cigarettes. "I apologize, but I've been wanting a smoke all day. En thinks I quit, and his nose is every bit as good as Jolie's when it comes to smoke in the house, so I have to sneak in my ciggies." She gave me an impish grin. "I can count on you not to tell, right?"

"Sure." She lit up, sucked in smoke, and smiled faintly at the rush it provided. It reminded me of when Faye was a smoker and how I used to worry about her health. I decided Enright must really care about Diane, because nagging our loved ones into quitting that nasty habit is the best thing we can do for them.

"Tell me how you and Enright met. He seems too shy to have ever asked a woman out on a date."

"Oh, he knows what he wants when it matters," Diane said cryptically. Gesturing around us she went on, "Imagine a place the exact opposite of this—a factory with gray walls stuffed with noisy conveyer belts that shake the whole place. I spent eight hours a day checking seals on bottles that passed by." She made a disdainful click with her tongue. "Not rocket science, trust me."

"But Cinderella dreamed of going to the ball."

She chuckled. "I sure did. I'd look up to the admin section and think, 'What have those people got that I haven't got?'"

"And the answer was—?"

Her voice was light. "Brains. Education. Class."

Truth shone through her light tone, and I felt sorry for her. "I think you're very classy."

Tossing the cigarette butt to the ground, she crushed it with her toe. "You didn't see me back then. I was hopeless!"

Though Enright had brains and education, he couldn't be considered classy. Still, I imagined him visiting the factory floor, seeing the lovely Diane, and being smitten. Had she settled for brains, education, and no class because she wanted so badly to have the life she'd always dreamed about?

Since she didn't pick up the butt, I stooped to retrieve it, wrapping it in a tissue and stuffing it into my pocket for disposal later. "Enright must have seen something in you."

Diane wasn't one to kid herself. "What does a man see in a woman?" She glanced at me sideways. "I know people make nasty comments about trophy wives and gold-diggers, but if our marriage works for us, what business is it of theirs?"

Jolie strained at the leash, pulling Diane ahead a step. So the lovely worker bee had set her cap for the shy but well-paid engineer, just like in a romance novel. How had it worked out for them? Diane might be a little bored in this new location with her husband gone so much, but she didn't seem unhappy. She had a lovely home and beautiful clothes. Having seen how Enright brought take-out food so she didn't have to cook, I guessed he was putty in his attractive wife's hands. The marriage might not be based on mutual passion or traditional love, but Diane was correct: a match is a match if it works for those involved.

Diane's phone sang a few bars of Kanye West, and she answered. "Hey, babe. How are things?"

Listening for a few seconds, she said, "That's all right." She rolled her eyes at me. "Just bring home something great for dinner. You know I'm not about to cook."

She put the phone in her pocket. "Working late again. What a surprise." She sounded resigned but not angry.

We walked on for a while. "I assume when you and Enright married, your career in water bottling came to an end."

Diane shivered delicately. "En didn't want me to ever go back to that place." She curled her lips under her teeth for a moment before adding, "He didn't even want me to hang around with the girls I used to work with. He said women with nose rings and tats are poor examples of the feminine ideal."

I tried to imagine Don telling me who I could hang around with. "If they were your friends, why did he care?"

"En said I should make new ones." She must have seen disapproval on my face, because she added, "That was another reason it was better we moved away and got a fresh start."

"From what he said last night, I gather your husband doesn't approve of the bottled water industry."

She shook her head. "He says it's ridiculous."

"So he's happier working at WOZ."

"Happy?" She gave me a wry look. "Does En look like a guy who understands happiness? He's all about science."

Unsure if that was a criticism or simply a statement of fact, I said, "I guess that's good, because the EPA and the state of Michigan are interested in how WOZ treats the lakeshore."

"It sounds to me like he's doing different work with the same result." With a jerk on the leash, she pulled Jolie away from a discarded hot dog bun. "I think it's all as dull as science."

Chapter Thirty-one

Faye

Barb had gone to put her beloved Chevy into winter storage, with Dale following in her more modern Ford Edge. Together they had washed and waxed the old car, changed the oil and added stabilizer, and checked the air in the tires. Once they reached the storage unit, Dale would help her put carpet strips under the tires and cover it with a drop cloth.

Though Dale didn't often drive anymore, he enjoyed helping Barb and loved that old car almost as much as she did. The distance they had to travel was short and it wasn't raining or snowing, so the task wouldn't strain Dale's abilities. As usual, he checked the weather several times before they set off.

I admitted to myself that I was glad to see the Chevy gone for the next few months. Retta was always going on about how it was sure to break down when Barb was out in the middle of nowhere, and there's a lot of nowhere in northern Michigan. While I didn't criticize Barb's baby out loud, I did worry.

Barb sometimes went out at night, after we were in bed. She was very quiet, but old houses aren't silent places. Stairs creaked, doors squeaked, and floors shifted, no matter how lightly she treaded. When we first began sharing the house, I thought she was meeting some man she didn't want us to know about. Now she had Rory, and everyone in town knew it. Barb didn't have to sneak away at midnight to see him, but she still went out, at least once a month. Where did she go?

I'd conjured up all kinds of theories, but none of them convinced me for long. My sister wasn't a spy or a cat burglar or one who'd go looking for UFOs in the night sky. She was much too responsible, too practical, for such silliness. I'd thought about telling Retta, but I couldn't predict how she'd react. She might simply say, "Barb, Faye wants to know where you go in the middle of the night." On the other end of the spectrum, she might roll her eyes and tell me to keep my nose out of Barbara's affairs.

Since Barb's secret outings were none of my business, and since I didn't have the nerve to come out and ask what the midnight absences were about, I worried around the edges of the problem. Her car might break down. She might get lost on some dark road on a starless night. A violent man might follow her and hurt her. Worry is what I do, and believe me, I'm good at it.

When she drove her newer vehicle, I had one less worry. Not that it helped much.

Rick Chou visited the office just before closing time, stepping inside quickly and closing the door with a firm bang to keep out the sharp wind. He seemed faintly disappointed to find I was the only one there. "I wondered if Ms. Evans has found Candice yet."

His assumption I was office staff and no more was faintly annoying, but I was used to it. "We've made contact," I told him. "It's a matter of working out how the signing will be handled."

"Good. My real estate agent has a bite on the property, so I'd like to get this wrapped up in the next week or so." With a smile he apparently thought would melt my female heart he added, "Candice is a great person, but she has problems with men. I guess her dad was real hard on her."

When I didn't respond, he abandoned the it-wasn't-anything-I-did-wrong attempt. Fiddling with a button on his coat he said, "Retta tells me you've got a case of suspected elder abuse. I suppose that's more interesting than locating a stubborn ex-wife."

I tried to read the intent behind the question. Was it idle curiosity, or was Chou trying to wheedle information out of me? I made a mental note to caution Retta about discussing our cases with anyone. Even an offhand comment made to the wrong person could create problems in such matters.

"All of our cases are interesting, Mr. Chou." I said primly.

He shoved his hands into his pants pockets, jingling the change there. The look that passed over his face might have been anger, but it might also have been irritation that his charm didn't work on me. Guys like Chou aren't used to that.

In the end he forced a smile. "Well, I appreciate what you ladies are doing. My agent says these buyers are motivated."

"Do you mind telling me who your agent is?" It was a hunch.

"The property's listed with a couple of online realties," he replied, "but up here I'm working with Gail Sherman at So-Rite."

CHAPTER THIRTY-TWO

Barb

Checking the email on Friday morning, I told Faye, "Candice Chou is willing to meet us on Monday."

"Where?"

"She'll be passing through the Madison, Wisconsin, airport in the afternoon and has a two-hour layover."

"Still not taking any chances, huh?"

"I assume Retta's willing to go?"

"She's on her way here now," Faye said. "I'll get her a flight and pull the documents together—" She paused as scratching sounded from the back of the house. "—as soon as I let Buddy out of the entryway."

My cell buzzed, and I saw the call was from my nephew. As soon as Faye was gone, I picked up. "Hi, Cramer."

"Aunt Barb, I've got stuff on Chief Neuencamp's problem."

"Great." I rattled around in my desk drawer for a pen. "I'm ready—give me the name."

A noise in the outer office alerted me, and I peeked out. Retta came in the front door, accompanied by a dozen leaves the blustery wind blew in. Taking a broom from the closet she swept them up, listening to my end of the conversation as she worked.

"Name?"

"Harold Gager, twenty-six years old."

"A man? But the phone calls—"

"There are at least two people involved. The guy at Subway says Gager comes in all the time to use the free Wi-Fi. He sends the emails. A partner must make the calls."

"Is this guy employed?"

"Works at the Ugly Bar. Nights."

"Any idea why he's doing this?"

"He filled out an application online to be an officer on the APD last July. Maybe the chief was rude to him or something."

"Rory isn't like that."

"Yeah, I guess you're right. The chief's a really good guy."

"I didn't know you'd ever met him."

"Yeah, well, April had a little problem a few months back."

"Oh." Cramer's ex-wife had had several "little problems," usually stemming from her tendency to drink too many Mojitos.

"She got into it with this other girl. April poured a pitcher of beer over her head, and the girl called the cops. The chief had taken a shift, like he does sometimes, and he took April in so she could sober up." Cramer paused, but I knew what was coming. "The next morning she called me to come and drive her home."

"And you went."

"I did." He sounded ashamed. "Chief Neuencamp didn't see any sense in charging her, but he said she can't keep doing this stuff. I paid for the things that got broken in the scuffle, and he let her off with a warning."

"And what happened after that?"

I heard scuffling on the other end and pictured Cramer scraping his foot like a kid ashamed to tell what he knows. "April didn't like what he said, but as far as I know she hasn't been in trouble since."

"You know you aren't responsible for her." I glanced at Retta, who was removing brown leaves from one of Faye's plants. She didn't know it was Cramer on the other end of the call, although she might be able to guess from what she was hearing.

Cramer sighed. "I know. It's just hard when someone could be different—happier—and you can't get them to see it."

"I understand." I got back to business. "So what's the information you have for me?"

Cramer provided a short bio and addresses, both work and home, for Mr. Gager. He'd come to Allport from Indiana with a woman who had since tossed him out and moved on with her life. He lived alone in a trailer park just out of town and worked nights tending bar. When I'd copied the details down, I thanked Cramer and ended the call.

"Is somebody picking on Rory?" Retta took a seat on the chair closest to my desk.

I paused, wondering how much to tell her. On one hand, Retta's nosiness was irritating, as always. On the other, she knew the Allport undercurrents. She might even know the man Cramer had identified and why he was angry at Rory. Without saying who'd done the work of tracking Harold Gager down, I told her what he was up to. She was outraged at the insult to Rory's character. "We are so lucky to have a decent, experienced chief of police in this town. I can't believe somebody's trying to get him fired."

"Apparently Gager wanted a job but wasn't chosen."

Retta slapped the desktop. "So naturally it's Rory's fault. Like school kids who blame the principal for rules they don't like."

I said what Rory would have said had he been present. "Those who aren't smart enough to think those things through blame the person they see, not the system he works for."

She made a rude noise. “And you can’t reason with them, because they love having someone to hate.”

“Well, now that I’ve found out who it is, I intend to stop him. I want to be there when he’s caught. I want to look him in the eye when he realizes his plans are ruined.” I sounded like some B movie hero, but that was how I felt. This was personal, and I intended to see these people fail in their attempts to ruin Rory.

Retta leaned closer. “What are you going to do?”

“I don’t know,” I told her. “But it will be diabolically clever.”

“I’ll help,” she said. “I can be diabolically clever, too.”

***

Rory was out of the office when I dropped in, which I’d known ahead of time. When no one else was nearby and the buzz of other conversations covered ours, I asked the secretary casually if anyone she knew of seemed particularly angry with Rory.

Janet’s eyes narrowed as she thought about it. “A guy called after they hired Patrick last summer, demanding to know why he didn’t get the job. I explained I have nothing to do with hiring, but he wouldn’t shut up. Finally I said I had work to do even if he didn’t, and I hung up.”

“Did he blame Rory?”

She chewed on the end of her pen for a moment. “He did ask what the chief had against him. I told him Chief Neuencamp isn’t like that, but he wasn’t about to believe me.” She paused as things came together in her head. “You do know the calls about Rory slacking on the job are made by a woman, right?”

“Yes, but that could be to throw us off.”

“You think we might have an angry pair, working together?”

“It’s possible.”

Janet had come to know me pretty well. “Who is it, Barb?”

"I have a lead on the man. No idea who the woman is."

"It would be great if you could stop them." Janet brushed overlong bangs away from her eyes. "Why are people like that?"

"Maybe they blame others for their failures because they don't want to blame themselves."

Janet nodded agreement. "So are you going to tell the chief you know one of the people who's trying to sabotage him?"

"I'm not sure what I'll do. I'd appreciate it if you keep this to yourself for now."

"Not a problem," Her dark eyes flashed. "I have a feeling you can handle this jerk—and his jerkette, too."

***

When I returned home the landline phone was ringing. "Smart Detective Agency."

"Stan Wozniak here. I need to speak with Ms. Evans."

"This is Barb Evans. What can I do for you, Mr. Wozniak?"

"You can explain why you asked Enright Landon those questions the other day."

His tone made my hackles rise. How much paranoia did the man hold in his cramped little soul? Apparently, because of a few questions he'd become suspicious of his new employee.

I cleared my throat, banishing the snotty response that first arose. "You heard everything Landon and I said. Is there a problem I'm unaware of?"

"I didn't get where I am today by blindly trusting others, Ms. Evans." Without skipping a beat he asked, "Are you currently investigating a case?"

"Several, actually." *Several is vague enough to mean two.*

His pause was brief. "But you multi-task, right? Isn't that what the modern woman is noted for?"

"You know what they say. We have to work twice as hard to be considered half as good." *Especially by men like you.*

His next words surprised me. "Can we meet somewhere? I'd like to run a problem by someone familiar with the criminal mind."

Was Wozniak losing it, or did he know something I didn't? *Only one way to find out.* "Where would you like to meet?"

"There's a diner on 12th and Main. Do you know it?"

"Yes. When?"

"Now if you can manage it. I'm already there."

How like him to assume I'd dance to his tune. He was clever, though, because I was intrigued enough to meet him. "Give me fifteen minutes."

Fall in Michigan is a time when each day—sometimes various parts of a day—requires a different coat: light, medium, rain, wind, or heavy. I'd walked to Rory's office earlier, so the question I had to ask myself was which coat I'd left my car keys in the last time I drove somewhere. Faye came into the office as I was checking pockets.

When I told her where I was going, her eyes widened. "Really? Stanley Wozniak?"

"I'll tell you all about it when I get back."

***

Wozniak was sitting at a table in the classic Wyatt Earp position: facing the room, back to the wall. Before him was a platter, empty except for stains of egg yolk and toast crumbs. He rose as I approached. "What would you like, Ms. Evans?"

I spoke to the waitress. "Coffee, please."

He tried to interest me in a pastry, but I refused. Taking his platter, the woman went off to get the coffee pot.

Wozniak regarded me with his usual direct gaze, so I looked right back. He was a few years older than I with gray hair cut GI short and a lean body that hinted at either an exercise regimen or high metabolism. From Retta I knew Stan had been married three times and was known nowadays for temporary liaisons with women who were physically attractive but not terribly smart.

"You're wondering why I asked you here."

"It sounds to me like you distrust the man you recently hired."

The waitress returned to pour my coffee and refill Wozniak's. It smelled good, and I smiled at her in thanks. Wozniak waited until she was gone before he spoke.

"Shortly after you came to the office, a woman from the human resources office at Landon's last place of employment called. He was out at the quarry, so I took the call. She wanted to ask him something about his 401K, and I told her what time she could call back later and speak to him." Stan sipped his coffee. "Since your visit was fresh in my mind, I asked the woman if they'd ever had any questions as to Landon's character." He paused to give me a lesson in business. "They all write glowing reference letters, but they never tell you what they left out."

"Hard to get rid of an unsatisfactory employee if you admit he's unsatisfactory," I agreed.

"Yes. Well, this woman assured me Landon was an excellent engineer and a hard worker, uninspired but honest. The only hiccup came when the company credit card he was given got charged for a bunch of cash withdrawals he couldn't have made."

"Couldn't have?"

"While Landon was at work, someone visited multiple ATMs and took the maximum amount from each one."

"Stealing from the company?"

Wozniak shrugged. "It wasn't Landon. He was at the plant on the days it happened, and the card was in his wallet."

"Identity theft, then."

He nodded. "The police found security camera footage of a young man in a hoodie with lots of facial hair and tattoos making the withdrawals, but they never located him."

"So Landon was never a suspect."

"No." Wozniak seemed certain. "The card was used repeatedly over a month's time. It wasn't until the bookkeeper reconciled employee record sheets with the credit card statements that the theft was discovered."

"And steps were taken to stop it."

"Of course." He shifted in his chair, setting his elbows heavily on the table. "The authorities were alerted and the card was flagged, but it was never used again. The police believe the thief was a lone wolf who seized an opportunity and made the most of the information until discovery of his withdrawals became likely."

"How much did the company lose?"

"Fifty thousand dollars."

I set my cup down on the coaster with a soft ceramic clunk. "The thief must have been pretty busy for a while."

"That's why I'd like to hire you to check on Landon—discreetly—and see if he's the type who might have taken some fast cash from his employer."

Remembering the shy engineer's demeanor I asked, "Do you suspect he isn't what he seems to be?"

Wozniak grinned mirthlessly. "It's hard for me to believe anyone is as mild-mannered and self-effacing as Enright Landon. If I said I wanted him to personally get Lake Huron water samples from a mile off-shore, he'd nod that big old head of his and start wading." He shrugged. "I suppose it could be an act."

Neither of us mentioned a former, trusted WOZ employee who'd turned out to be dishonest. The fact that I'd exposed his crimes made Wozniak willing to trust me, even if he didn't like me. To men like Stan, liking has nothing to do with business.

I considered his offer. "I'm not sure if we can help you. If the case we have now should connect to Landon, we'd run into a conflict of interest."

As I said it, my brain took that idea a step further. What if Stan himself was behind this? He had the money to buy the properties, he had the resources to build a bottling plant, and he was always looking for ways to expand WOZ Industries. Had he hired Landon with an eye to diversifying into bottled water?

Then why would he want me to investigate him?

That answer came quickly: to keep his finger on the pulse of our activities. If Wozniak wanted to know what the Smart Detectives were up to, our best way to learn what *he* was up to might be to agree to his proposal.

He was waiting, and it felt like those gray-blue eyes were reading my thoughts. "Tell you what. If something we learn points to the possibility that Landon is dishonest, I'll make sure you're made aware of it."

I didn't say how he'd be made aware. He might learn of it when the police came with a warrant to search his offices. If Wozniak was involved in property crimes, elder abuse, and possibly murder, he'd get no sympathy from me.

"Fair enough." He set his cup down and slid it off to the side, as if closing the topic. Looking over my shoulder at nothing he said, "I see her sometimes."

The abrupt change of subject caught me by surprise, and I stared at him blankly.

“Brooke. We get together whenever I’m up here.”

It took me a second to recall that Brooke was the granddaughter he’d rejected, believing her father was a murderer. “She’s a good kid—got all A’s on her last report card.” His voice took on a wistful tone. “She looks just like my Carina did at that age.”

“I’m sure that’s a good thing—for both of you.” Sliding out of the booth, I took up the jacket I’d laid on the seat and pushed my arms into the sleeves. It had been my intention to remain aloof, but the fact that Stan was trying to be a grandfather to Brooke earned him a modicum of respect in my eyes.

“If what I learn about Landon has anything to do with his job at WOZ Industries,” I told Stan, “I’ll be in touch.”

CHAPTER THIRTY-THREE

Faye

While Barb met with Mr. Wozniak, I called a couple of contacts who'd promised to do some digging for me. A friend at the county records office had researched the current ownership of the Clausen property. "It was purchased by a corporation called S&S Incorporated," she reported, "but I couldn't find a single human associated with it, just a law office out of Detroit."

Sherry, who ran a local print shop, had a friend in Lansing knowledgeable enough to navigate the layers of government bureaucracy and locate paperwork making its way through the system. "A usage request has been made," she reported. "The owner of a property on Sweet Springs asked for an assessment, and it's scheduled for November 18th. The property owner is—some corporation." As she paused to check her notes I supplied, "The S&S Corporation."

"You've heard of them?"

"Not till a minute ago. Any people named on the application?"

After a few seconds she said, "Sydney Mellon is the contact person. Is that a name you recognize?"

"Nope." I shuffled through my notes on the case, but I was pretty sure that name hadn't come up.

"Then I guess what I found doesn't help much."

"We know there's interest in the water at Sweet Springs."

"I was out there once," Sherry said. "It would be a shame to build a plant next to all that natural beauty."

“I agree.” Knowing Sherry was an active member of the Allport grapevine I asked, “If I give you some names, will you tell me what comes to mind?”

“Sounds like a fun game.”

Unwilling to tip my hand too easily, I started with two Allport city councilmen. Sherry’s answers were predictable, and I tried the name of a man who considered himself an entrepreneur.

“Nobody likes George,” she said. “Avoid him like the plague.”

“How about Gail Sherman? She’s a realtor at—”

“I know of her,” Sherry interrupted. “They say she goes through men like the Kardashians go through eyeliner.”

“So who’s the current man?”

“Some tourist. That was last week, so it might be old news.”

Barb’s current location flitted through my mind. “How about Stan Wozniak? Did Gail ever date him?”

Sherry searched her memory, humming a little. “Can’t say yes for sure, but she’s definitely his type: big boobs, big eyes, limited comprehension of words of more than two syllables.”

“She’s dumb?”

“Not when it comes to making a buck, but she couldn’t tell the truth about a property if somebody tattooed it on her arm.”

“So, not crooked but definitely bent a little.”

“That’s about right. Come to think of it, Gail might be seeing Stan. Her car was at WOZ last week when I delivered stationery.”

“You’re sure it was her car?”

“She’s got one of those magnetic signs that says SO-RITE REALTY. If the Asian guy is in her past, she might go after Stan. She’d have to move fast, since he isn’t around much anymore.”

“The Asian guy?”

"The tourist. Can't think of his name—"

Rick Chou. Gail was dating—or had been dating—our client and Retta's new friend. How much had they talked about water bottling, elderly aunts, and the Smart Detective Agency?

The door opened just then and Barb came in, along with windblown dirt and leaves. Eager to know what she'd found out, I thanked Sherry and told her I'd catch up with her soon.

I turned to Barb expectantly. "What's with Mr. Wozniak?"

She frowned, making deep lines between her brows. "He wants us to check on Enright Landon, he says, but I'm wondering if he's got ulterior motives." She took out her phone. "I turned off the ringer during our meeting, and on the way home I saw I'd received this." She held out her phone so I could read the message. Rory wanted her to call him at the police station as soon as possible.

"Sounds serious."

Barb made the call. "Hi, Janet. It's Barb Evans returning Chief Neuencamp's call."

She waited briefly then said, "Rory? What's going on?" Her expression changed as she listened. Finally she said, "Thanks. I'll be in touch."

We both turned as the door opened and Retta came in. "I was right behind you. I thought we'd—" She stopped as the look on Barb's face registered. "What's wrong?"

"Gail Sherman's body was found floating in Sweet Springs this morning. Sheriff Brill called Rory, and he let me know."

***

News came in bits and pieces, some of it reliable, some typical of the small-town telegraph, overblown and edging on the ridiculous. Gail had been raped and strangled. Not true. She'd drowned saving a child but couldn't save herself. Also fiction. A passing motorist had seen her fall into the lake from the main road but couldn't get to her in time (geographically impossible).

I was reminded of when Dale got hurt. I'd learned afterwards that according to town gossip, I'd moved the fallen tree off him myself, powered by love and adrenalin, like the Cajun Queen who saved Big, Bad John in the song. Way wrong, though if I'd been there, I certainly would have tried.

The truth of Gail's death, Rory reported half an hour later, was that Fred Marsh had been at his grandfather's house and noticed something white floating near Clara's dock. Since the night had been windy, he'd thought a tarp might have blown into the lake. On his way home he'd stopped to fish it out but instead discovered Gail's body. "There's a wound on her head," Rory said over the speakerphone. "The coroner will have to determine if she was struck or hit her head when she fell into the water."

"According to both Fred Marsh and Clara, Gail was afraid of the lake," I told him. "She wouldn't go near it."

"I guess we'll know more when the autopsy's done."

After ending that call Barb mused, "If Gail had a partner, as Faye suggested, he might have begun to see her as a liability."

"Because we started looking into her activities?"

"Right." Spinning slowly left and right in her chair, she laid out a possible scenario. "Let's say Gail meets Mr. X, who's smarter than she about business but unaware of Sweet Springs. When Gail mentions her aunt's property, this person sees possibilities. Still, he knows local objections can delay projects like that and even derail them. Gail knows the Clausen place is for sale, and she says she can talk Aunt Clara into selling. He offers financial backing, and they form a partnership."

"Right," Retta said. "The corporation that bought the Clausen property is probably Gail and the partner, whoever he is."

"Or she," I put in.

Retta turned to me, one brow quirked. "It has to be one of two people, either Enright Landon or Stanley Wozniak. Enright has the technical know-how to deal with a water plant and Stanley has the business sense."

"And the drive to make a big profit," Barbara put in.

"Exactly." Retta had a new idea. "Maybe the corporation is actually Gail plus Wozniak *and* Landon."

"Which one of them murdered Gail?"

"We're not sure anyone did, Retta."

"Oh, come on, Barbara Ann. The woman was terrified of the lake. Why would she go down to the dock and just fall in?"

Barb shrugged. "There could be a dozen reasons. We need to deal in facts."

"But we should think outside the box, too."

"All right, let's do that. Are there other reasons why someone would want Gail dead—assuming she was murdered?"

We all thought about that for a while. "It depends how far the scheme to get the properties went," Retta finally said. "If Gail and her partners killed Caleb Marsh and burned the Warners' house down, one of them might have wanted to get back at them."

"But the Warners are in Detroit, and Fred Marsh isn't the type to push a defenseless woman off a dock," I argued.

"If Marsh learned Gail was partly to blame for his grandfather's death, he might have confronted her at Clara's."

"Killing her could have been an accident." Barb took off her glasses and polished the lenses with a wipe.

"Right. He chased her onto the dock. She fell, hit her head on a post, and died. He panicked and made up a story about finding her body." Retta's flair for the dramatic took it a step farther. "Or he killed her in a rage and threw her body in the water to make it look like she drowned."

I shook my head. "You're way outside the box now. How would Fred have found out Gail's scheme? How would he know she'd be at Clara's house? Why wouldn't he call the police if he thought she was involved in criminal activity?"

Retta fell silent, chastened a little by common sense, and I tossed out my own theory. "What about Rick Chou as the silent partner? According to rumor, he and Gail had some sort of relationship. He's got money, so he could provide the financing."

"And he's been keeping tabs on us by sticking close to Baby Sister." Though Barb's phrasing was more aggressive than I'd have chosen, I'd been thinking the same thing.

"Rick is no murderer." Retta's indignant expression contradicted her tone, which revealed she knew how weak her position was. "He doesn't even live here full time."

"That doesn't preclude his scheming to make a pile of money when the opportunity arises. If he had a fling with Gail—"

"Gossips saying they were an item doesn't make it true."

Knowing gossip, Barb and I had to acknowledge her point. Still, Retta didn't want to believe Chou might be different than she imagined him, which clouded her judgment.

"What's the scenario?" Barb asked. "If Gail was murdered, which we don't know yet, it would go like this: Gail is a minor crook. She meets a man—she's always meeting a man—and they hatch a scheme. When she becomes a liability, he kills her."

"If that's true, the coroner will find evidence of murder and his plan will be ruined."

"But if they don't find anything, he's good to go. If a crime is indicated at a future point, he can say he had no idea what Gail did to get the property. She'll take the blame for anything the police *can* prove."

"Not much chance of that," Retta put in. "There's no proof Mr. Marsh's death wasn't an accident. The Warners' house burned due to arson, but there's no evidence of who the arsonist was. Gail wasn't even in Michigan then." She began rearranging items on Barb's desk, caught herself, and buried her hands in her lap. "With her dead, no one can tie Mr. X to the scheme."

"Except that he's the one who profits," I argued.

"But we can't prove he committed crimes to put himself in that position. Getting the bottling plant going might be a little more difficult to pull off without Gail to hide behind, but it can be done. We have no way to stop him."

We argued, discussed, and puzzled over Gail's silent partner for the next half hour but got nowhere. When Retta finally went home, I asked Barb, "Should we cancel the Canada trip?"

"I don't see any reason to," she replied. "Rory isn't involved in the investigation of Gail's death. Lars is coming in tonight, and there isn't much we can do until the medical report is in, which will be Monday at the earliest." She bit her lip. "Did you tell Retta about the plans for tomorrow?"

"She thinks we're going to visit Clara." At her look, I raised a palm. "You can spring the trip on her at your convenience. I'm not telling Retta she has to be up and dressed by five."

Barb sighed, and I knew she was regretting the whole idea. "Okay. I just hope she reacts well when the guys show up at the railway station."

CHAPTER THIRTY-FOUR

Retta

On our dog-walking date, I had invited Diane Landon to go shopping with me on Friday. It's more fun to shop with someone else, I think, though Barbara disagrees. She shops only when necessary, and then with deadly precision and no sense of adventure whatsoever. Faye buys her clothes at second-hand stores, claiming it's ridiculous to pay full price. Though Diane was a lot younger than I and had less age-related flaws to hide, it would be nice to have a companion who appreciated good fabric and clever design.

We had a good time, talking about everything the way women do when they're getting to know each other. She'd lived in a lot of places, since her dad worked on oil rigs. "Name a state with oil, and I've lived there," she joked. She was very interested in what is was like to be a private detective, and though I explained it was nothing like the movies portray. I admitted we'd done well with the cases we'd had thus far.

"Now you're looking into something about water bottling?"

I shrugged. "It's one possibility in a case we took on."

"Sweet Springs, right?" She flipped her hair over her shoulders. "I heard you telling En the other night."

An image of Barbara Ann's disapproving face came to mind, and I gave a no-answer answer. "As I said, just a possibility."

"I see." Fingering the weave of a sweater on the sale rack, she wrinkled her nose. "Our agent mentioned the place once."

"Gail Sherman? What did she say about it?"

Her mouth twisted as she tried to remember. “Something personal. I think her grandmother or someone like that lived out there, but it wasn’t a good situation for her anymore.”

“Clara is Gail’s aunt. Was. You heard Gail is dead, right?”

“It was on the news. It’s terrible, an accident like that.”

I didn’t comment on that. “That’s all she said, that her aunt lived at Sweet Springs?”

She frowned again. “She said something about getting control of the property if the aunt was declared incompetent. She said she had some ideas about what to do with it.” Diane smiled ruefully. “That’s really all I remember.”

“Every little bit helps us,” I said encouragingly. “I don’t know what will happen to Clara’s property now that Gail’s dead, but it would be a shame if someone turned the area into a bottling plant. It’s really pretty out there.”

“Yes,” she agreed, “though that dirt road makes a mess of your car.”

I put the cropped pants I’d been looking at back on the table. The fabric was too stiff “Have you been out there?”

“No,” she said. “Gail said she had to take her car to the carwash after every trip out there.”

“When did you last speak to Gail?”

Diane considered. “Saturday, I think. She called to talk to Enright, who was home for once, and we chatted a little while I searched the house for him.” She chuckled. “He sets his phone down and walks away, so I’m always answering his calls.”

Saturday had been the day a strange man chased me off Clara’s property. I remembered seeing two cars drive by on Sweet Lane, too. Had Gail been out there with her partner? Had he been the one who’d threatened me with a hoe? Recalling his wiry build, I thought of the young man I'd seen outside Diane's house a few nights later. It could have been the same man, I decided.

"What time do you go to bed at night?" Diane gave me a funny look and I groped for a reason for asking. "I don't like calling people if they're early-to-bed types."

"Am I that easy to read?" She made a little duck-face. "I go to bed pretty early most nights. Usually around nine o'clock we head to our rooms, which are at separate ends of the house." Smiling in embarrassment she explained, "En snores like a diesel, so I sleep alone. Once I turn my white noise on, I'm out for the night."

Snoring does separate lots of couples, but separate rooms might mean Enright didn't want his wife knowing what he was up to. Mr. X might have hired a minion to do his dirty work.

If that was so, his choice of a wife like Diane was more calculating than I'd thought. She wasn't the type who'd question Enright or object when he worked all the time…and she wouldn't notice if a strange young man hung around their home after midnight.

Chapter Thirty-five

Barb

Since Lars' arrival was a surprise for Retta, and since Retta has radar that picks up almost everything that goes on in Allport, we'd decided Lars would stay at Rory's cabin Friday night. From what Rory told me, it sounded like they'd planned Lars' one-night stay like ten-year-olds in a backyard tent. In order to get the place ready, Rory and I drove out on Friday afternoon with enough supplies to get the Donner party out of trouble.

The roads became smaller and narrower as we headed for Rory's little piece of heaven, but at least we didn't have to travel by snowmobile, as we had the first time I visited. The drive was pleasant, evoking the sense we'd left the world behind. Modern structures gradually disappeared, and we saw only a few hunting camps, most of them deserted. The trees were bright with color, and because the road wasn't plowed in winter, they grew closer to the road, creating the illusion of traveling through a worm-hole to another dimension. I turned my cell phone off, since there was no reliable signal anyway. Rory and I were truly by ourselves.

Those who know me well might have been surprised to learn I spent time in a primitive cabin where meals were made over an open fire and an outhouse took the place of a real bathroom. It sometimes surprised me too, but I'd come to enjoy the quiet, the complete darkness at night, and the visits from deer, raccoons and other animals that regarded us gravely when we turned a light on them and then went back to what they were doing. At night the coyotes howled, far away and mournful, and I learned to sleep through the sound as I had learned to sleep through sirens in my years in the city.

The cabin sat along a river, below the road as it passed along a ridge. There was no place for a driveway, so we parked in the trees and made our way down a steep incline to reach the front door. We each took a load of groceries, but Rory said he'd fetch the rest after he got a fire going. My job would be to organize what we'd brought.

Entering brought the scent of wood smoke to my nose, and beyond that, dust. The structure was one room, no more than thirty by thirty, but it was tightly-built and had everything Rory wanted in a getaway. A fieldstone fireplace took up the center of one wall, and a wood box beside it held the makings of a fire.

Rory planned to cook what he called "linner," a meal halfway between lunch and dinner, for the two of us. "Once the fire takes hold," he said as he wadded paper for tinder, "we'll go for a walk while the place warms up. By the time we get back the heat will be just right for cooking pork steaks."

On the wall opposite the fireplace was a pump, which Rory had put into working order. Clean, in fact, very good water was available with a little effort on the handle. In the back corner was a bed with an iron frame and a comfortable mattress. It had replaced a fold-down wooden bunk on the other end of the comfort scale.

The center of the room held a small dining table with four chairs, an addition I was particularly proud of. Driving past the Salvation Army Red Store one day last summer, I'd seen it sitting outside and stopped. It was the right size, the chairs matched—though their seats were tattered—and the price wasn't bad. I'd bought the set, asked Faye to recover the seats, and presented it to Rory as a birthday gift.

The rest of the cabin's wall space was taken up with shelving, mostly cupboards. I sometimes chuckled at the things Rory had hauled out to the cabin "in case," things like extra socks and empty plastic bowls. If I hadn't known better, I might have imagined we were hundreds of miles from civilization.

The cabin's interior was colder than the air outside, which had dropped into the twenties, so the fire would be welcome. Rory set the crumpled newspaper in place and stacked kindling atop it, thin, dry wood that would burn easily. Using a grill lighter, he set the pile on fire. When the kindling started to crackle and turn black, he put two small logs on top. Soon the pungent odor of fresh smoke overlaid the stale smell of older fires.

Watching him work pleased me, bringing back memories of my father lighting our old wood-burning stove to provide extra warmth on the coldest nights of winter.

As the fire strengthened, Rory went to the truck for the rest of his purchases and I turned to stowing the supplies. Aside from the things kept in coolers outside the cabin, food items were stored in a metal cabinet with a strong latch, to keep out the critters. Rory was careful to see that no food was left out, no crumbs scattered around. "One or two little guests will get in no matter what we do," he acknowledged, "but if they find something to eat, they invite all their friends and family to join them."

In late spring, Rory and I had installed a new window to replace the one broken in a struggle with men who'd meant to kill us. Rory and Lars had done more work recently, so I was treated to a tour of the renovations. New to me was a quaint apparatus in the corner next to the fireplace, framed with two by fours. On an overhead shelf sat a large, collapsible plastic bag with a hose and shower head attached. Rory explained we could heat water, transfer it to the bag, and enjoy warm showers. Peering through a plastic curtain hung across the space, I saw a drain in the floor.

"Primitive, but it works."

"Well done, Ranger Neuencamp. I can't wait to try it."

"Lars helped with the base, which weighs a ton. And he rigged the curtain for privacy."

Once we'd stored the provisions, we went for a walk along the river, which wasn't much of a river at this point. Still, the stream made a happy little sound as it hurried along its way. On the shady side, ice had begun to build at the turns, so thin it was merely a glaze hanging above the water.

We let the quiet settle on our heads like a comforting blanket. Rory claimed his blood pressure dropped twenty points each time he came here, and I believed him.

There was no path along the stream, and after a half mile or so, the way got difficult. We had to step over twisted branches and skirt swampy spots, and our hiking boots made sucking sounds as the half-frozen, half viscous muck worked to pull them off our feet. Finally, thick undergrowth forced us to turn around and head back the way we'd come. "It's time to make linner anyway," Rory said. "We've got just enough time to dine before we have to get back to town and meet Lars at the airport."

As Rory prepared our meal in a skillet over the fire, we turned to talk of the day's events. Gail Sherman's autopsy wasn't complete, but preliminary reports indicated her head wound contained wood splinters. "The doc says she might have hit the one of the pilings on Clara's dock."

"Which means—?"

He shrugged. "Maybe she was in a hurry and caught the heel of her shoe, which was too high for walking around on a dock safely. She fell, striking her head as she stumbled into the water."

"And if she didn't stumble?"

He knew where I was going. "Then someone pushed her."

"Is it similar to what happened to Caleb Marsh?"

He nodded. "Both deaths are conceivably accidents, but my guess is they're a little too convenient for you."

"Don't you agree?"

"I do. It's just that it's going to be hard to prove." He turned the meat with a fork the length of a yardstick. "If Marsh was murdered, Gail is your number one suspect."

"She wanted his property. She went right to the heirs and offered to buy it."

Using his shirt-tail as a pot-holder, Rory removed the skillet from the fire. "Well, she's dead now. If Marsh was pushed, Gail probably did the pushing."

"I don't know about that." I readied the plates, one in each hand, and Rory speared the meat onto them then took up a can of beans he'd set at the side of the fire to warm. He poured a serving onto each plate, and we retreated to the table to eat our meal. "I met Gail Sherman, and while I would never say who could or could not be a murderer, I doubt she cold-bloodedly pushed an old man she'd known all her life to his death. She struck me as the kind of person who might advocate bombing unknown people in a foreign country with some vague idea that they're her enemies. That doesn't mean she could look someone in the eye and murder him."

"Just about anyone can kill in a fit of anger," Rory argued. "If the old guy refused her offer once too often, or if he ordered her off his land, she might have lost it."

"True. But the fact that Gail is now dead, also pushed, indicates there's another person involved, someone who stayed out of the spotlight while Gail did her part."

"Buying the properties."

"Right."

"But she hadn't finished."

"No." I took a drink of the icy water Rory had provided from the hand pump. "What if Gail didn't know there'd be murder and arson involved? What if she thought they were going to quietly buy up the land over the next year or two by negotiating with Marsh and the Warners?"

"You think she was greedy but not necessarily homicidal."

"Right. I can see her justifying what she did to Clara, telling herself it was necessary." Taking a bite of perfectly done meat, I chewed before going on. "Gail might have believed the fire was an accident, but when the old man died so conveniently, she'd have to have been suspicious. She calls her partner and says, 'We need to talk.' He arranges to meet her at Clara's house and kills her when she refuses to be part of the scheme anymore."

Rory sighed. "You make a good case, but again, the only provable case is against Gail, who's dead."

"Once we find out who the partner is, we can set about proving it."

We'd finished our meal, and I cleaned up while Rory banked the fire. Since he hadn't volunteered the information, I brought up the anonymous calls and emails. A shadow crossed his eyes, and I saw that what had been a joke was now something else. "She's accused me of sexual harassment."

I was so shocked I couldn't respond for a moment. I knew "she" was two people, but I wasn't ready to let Rory know I'd taken up his cause. Old-fashioned in some ways, I was afraid he wouldn't approve of his girlfriend defending him, and he'd certainly object to Cramer's method of learning Gager's identity.

"No one who knows you will take that allegation seriously."

He sighed. "But they still have to investigate it."

"Tell me what was said."

"The complaint is that I man-handled a couple of women we had in the lockup—" He paused before finishing, "—in a sexually inappropriate way."

"Do these women support the claim?"

"Not so far, but what if one or the other realizes the crime she's charged with could be dismissed if I did something wrong?"

"But it isn't true."

He grimaced. "You know I take a shift sometimes. We're always short-handed, and it does any boss good to do once in a while what his staff does every day."

I nodded. "It's easy to forget what it's like in the trenches, no matter what the organization."

"Well, I arrested a woman who keyed her boyfriend's car, and according to our caller, I groped her in the process. The other woman was in lockup when I got to work. The state police got an email claiming I offered to drop the charges in return for sexual favors." His eyes had turned even darker.

I wanted to put my arm around him, touch the rough fabric of his shirt, and tell him things would work out, but I sensed it wasn't the right time. I let him finish in his own way. "Of course they sent a detective to interview the women. He kept it general, asking if anything unusual had happened during their recent encounter with the Allport police." Rory's tone was matter-of-fact, but I could see it was killing him to say it aloud. "One woman said no right away, but the other one, the car-keyer, played it a little, trying to find out what the detective was talking about."

"Smart enough to see an advantage in spinning a story."

"She stopped short of making specific charges, and she blew a .13, so her word is suspect." He stared into the fire. "But I was the arresting officer, so she knew who they were looking at."

I was so upset by the situation that I hardly noticed Rory's misuse of *who* for *whom.*

When we'd finished eating, we swept the cobwebs out of the cabin's corners, which always made me sneeze. Dust never gets completely removed from cabins; it only rises briefly during cleaning then falls back into place.

That done, we drove back into town to meet Lars. Allport's version of an air-travel hub didn't require an early arrival or fighting our way through a crowd. There was only one gate and seldom more than half a dozen people waiting for an arriving flight. The same person took tickets, checked passengers at boarding, and answered the phone. One became quite well acquainted with her over the course of a single trip.

We watched the little plane land and saw four people exit before it turned around and taxied away, headed for its next drop-off point. Lars entered the terminal with a carry-on slung over his shoulder. Beside him walked an elderly woman who was telling him something that required wide gestures. He smiled politely, waited until she'd finished her story, and touched her arm in farewell. She stood smiling after him as he approached us, clearly impressed with the nice "young man."

Lars did look good. Though I knew he was fifty, he might have passed for forty. Between his Scandinavian heritage and the fitness required by his profession, he made female hearts flutter, Retta's included. She just forgot sometimes how much she liked Lars. The woman had a short attention span.

After picking up the rental car he'd arranged, Lars followed Rory and me to the cabin. Rory joked that Lars would get lost without a guide, being a city slicker, and Lars replied he could always call in an FBI drone to locate any place on the planet. When we arrived, Lars was like a kid at summer camp, running his hands over the backs of the chairs, the mantel, and even the water pump, as if marking them with his scent.

Since it was his first time staying at the cabin alone, Rory explained how to keep the fire going and how to work the generator. Lars' expression as he listened was serious, as if it were February and not October.

I hoped to have time to tell Lars about the harassment Rory had been receiving. Since things had become more serious, I wanted advice on how to proceed. It only took a suggestion that there might not be enough wood in the cabin to get Rory on his feet. Lars rose to help, but I shook my head, signaling I wanted him to stay. Catching on, Lars went to the pump instead and refilled his cup with water.

While Rory was gone, I explained the situation. "I've tracked down one of the perpetrators," I said in conclusion, "but I don't know what to do next. Do I tell Rory what I've got and let him take over? Do I give the information to the state police?"

Lars thought about it. "There's a second person involved but you don't know who she is?"

"My source thinks Harold Gager does the on-line stuff and a woman makes the calls. It's possible they're operating separately but more likely they're cooperating."

"I'm guessing you found this guy in a way that won't be admissible as evidence in court."

I felt my face flush. "Yes."

He didn't seem bothered by that. "If you identify one of them the other could keep it going. When that happens, a lawyer will argue it wasn't him in the first place. We need to get them both."

I liked that he said *we*. Lars was already on board.

"Let me think on this for a while and see what I come up with." He put a strong hand on my arm, and I felt as if I'd entered into a solid, firm alliance.

Rory entered with an armload of wood and dumped it into the wood box, making a terrible clatter. "There. If the fire should go out, you know how to get it started again."

"Sure."

There was further discussion of problems that might arise, but Lars contended he could handle them. After he'd asked three times if Lars would be okay, Rory turned to me. "Let's go, Barb."

As we left, our favorite FBI man's frame filled the cabin doorway, a boyish grin on his face. Mom and Dad were trusting little Lars to stay home alone, and he was thrilled about it.

Chapter Thirty-six

Retta

It was hard to believe Barbara had chosen to tell me and not Faye about her plan to rescue Rory's reputation, but it was probably due more to timing than anything else. The only thing she hadn't revealed was her source, but that hadn't stopped me for long. I simply expressed a desire for a Coke, and while she went to get it, peeked at her phone. (Her code is her birthday, which I'm sure she thinks is really clever.) Her last caller was Cramer, which surprised me. I've never seen Faye's boys as go-getters, though it wasn't for lack of brains. It was more a tendency to be satisfied with where they were and what they had.

I was angry that someone was harassing Rory, who was a darned good police chief. When he'd arrived in Allport the year before, he had interested me as a man, and I'd done a little flirting in those first few weeks. As soon as I figured out he wasn't my type, I'd set to work getting him and Barbara together. They're two of a kind: so honest and dutiful they're kind of boring.

If some low-life people were making trouble for Rory, we had to stop them. I considered how it might be done, but nothing I came up with seemed workable. We didn't have the power to order them to stop, and if we turned the name Cramer had found over to the state police, Rory's reputation would get dragged through the mud when the case went to court. Like our dad used to say, "Throw enough mud at a person and some of it will stick."

Barbara and I were apparently thinking along the same lines, because she called me after supper. "Faye and I have been talking, Retta, and we'd like to do something tomorrow."

"Good," I responded. "Let's stop these people who are threatening Rory's job."

In response she said the oddest thing ever. "That wasn't what I meant. We're going to take a trip."

"What?"

"The three of us should go away for the day." She cleared her throat. "With time away, maybe we'll figure something out."

Miss I-plan-everything-six-weeks-ahead was asking me to drop everything for a girls' day out? "We're in the middle of two cases, Barbara Ann. Rory's being harassed and you know who one of the culprits is. And you want to take a trip?"

"Nothing's going to happen before Monday."

"And I have to fly to Wisconsin on Monday."

"Right, but if we figure out what we're going to do over the weekend, Faye and I can handle it between her trips to feed the chickens. Why shouldn't we enjoy the fall colors for a day?"

She sounded so weird, so un-Barbara-like, that I became suspicious. "So when Faye asked me to go to the Meadows with her tomorrow, she was setting me up for this sisters' day out?"

"Maybe."

I tapped my fingers on the doorframe, puzzled. "Barbara, what's this really all about?"

"Can't we just have a nice time without you getting all fussy?" Calming herself with a little cough, she started over. "I thought we'd ride the Algoma Railway. Faye's always wanted to go, and it's the perfect time of year. On the way up there, we'll decide what to do about Rory's problem."

Letting out a sigh, I said, "I guess that works." There was more to it than she was letting on, but at least my sisters weren't leaving me behind, like they used to when we were kids. I was part of their plan, though I wasn't sure why.

I hadn't answered Barbara's last attempt to defend the Oxford comma, a text she'd sent without explanation. AMONG THOSE INTERVIEWED WERE MERLE HAGGARD'S TWO EX-WIVES, KRIS KRISTOFFERSON AND ROBERT DUVAL.

Though I saw her point, strict grammarians like Barbara never give people credit for being able to figure out what a sentence is trying to get across. They're as bad as those people who put CONTAINS NUTS on a bag of cashews.

I was eating a piece of pie when the phone rang. Pie is my specialty and my weakness, and I'd made pumpkin in honor of October and chocolate because it's my favorite. I'd cut myself a tiny slice of each. Who can decide which is better? Not me!

It was Rick Chou calling, and it was cute how eager he was to get another chance to see me. I toyed with the idea of inviting him over for pie, but I said, "Can't see you tonight. I've got to go to bed early so I can get up before dawn."

"That's not a problem for me."

His tone was suggestive, but I just laughed. "I meant I've got to go to *sleep* early."

"I was hoping you could give me a better end to the day than I had at the beginning," he said, sounding pouty.

"What happened?"

"One of Allport's finest gave me a ticket."

"Oh, no! What for?"

"This old woman with a cane was crossing the street right there near the movie theater. I was waiting to make a turn, and she held me up till the light turned red. I honked the horn to let her know about it before I scooted down the street. I didn't see the cop sitting across the intersection."

"But he saw you."

"Gave me a ticket for an unsafe turn." He was still angry. "Old people shouldn't leave the house if they can't keep up with traffic patterns."

"Don't be such a grump," I chided. "Even old people have to get out sometimes."

"I suppose." He changed the subject. "Did you hear about the real estate agent who drowned?"

"Yes. I met her recently." The pie was calling to me, and I wondered if I had time to take a bite between conversational turns. It was still warm, for pity's sake.

"She'd listed my house. I've asked the other woman in the office to take over, but I hope it doesn't slow things down."

"That might be a good thing if it keeps you here longer."

"Not possible," he said, then he picked up on my flirtatious tone. "Oh, I get what you mean. I wouldn't mind if I got to see a little more of you." He let the double entendre sit there for a second before adding, "Still, I have things to do in Grand Rapids."

"Busy, busy?"

He sighed. "If the sale doesn't go through next week, I'll have to come back later in the month to finalize things."

Faye's suspicion that Rick might have been Gail's partner came to mind and I asked innocently, "And after that? Will you have any reason to come back to Allport once the house sells?"

"None," he said, "unless a certain lady makes it worth my while to drive up here."

"You don't like this area?"

"To tell you the truth, I'm a city boy. My first wife was the one who wanted a house on Lake Huron, and it's been nothing but a money pit. I'll be glad to see it gone."

"Your first wife?"

There was a long pause. "She died."

"Oh, Rick, I'm so sorry." Now the pie didn't seem so important, and I shoved the plate away. The poor man!

"Thank you."

I switched the conversation to more pleasant things, promising to call him soon so we could get together. Faye was wrong about Rick, I thought as we ended the call. He wasn't interested in anything in Allport—except maybe me. He'd dealt with a lot of sorrow, too, a dead first wife and a second one with mental issues. He deserved a little fun, and if I could provide it, I was willing. Out of respect for Barbara's opinion, though, I decided I'd finish the case first. Once Rick was no longer a client of the Smart Detective Agency, I could say for myself what he'd be to Retta Stilson.

CHAPTER THIRTY-SEVEN

Faye

The Algoma Central Railway provides the opportunity for a beautiful ride through the Canadian wilderness. I'll say that up front. As for the rest of Barb's idea, it wasn't the greatest.

In the first place, the train left at eight a.m., which meant we had to leave Allport before five. When we stopped at her house, Retta came out dressed but hardly awake, crawled into the back seat of Barb's car with her pillow and blanket, and promptly went back to sleep.

The ride was dark for most of the way. Barb was uneasy about the surprise she'd arranged, and it showed. Luckily, Retta was too busy napping to notice. We crossed the Mackinac Bridge to Michigan's Upper Peninsula, often known simply as the U.P. Continuing due north, we took the Ambassador Bridge into Canada. Our entry was uneventful, since I'd remembered when we picked her up to ask Retta if she had her passport. She'd forgotten, but it hadn't taken me long to run into her house, find it, and put it with Barb's and mine in an envelope I'd brought along for that purpose. That made crossing into Canada easy, and we got to the railway station on time. The train was waiting, making little huffs and hisses as people moved busily around it, preparing for departure.

The mood changed when we entered the building and saw the three guys sitting there. Retta made a little gasp, and the look she turned on us was accusing.

"Surprise." Barb's smile was weak.

For once Retta was speechless, but it didn't matter. Lars was on his feet, approaching with arms raised. "Hey, there, lady. Are you glad to see me?"

In a performance worthy of an Oscar, Retta squelched the anger I'd seen oh-so-briefly and put on a smile. "Lars Johannsen, you devil! I'm totally shocked." Turning her face slightly toward Barb she added, "I can't believe you pulled this off."

Rory and Dale had come up behind Lars, and I saw relief on their faces. Being men, they'd concluded things were going to be all right. Being Retta's sister, I knew they weren't.

If I hadn't known better, the day would have been completely relaxing. We got on the train. We rode through beautiful country, tracing colorful hills and a wide river. We saw waterfalls. We crossed trestle bridges. It was quite a journey.

At the park, we broke off as couples to explore. I'd made sandwiches, coleslaw, and peanut butter cookies and arranged portions in three different cooler bags. The others planned to do some hiking, but Dale and I stayed on the level ground close to the station. After walking around a little we settled at a table and ate our lunch, enjoying the peaceful quiet.

Rory and Barb took the River Trail, which according to the signs went past a couple of waterfalls. Somewhere along the way they would stop and eat their lunch, probably with the roar of water just over their shoulders. It would be lovely, but Barb would be distracted, wondering what Retta would do to repay her for interfering in her love life. Hiking was probably good as she worked off her worry with physical exertion.

Retta and Lars took the most energetic trail, Lookout. Just reading the pamphlet made me tired: *A challenge for the adventurous and energetic, this trail ascends 250 feet above the tracks to provide a breathtaking, panoramic view of the canyon...over 300 stairs that lead you to large wooden viewing platforms, where you can catch your breath until the view takes it away again.*

They said it would be fun. I told them I thought it would be torture. Still, it gave them time together, which after all was why Barb had planned the trip. Not that Retta would forgive her just because we all had a day of fun.

Barb had learned the name of the man she thought was telling lies about Rory, though she didn't tell me how she knew. We'd talked on the ride north about how he might be stopped, but neither of us had a workable idea. Of course, once Rory was present, the subject was dropped. I wondered who knew what in our little group. Was Rory aware that Retta and I knew about his problem? Did Lars know? It might have been easier if we'd all laid our cards on the table and attacked the problem together, but sadly, that's not how people do things most of the time.

The ride back was pretty quiet. Dale napped, and Lars, Rory, and Barb kept checking their phones for a signal. Once the train's motion settled into a smooth, gentle rock, Retta announced she needed to find the rest room and wanted me to guard the door. Of course I knew she really wanted to talk to me, so I agreed without pointing out that the train's bathroom doors had perfectly good closure devices. As I left my seat, Barb shot me a helpless glance, but I simply rolled my eyes in response. There was no avoiding Retta's revenge, whatever it turned out to be.

To my surprise, there were no questions about why or how or who was to blame. Retta was on a completely different tack.

"Lars and I talked about Rory's stalkers," she began. "He thinks we should confront them privately rather than arresting them and making the whole thing public."

That seemed an odd position for an FBI man to take until I thought it through. "If they're arrested and tried, people will take sides. Their lawyers will accuse the mayor and the police of protecting their own, and they'll have to bend over backward to prove they aren't doing that."

"Exactly," Retta agreed. "If half of Allport believes a quarter of what they say, Rory's reputation will be damaged beyond repair."

Glancing out the window at miles and miles of trees, I thought of the whispers that would persist, even if Miss Tattletale and her partner were found guilty. "It's sad, but many people believe the worst of others, especially when they're cops." I returned my gaze to Retta. "Does Lars know how to stop them?"

Retta grinned. "I think I do, but here's the deal: Barbara Ann isn't going to know a thing about it till it's over."

I raised a hand in a gesture that ended up looking as if I were fending off a blow. "Retta—"

"What, Faye? She went behind my back to do something she intended to be a good thing, right?"

"She just wanted to—"

"—let me know she disapproves of my behavior." An abrupt wave dismissed Barb's wants. "I can't say I'm not glad to see Lars. But she needs to know what it feels like to be left out of things. Lars and I are going to take care of Rory's problem, and Barbara Ann will find out about it when it's done."

"I wish you wouldn't—"

"What? Help Rory save his job?"

"Well, no, but it might be dangerous."

"I've got Lars, which is almost as good as the whole FBI. We can handle this." With that, Retta stepped into the bathroom and closed the door in my face.

CHAPTER THIRTY-EIGHT

Retta

Barbara Ann thought she was clever, and I let her think it—temporarily. Because she liked Lars and didn't approve of Rick, she'd set me up for a weekend reconciliation. Talk about acting like my mother!

I looked a mess when we arrived in Algoma, which gave me more reason to be mad at her. My snooze in the back seat had made my hair flat on one side and rubbed off most of my makeup. I had dressed in jeans and a sweatshirt, not what I'd have chosen if I'd known Lars would be seeing me.

Barbara's interference backfired, as interference usually does. Even as I hugged Lars and acted pleased with the surprise, I was deciding I would definitely see Rick again as soon as Lars went back to New Mexico. In the first place, Rick was sweet, too, and in the second place, Barbara needed to learn to keep her nose out of my business.

For the record, I wasn't upset with Faye. It was obvious to me that Barbara had masterminded the surprise and Faye had done as she was told, as usual.

I had to admit it was good to see him. Lars is handsome, fun to be with and the type of manly man my Don was. The problem was that I like to be the one doing the inviting. Barbara Ann was going to pay for trying to micro-manage my love life.

Weaseling the details out of Lars as we hiked the trail was easy, because as long as you're nice to a man, he will spill his guts. As Lars recounted how they'd set me up, I realized he'd come to Michigan only because Barbara invited him. He was clueless about Rick and so pleased with his part in the plan that I couldn't be angry at him.

When we reached the end of the railroad line, Barbara suggested Lars and I ride back together in his rental car because she, Dale, Rory, and Faye were all going into Allport. The implication was that Lars would be staying at my house, but I didn't comment on that one way or another. Let her wonder if her little scheme was working.

On the ride back to Allport, we discussed Rory's problem again. I'd told Lars everything I knew except Cramer's name, but he had me repeat the story in more detail.

"Are you certain her source is good?" Lars asked when I finished.

"I'm not one to go off half-cocked," I replied. "I used Barbara Ann's phone and called him myself to make sure he knew what he was talking about."

"Who is it?"

I licked my lips. "Lars, what he did isn't exactly legal. He was trying to help, but—"

Lars chuckled. "What we're going to do won't be completely legal either. I won't tell on your guy if you don't tell on me."

It was both scary and exhilarating to hear him say that. We were going to save Rory's career, but the method wouldn't be "completely legal."

"Faye's son Cramer is a whiz at computers," I replied. "He hacked the email server and figured out who's sending them."

"Cramer," Lars repeated. "Tell me everything he said."

I tried to be thorough. "Cramer said this Gager's pretty good at hiding, but Cramer's good, too. He said something about IPs, or maybe it was IGs. I get confused when people start using all those letters. Cramer would know, though."

Something Cramer had said in our conversation came back to me, though I didn't pass it on to Lars. "I knew you could fix computers, Sweetie," I'd said to him, "but I didn't know you understood internet stuff."

"I kinda wish I didn't sometimes." It had been an odd statement, and I'd waited to see if he was going to explain it, but he didn't. Cramer was a real introvert, and I didn't always know how to communicate with him. It always seemed the more questions I asked, the fewer words he used in answer.

Lars seemed ready to accept Cramer's word, but he was anxious about the timeline. "I have to fly back to Albuquerque on Monday." He scratched his wide, rather pale forehead. "I can hunt the guy down and threaten him with prosecution. He won't know I'm out of my jurisdiction, and that might end it."

"What about the woman? We have to stop her, too."

Lars nodded. "I know, but like I said, time isn't on our side."

We both thought about the matter as the miles slid by. The day was dying, and clouds scattered in the west were turning pink and orange as the sun passed behind them.

How could we get Gager to lead us to Ms. Tattletale?

"I have an idea." As I explained my plan, Lars asked a couple of questions. After some thought, he added some things that would make it work better.

"We'll need help. We can get Barb and Faye to—"

"Not them." When he looked at me, his eyes wide with a question, I told half a lie, half the truth. "Faye couldn't play a part if you paid her to. She's too honest. And Barbara…is busy with another case we're working on. I'll get someone to help."

We talked about it all the way through the U.P., across the bridge, and down US-23. It was nice to have Lars with me, and I couldn't help thinking that we made a great team.

Once we had the details worked out, I made two calls to set things up. Cramer said Gager was scheduled to work at the bar, and he agreed to be half of our back-up team. Gabe and I engaged in a lengthy argument about whether he would step across the threshold of an establishment focused on the consumption of alcohol. First I heard that Mindy wouldn't like it. Then I heard that Mindy's mother wouldn't like it. Finally I heard that Jesus wouldn't like it.

I salved Gabe's conscience by offering fifty bucks, assuring him neither Mindy nor her mother had to know where he was going, and arguing that Jesus, though he would definitely know, would approve of Gabe helping Agent Johannsen and me stop a despicable criminal.

When I ended the call, Lars gave me a smile. "You're really something, you know that, Retta?"

I fished a little. "Is that something good, or something else?"

He reached over and patted my thigh. "Oh, you're something good *and* something else."

Okay, maybe Barbara's expectation that Lars would be spending the night was correct. Not that I'd ever tell her.

CHAPTER THIRTY-NINE

Faye

Rory dropped Dale and me off at home, and he and Barb went on to his place. I guessed they needed each other for comfort, he for his trials at work and Barb for awareness that Retta was probably at this very moment arranging some sort of payback.

I had missed my Saturday at the farm, but I drove out early Sunday morning to get the girls for church. Afterward we stopped for Dale and Buddy and drove back out for the afternoon. My car was full, which reminded me of our kid-raising days, though without the punches boys seem compelled to engage in when confined in the back seat. As we traveled Dale pointed out the farm where he grew up. He did that nearly every time, but the girls were always polite.

"Were you and Aunt Faye childhood sweethearts?" Iris asked.

"Not until senior year," Dale replied. "We lived just a couple of miles apart, but the Evans girls were way above me on the social scale."

"Dale, that's crazy!" Too late, I realized that was a bad thing to say to a man with a brain injury.

He put a hand on mine, and I felt the familiar roughness of his fingertips. "I was a woods rat from day one. You could have found somebody who would have made a lot more money."

"I never wanted money."

"You never had the chance to find out what it would be like to have it, did you?" The look he gave me said what he was thinking: I'd gotten pregnant with Jimmy at eighteen, and that was the end of my choices.

It was partly true. The pregnancy had narrowed my options, but I'd had options nevertheless. I'd never looked forward to college. All I ever wanted was Dale. Despite the embarrassment, the pain I caused my parents, and his mother's undying resentment, I wouldn't have changed a thing.

The girls had returned to whispering among themselves, and I let the subject drop. Dale and I would discuss this further when we were alone.

When we arrived at the farm, Dale and Bill disappeared into the tractor shed to do whatever men do where there are tractors. The girls went to change their clothes, and I began helping Carla with some canning. There's a great sense of accomplishment in seeing rows and rows of vegetables neatly packed into glass jars lined up on the kitchen counter, waiting to hear the pops that signal they've sealed. It's work, of course, and we'd been through it many times already this fall, with green beans, corn, carrots, tomatoes, asparagus, peas, and beets. Knowing we'd have nutritious, tasty food on hand was worth the effort, and the cooler temperature outside meant we could open the doors and get a breeze through when all that steam started building up.

Carla was an eager student, and my mother's secrets had come back to me, though I hadn't canned in years. We worked together amicably, and I realized how happy I was to have her as my daughter-in-law. I hardly knew Jimmy's wife, but what I'd seen of her left me unmoved. I'd tried to be kind to Cramer's wife April, but she was so self-centered it was hard to know how she felt toward me. I'd felt guilt but also relief when he finally admitted she was hopeless and refused to take her back a third time.

I liked and admired Carla, and I thought she liked me. I hoped she felt she'd been lucky to get me as mother-in-law, since we don't have much choice there.

CHAPTER FORTY

Barb

I came home to an empty house. As soon as I entered my apartment, however, I found that I wasn't alone. The cat was waiting, and she clawed at the window screen, obviously unhappy with me. I hurried to replenish her food dish. Hungry as she always was, she refused anything that wasn't fresh.

Once I'd fed her and been allowed my three pets, she darted off. I wandered down to the office and checked for voice mails on our business line. There was one, and I heard a slightly familiar voice. "This message is for Ms. Evans. It's Enright Landon, the person you spoke to at WOZ Industries. Something occurred to me when I saw the local newspaper tonight, and I thought perhaps I should tell you about it."

He gave a number where I could reach him, and I thought about it for a moment. It was Sunday morning, but he'd called us at ten on a Saturday night. I decided it was permissible to return his call right away.

"Mr. Landon," I said when he answered. "It's Barb Evans."

"Oh, yes, Ms. Evans. You got my message."

"I was away overnight. I should have given you my cell number."

"Not necessary. I'm not sure this information is valuable in your investigation, but I saw the report last evening that Gail Sherman died recently on the springs your other operative, Mrs. Stilson, mentioned to me."

"Yes. She was arranging property sales out there."

"Ms. Sherman was our agent when we bought this house. My wife and she became acquainted."

I wondered where this was going. "Did Ms. Sherman even mention Sweet Springs to you?"

"Not that I recall."

He didn't say more, and I wondered again what his purpose was in calling. "The news report reminded you of something?"

"Only that Mrs. Sherman was an acquaintance. I'd seen her at work and at my home. And of course she sold us our house."

He seemed to be finished. "I appreciate the information."

"Yes, well, I just wanted you to know. Have a good day." He ended the call.

Well, that was odd.

I paced the width of the office a few times, turning abruptly on my heel as I reached each wall. What was Landon trying to tell me? Did he suspect his boss of conniving with Gail Sherman? Did he think Gail had tried to engage him in her illegal activities? Or had he colluded with Gail and was now trying to distance himself from her? Was he afraid he'd be a suspect in her death?

He'd made a point of saying that his wife and Gail had become acquainted, whatever that meant.

That was it. He knew we'd uncover connections, and he didn't want us to link Gail to him. He'd called to convince us that she'd been his wife's friend, not his partner in crime.

CHAPTER FORTY-ONE

Retta

The Ugly Bar was aptly named: no frills and no atmosphere, unless you count the odor of stale sweat. A beat-up pool table in a corner was too close to the walls, so black marks showed where the cue-butts bumped them as players lined up shots. I'd have bet the cheap brown carpet underfoot was filthy, but it was too dark in there to tell.

I entered wearing an outfit Mom would have called trashy, an off-shoulder top I'd bought on a whim and never worn, tight black jeans I'd found in stuff my daughter left behind when she went to college, and boots that came up to my knees. I'd added Don's old motorcycle jacket, slopped on too much eyeliner, and covered my hair with a knitted hat. I hoped no one I knew would be in the bar, but it was a pretty good bet they wouldn't be. Even if a friend was slumming, I hoped he or she would have a hard time recognizing me in that getup.

Taking a seat at the bar, I ordered a screwdriver and slumped on my elbow, looking sad. Gager was waiting on someone at the far end. He was slight, blond, and just handsome enough to get by. His nose was a little too big, his jaw slightly too far back, but he moved with confidence and had Christian Bale eyes. He needed some fashion help, but most men in Allport did. I found myself comparing Gager's khakis and T-shirt to Rick Chou's silk shirts and perfectly-fitted trousers. Rick did without the sweat-stains, too.

Gager paid no attention to me after serving my drink, but that was okay. When he went to clear some tables, I reached over the bar and poured it into the basin of soapy water used for washing glasses. When he came back, I ordered another.

After he'd served me a third round in fifteen minutes, he asked, "Rough day?"

I rolled my eyes. "It's turning into a rough life."

He raised a brow. "That's harsh."

Turning slightly, I nodded over my shoulder. "See that guy?"

"The big dude in the suit? Yeah."

I spoke with exaggerated lip movements. "F.B.I."

Gager's forehead wrinkled as he examined Lars, who sat facing us at a table in the corner. He was listening intently to a man whose back was to us. "For real?"

"For real. He says he's in town to investigate some cyber-crime, but I don't believe it."

"Cyber?"

"If it's cyber-crime, then why is he asking about stuff that's got nothing to do with computers?"

Gager lifted one corner of his lip, Elvis style. "Like what?"

"Like sexual harassment. He wanted to know if the chief of police ever gave me a hard time."

"The chief?"

"Yeah. Neuencamp stopped me a month back and accused me of driving drunk." I slapped a palm on the bar. "I had one glass of wine with a friend, but the chief got all nosy about it. Anyway, that FBI guy wanted to know if he did anything inappropriate during the arrest." I shrugged. "I should have said yes. Maybe I coulda got the charges thrown out."

"The FBI is investigating Chief Neuencamp?" He couldn't keep the smugness out of his tone.

I leaned toward him. "That's just it. I don't think it's about him. The agent asked how much I knew about computers." I gave him a slushy smile. "I told him I can turn anything on, even a PC."

A voice sounded from over my shoulder. "There you are."

Turning, I faced Gabe, who'd done his best to create a deep-cover persona. He wore black jeans, a black leather jacket with studs everywhere, a black leather cap that looked like it had been run over by three semis and a Harley, and a black T-shirt that said, DAYTONA BIKE WEEK—2003. His scent was something that should have said CHEAP BUT STRONG on the bottle.

It was hard to believe this was the guy who'd claimed he couldn't possibly come to the Ugly Bar and play my brother. For the record, at no time had I said he should arrive looking like Easy Rider.

While I recovered from the costume, Gabe said his next line. "You know you ain't supposed to be seen in a bar."

"I was just telling this guy about the fed over there," I replied. "I'll be glad when he goes back to Detroit or wherever."

Gabe's tone grew more irritated. "You ain't supposed to be drinking in public until your case is settled." With a glare worthy of an Oscar, he inclined his head at Gager. "And you sure don't need to blab your business to some bartender."

Slurring my words a little, I gestured toward Lars. "He's not investigating my drunk driving thing. He's here for—"

"You don't want to be part of what he's here for." Warming to the role, Gabe glared at me. "Keep talking—you'll get subpoenaed to testify against those people when they catch them."

I flashed Gager a nervous look and he asked, "He's after two people—that FBI guy?"

I bit my lip like I'd really screwed up. "Forget what I said, okay?"

His smile was casual but a little off. "Hey, I'm a bartender. We listen, but we don't really hear."

From the look on Gager's face as we left, I knew that was a lie. He'd heard, and he was worried.

Gabe insisted on waiting outside with me, but he shivered like a sapling and yawned loudly every few minutes. Finally Lars and Cramer came out of the bar.

"How did it go?" I asked.

Lars chuckled. "The guy practically turned himself inside out trying to hear what we were saying."

He turned to Cramer, who added, "When I went to the rest room, he caught me in the hallway and asked if that really was a fed I was talking to."

"And you said?"

"Just what you told me to," Cramer replied. "That Agent Johannsen is looking into cyber-crimes in the Allport area. I said I was a suspect because of my computer background and my acquaintance with the victim, but I was in the clear now. I made like it was a big relief but told him I couldn't say anymore, because the investigation is on-going."

"Perfect," I said. "Now you two should go. Lars and I will wait to see where Mr. Gager goes after work, which we hope will be directly to his partner's house."

Though reluctant to leave the scene of the action, the boys headed to their respective pickup trucks. Lars and I scrunched down in the seats of his rental and waited. It was one of those crispy nights when the cold feels like it's trying to get under your skin, and soon Lars turned on the ignition. Fiddling with the gauges, he warmed his hands in the blower. "Boy, the temperature sure dropped when the sun went down."

We talked a little at first, comparing impressions of Gager, but after a while we just waited. I kept shifting in my seat, but Lars seemed used to it. After twenty-eight minutes of silence I asked, "What if he called and told her about this on the phone?"

"If he's as paranoid as most cyber-crooks I've known, he'll be convinced the Bureau is listening in."

The windows started fogging up, and I turned the dial so the warm air blew on the windshield. As it cleared, we saw Gager with his back to us as he locked the bar's back door. Crossing the parking lot, he climbed into a light-colored car that had duct tape holding one of the tail-lights together. He'd lit a cigarette as soon as he left the building, so when he got in, he rolled the car window down. The car didn't want to start, and we heard him swear at it with no originality whatsoever. Either the oaths or the repeated attempts paid off, and the vehicle finally started with a roar and a puff of smoke.

We'd parked out of reach of the street lamp's glow. When he turned at the first corner and went north, Lars put the car into gear. It wasn't difficult to follow, since it was after midnight in Allport. The streets were silent, and there was only one set of tail-lights ahead of us.

Cramer had given me Gager's address, but he didn't head for the trailer park. "We're two lucky ducks," I told Lars. "He's going to go see the woman."

Lars played devil's advocate. "At midnight?"

"The Burners and the chickens are asleep at ten," I replied. "That doesn't mean everyone in Allport is."

Gager went up US-23, Allport's main road, then turned into a residential neighborhood. Lars turned off the headlights. "We can see well enough by the streetlights, and we don't want him to notice we're back here."

When Gager finally slowed, he turned into a drive where a sign said WINDSWEPT APARTMENTS. Knowing the place slightly from a previous case, I directed Lars to pull into a dark corner. "We have to go on foot from here or he'll see us."

"I'll go on foot. You'll wait here." Lars spoke in his FBI voice. We'd talked earlier about whether I could be in on this part, and my arguments had been sound. I knew the area and the people better than Lars did. When women make logical statements, men tend to fall back on a flat, "No." That's what Lars had done.

I didn't see how he was going to stop me.

"Wish I'd known there'd be surveillance," Lars complained as Gager finished a second cigarette before exiting his car. "I could have brought things to make the whole process easier."

"Would that have been legal, since this isn't an FBI case?"

He sniffed once. "No."

"Then we go with what we've got," I said. "Brainpower."

One of those parabolic microphones would have been nice, it was true. As it was, we probably wouldn't hear anything.

When Gager left his car and headed for the apartments, Lars got out and followed, staying in the shadows.

As soon as Lars was far enough away, I went after him, also staying out of the lights. When Lars saw I'd followed, his choices would be to let me stay or give up on the mission. I knew him well enough to guess which he'd choose.

I caught up with him at the front corner of Building C, where Harold Gager was knocking on a door three apartments down. Lars glared, but I wasn't about to turn around and go back to the car because of a dirty look. With a grimace that said he should have known, he made the universal sign for silence, a finger to his lips. Like I was going to start singing "The Star-spangled Banner" at the top of my voice!

When Gager knocked a second time, louder and with impatience, the door opened. Lars leaned back, and we strained our ears to hear what was said. Since I was around a corner and behind a large man, I wasn't in an optimal position for eaves-dropping. I caught only a few words.

"She's sleeping. —can't come in." It was a female voice, petulant and vaguely familiar.

Gager rumbled something in a low voice, and the woman made a noise that might have been disagreement. He said something else, and she replied, "—minute. —coat."

Lars heard better than I could. "They're coming outside."

"Come on." I started for the parking lot where Gager had left his car. If they were going to talk outside on a cold night, they'd probably choose to sit in a warm vehicle rather than stand out in the wind. We had to get there first, get out of sight, and pray we could hear what was said.

I zig-zagged through the shadows with Lars close behind. Seconds later the apartment door closed, and we doubled our pace.

Gager had left his car between two others. Lars took a crouched position behind one and pointed me toward the other. I hurried into place as two people approached the battered Ford and got in. Gager started the engine, which only took two tries this time, since it had warmed on the way over. The noise it made dashed any hopes I'd had of hearing what they had to say. The thing sounded like a dryer with tennis shoes inside.

Then the miracle we needed happened: Gager lit yet another cigarette. In seconds the woman rolled down her window, waving a hand to push the smoke outside. "Do you have to burn one every three minutes?" she said angrily.

Since I was on her side of the vehicle, I heard her clearly and even smelled the acrid smoke she was complaining about. More than that, I recognized the voice. It was Cramer's ex-wife, April.

Without going too deeply into family history, here's the condensed version. Cramer and April married just out of high school. She quickly grew bored with having a husband who—make that bored with having a husband. She left Cramer for some guy she met on the internet. When that and a few other relationships didn't work out, April returned to Cramer, who took her back for reasons the rest of us didn't understand. The last time, when she'd left again to take up residence with a hard-drinking trucker, Cramer had finally summoned the gumption to end it. Despite offers to return and promises to do better, Cramer had filed for divorce, and April no longer had a husband to come home to when she needed a rest.

The trucker had moved on, and for the last few months April had been tending bar. It occurred to me now that it was probably at the Ugly. I recalled hearing she'd been arrested after a catfight there, but I'd never learned how it turned out.

Now here she was with Harold Gager. I was dying to hear what they were saying. Though Lars made frantic gestures of discouragement, I got down on my hands and knees and crawled toward the passenger-side window.

Gager was doing most of the talking, and I caught the end of a sentence. "—that's what the old broad said."

Old broad? Really?

"They don't know who it is," April said. "They're fishing."

"Well, if the FBI is fishing in Allport, I'm going to be someplace else."

She huffed in disgust. “You’re just going to take off? Quit your job and—”

“My job?” Gager interrupted, raising his voice. “You call pouring drinks and cleaning up vomit in the bathrooms a job?”

“Yeah, yeah, I know. You should be in law enforcement.” Her tone was disdainful. “You got all jacked out of shape because Neuencamp didn’t pick you for the good guys’ team. It was kind of fun giving him a hard time, but now we have to stop. How hard is that to figure out?”

“You don’t get it. Everything you do on the internet leaves a mark, and with the resources the FBI’s got, they’ll find me.” He paused, apparently aware his problems didn’t move her. “The same with phone calls. They’ve probably got your voice stored digitally. If they dig into who I’ve been with, they’ll get to you sooner or later.”

“Oh.” Disdain left her voice. “What do we do?”

“I told you. I go someplace else.”

“What about me?”

“You can come if you want.”

She thought about that. “My mom’s here, and all my friends.”

“Yeah.” He didn’t care much one way or the other.

“Sir, could you step out of the car, please?”

Three of the four of us made noises of surprise. April let out a little squeak, Gager said the word you’d expect a sleaze like him to say in such a situation, and I gasped like a landed flounder. Listening closely, I hadn’t seen Lars leave his hiding place and approach the driver’s side window.

Without giving Gager time to think about what to do next Lars ordered, “Step out of the car, now.”

Gager started to obey, moving slowly as if petrified with fear. I stood, craning my neck to see what was happening at the front of the car. Lars unlatched the door and took a step back. Gager put one foot on the ground, still moving in extreme slo-mo. When the dome light came on, I saw something under the steering column that didn't belong there. Gager's right hand moved toward it.

"Gun, Lars!"

As I spoke, Gager pulled the pistol out of its holster, at the same time pushing the car door toward Lars in an attempt to knock him off balance. Raising the pistol with his right hand, Gager tried to launch himself out of the car.

In one smooth movement, Lars reached in and took the gun as easily as if he were relieving a toddler of a lollipop. At the same time, he smashed the car door onto Gager's leg, making him roar with pain. Before I was quite sure what had happened, Lars held the gun loosely in one hand as Gager groaned, "My leg! My leg!"

"Amateurs want to go around armed," Lars said calmly, "but they don't put in the work it takes to learn how to handle guns."

April had started crying the moment she saw the pistol, but I put a hand on her arm. "Shut up," I ordered. "You're in a lot of trouble, so do what Agent Johannsen says."

In order to avoid residents who might have heard the noise we'd made, Lars ordered Gager and April to precede us to his rental car. If anyone in the apartments looked out a window, he'd merely have seen two couples crossing the parking area. When we reached the car, April and I took the back seat and Lars and Gager got in front.

It took a while to get the story out of them. There was a lot of blaming each other, but we got the basics. Gager blamed Rory for not giving him a job with the Allport PD. April had been angry with him since her arrest in August. They'd met through their jobs at the Ugly, discovered each other's secret desire to punish the chief, and cooked up the scheme, believing they wouldn't get caught because they'd been so clever about it.

"I can't believe you'd do this, April," I scolded.

"He treated me like I was fourteen," she insisted. "He said really mean things to me with Cramer standing right there!"

"If you didn't act like a child, maybe he wouldn't have treated you like one," I responded. Lars shot me a glance, indicating he'd handle the situation.

"Here's what can happen," he told Gager in a business-like tone. "I can arrest you for cyber-crimes and assaulting a federal officer with what's probably an illegal weapon, along with whatever else I think of on the way to the police station. You'll go to jail tonight, and I doubt you'll see the outside of a cell for a decade or so."

Gager started to protest, but Lars gave him a smack on the shoulder with the heel of his hand. "Listen to me, jerk-face! You can go to jail, like I said, *or*, you can leave Allport—in fact, leave the state of Michigan. I'm willing to give you one chance. Get a new start somewhere, and don't break any laws." He held the gun up, by the trigger guard. "No more toys. I intend to put your name into our national database. If you get anything worse than a parking ticket, you will suffer the full penalty for what you've done here *plus* whatever you're guilty of somewhere else."

"That ain't right—" Gager began, but Lars interrupted.

"What's not right, dirt-bag, is trying to ruin the name of a decent man who did nothing to you."

Gager shut up then, which showed at least an iota of common sense.

As April listened to Gager's choices, fear showed on her face. She was a pretty girl—woman—but her attractiveness was fading fast. Too many days of too much alcohol made her face look bloated. She looked hard-eyed and cold-hearted, the opposite of what an adult woman wants unless she's the villainess in a Bond movie.

April's gaze turned to me. She knew who I was, and I guessed she was trying to figure out how to turn the situation to her advantage.

The method she chose was laughable. "Aunt Retta—"

"Don't go there," I ordered. "You lost any respect I might have had for you the first time you ditched your husband to become the life of some drunken loser's party."

Her lip trembled, but I didn't believe it for a minute. "What are we going to do with this one, Agent Johannsen?"

"Same deal, you think?"

Whimpering, April put out a pleading hand. "I'm not like Harold. I can't spend my life moving from place to place."

"No, just from man to man," I commented.

"All right," Lars said. "I'll offer you a different deal. You stay in town, but you call the city offices and the state police post tomorrow and explain that this whole thing was a bad joke. Apologize and promise it will never happen again."

As she thought about it, her jaw jutted stubbornly. Lars went on. "It's time you grew up and stopped blaming other people for your problems." He glanced at me, and I thought humor glinted in his eye, though it was too dark to tell. "Ms. Stilson here will let me know when you've done as ordered. When I hear from her, I'll move your file to the FBI's inactive section."

"You can do that?"

"Ma'am, we're the FBI. We do whatever we want." Now there was definitely humor in the glance he shot at me, but his tone and that manly jaw of his were firm.

They agreed to Lars' terms, Gager angrily, April with a flirty smile that said she hoped to make him like her a little. Without reacting to either, Lars dismissed them. April walked away from Gager as if she'd never met him, hurrying across the windy parking lot to her apartment. Gager started his noisy vehicle one more time and sped away with a defiant squeal of tires. When they were out of sight, I climbed out of the back seat and got in front. Putting the car into gear, Lars started for my house.

"Do you think they'll do as you said?" I asked.

"Mostly, yeah," he replied. "Gager will always be a small-time hood, so I will enter him in the database. Most geeks, your nephew, for example, hack because they can, not because they want to hurt anybody. The fact that Gager used the computer to attack Rory and his habit of carrying a gun make him more dangerous. If his name comes up again, we'll know he's a bad apple. As for the girl, we might have scared her straight, but as selfish as she is, it's hard to predict how she'll view herself in the morning." He looked at me. "I guess you know her pretty well?"

I sighed. "Once upon a time, April was Cramer's wife."

When I told Lars their history, he whistled softly. "Why do decent men pick losers then keep making excuses for them?"

"It isn't only men." I chewed on my lip for a second. "I have to tell Cramer about this, and since I'm flying to Madison tomorrow, it has to be soon. She might call him with some made-up story."

"He told me he's a night owl. Why don't you call now?"

I did as he suggested, though I dreaded doing it. As I waited for him to answer, Cramer's remark about wishing he weren't so good with computers came to mind. Maybe he'd suspected it was April all along.

CHAPTER FORTY-TWO

Faye

The phone rang so early Monday morning I was surprised, and it was even more of a shock when I saw the caller I.D.

"Cramer, you're up early—or is it the opposite?"

"I had some things on my mind, so I couldn't sleep."

"What's up, hon?"

He told me the story of the night's activities. Retta had acted quickly, but Lars' presence was a golden opportunity to end the harassment Rory had been suffering. When Cramer said Retta wanted me to tell Barb the situation had been handled, I pictured her casually dropping it in at the end of their conversation. Retta knew Barb would be angry about her interference, so I got to be in the middle, as usual.

I had to hand it to her for solving the problem, though. "You're sure Lars scared them into giving up?"

"Yeah, he did. Gager is leaving Allport completely."

"That's good. What about the woman?"

"That's why I didn't sleep last night. The woman is April."

"Oh, no, honey. I'm so sorry."

He blew out a breath, and my hand tightened on the phone in sympathy. "Aunt Retta thinks April will behave herself knowing the FBI is paying attention. She's supposed to call the city offices today and apologize."

"Anonymously, I assume."

"Right. She thinks Lars and Retta are the only ones who know it was her. Retta thought I should know, and I—" He gave a dry chuckle. "—I wanted to talk it over with my mom."

There wasn't much I could say. Mothers cannot criticize spouses, even ex-spouses, without creating trouble. If we agree that a woman is worthless and cruel, our sons might conclude we think they're poor judges of character. And too many times, the cleft in the relationship is mended at some point in the future. Then you're the mom who said terrible things about the woman your son loves.

I said the only thing I could say, though it was repetitious. "I'm so sorry, hon."

"The funny thing is that I knew—at least I sorta knew. When I was researching Gager and found out he worked at the Ugly Bar, I thought, 'April works there.' I didn't let myself go on from there, at least consciously, but I think I knew right then." His voice sounded strained as he went on. "You think you know the person you married, you know?"

Recalling Dale's belief he'd ruined my chances at a good life, I said, "Sometimes you don't, even after decades of marriage."

"People always say I'm a nice guy." Cramer made it sound like a curse. "That's what some women look for, I guess, a nice guy with a steady paycheck—until they find one they like better."

"If it helps, you aren't the first man to be taken in by a pretty face, and you certainly won't be the last."

His answering murmur indicated intellectual understanding, but it had to be tough to comprehend with his heart. "I'll feel better when she admits to everyone that the stuff they said about Chief Neuencamp isn't true. I'd appreciate a call when you hear, so I know April did the right thing."

"I'll text you. Now go get some sleep."

"Thanks, Mom—Oh, one more thing. Aunt Barb told me about the case you're working on out at Sweet Springs."

I wondered briefly where he'd seen Barb. Apparently Cramer had had more conversation with his aunts in the last few days than he'd had in a year.

"She mentioned that Stan Wozniak out at WOZ Industries might be involved, so I did a little checking. Someone out there has been emailing the Clear-Cold Water Company. I didn't read the emails," he said as if to reassure me. "I just looked at their sent list." After a pause he added, "I can open them if you want me to."

My mind was making connections all over the place. Someone at WOZ Industries could be Stan Wozniak, could be Enright Landon. One of them was trying to connect Sweet Springs with a bottler. And my son was snooping into WOZ emails, which was undoubtedly illegal. I sat down in my chair with a plop, trying to think.

After a moment I said, "We should do this the legal way if at all possible. Then what we uncover, if anything, can be used against whoever the criminals are out there."

"I don't get the whole water thing. Why's the water at Sweet Springs so important?"

"I have a theory. Now that bottlers have sold most of America on bottled water, they're taking the next step and marketing lines of "better" water. Spring water is supposed to be healthier, so they can charge more for it."

"I see." He didn't see, but then Cramer had probably never paid for water in his life.

"You've been helpful, and Barb and I will get on this right away." I wanted to add, "Don't do it again," but I bit my tongue.

"I tried to call Aunt Barb all day Saturday, but the phone kept going to voicemail. Then I tried you and Aunt Retta. Same thing."

"We were in Canada, the three of us," I told him.

"That's cool. Was it a good trip?"

I wiped a film of perspiration off from my upper lip with a tissue. "It's really too soon to tell."

"I should have told Aunt Retta last night, but I kind of forgot about it when she called and said we were going to sting the people who were harassing the chief." He'd begun to sound less stressed. I guess talking things over with your mom can be helpful, even if the things you tell her make her shiver. "It was kind of fun helping Agent Johannsen, even if—" He'd reminded himself of his ex-wife's low standards.

"I'm sorry April did what she did, but she got what she deserved. It can't be fun to face Lars Johannsen when you're guilty and he knows it."

Cramer's sense of humor returned. "Don't forget Aunt Retta. I bet she didn't cut April any slack, either."

Chapter Forty-three

Barb

Faye and I acted on Cramer's information immediately. I put in a call to Cold-Clear and, with some fast talking, got an appointment with their resource development director. Since Cold-Clear was headquartered in Bay City, it meant a long drive for me, but I doubted they'd reveal company business over the phone. Face-to-face I could use my lawyer skills to elicit information. Even if they wouldn't give me a name, I could perhaps read between the lines.

Antoinette Nash was round-faced, stocky, and direct. Her office smelled of roses, and I saw a bouquet of at least two dozen on a table to one side. A gift for Sweetest Day, it appeared. I always wondered who observed that made-up holiday.

I liked Ms. Nash right away, and she seemed to respond to me as well. We spent a few minutes discussing our backgrounds, recognizing without stating outright that we'd fought for our positions in a world dominated by men. I had retired from the field of corporate battle, but she seemed capable of holding her own in hers.

I explained that we'd "stumbled" on the company's name as we investigated a case. Figuring Cold-Clear wouldn't want to associate itself with shady dealings, I told her our theory that a person or people was attempting to buy up the Sweet Springs properties in order to gain complete water rights. "One name we're pretty sure of is Gail Sherman."

Frowning, she opened a folder on her desk, flipped quickly through several sheets with a moistened finger, and scanned one near the bottom. "I have no record of anyone with that name."

I breathed an inward sigh of relief when she answered. We weren't going the "Contact our lawyers" route, at least not yet.

"Ms. Sherman was a real estate agent who might have been working with someone acquainted with the bottling industry—combining their talents, as it were."

She picked up on the verb tense. "She *was* an agent?"

"Ms. Sherman's body was found in the springs last week."

Nash sucked in a breath. "That's terrible."

"You can see why we'd like to know with whom she might have been working."

"We can't reveal details of an on-going negotiation."

That was what I'd expected. "I understand." After a pause I said, "Perhaps you could confirm some of what we know." When she hesitated, I added, "Ms. Sherman was probably murdered. There was another suspicious death, an arson, and an innocent woman who is confined to a nursing home, all so someone can get control of this property."

That information dismayed her, so I went on quickly. "You can simply nod your head to let me know we're on the right path."

After a moment, she nodded once.

"All right," I said. "Someone contacted you recently with an offer to sell Sweet Springs to Cold-Clear."

When she merely looked at me, I revised the statement. "Someone wants to lease Sweet Springs to Cold-Clear." That time I got a nod.

"Last week you sent one of your engineers to test the water."

Another nod. Retta had told Faye, who'd told me, that she'd been out to the springs last week and seen two vehicles leaving the area. What Retta had been doing out there I didn't know. Faye had convinced me it was best not to ask.

If bottling was the issue, which it seemed to be, people with scientific know-how would be poking around the springs, testing and devising methods for water withdrawal.

Now I used my semantic skills. "The offer to provide water rights came by email, from an account listed as WOZ Industries."

Nash hesitated but finally gave a quick nod.

"Can you provide a name?"

"I can't." She sounded genuinely sorry.

"Can you tell me if the person has visited this office?" My thought was I could check recent trips to Bay City made by everyone involved with Gail Sherman.

Twirling her pen between her fingers, Nash thought about the repercussions of answering that question. "No."

"Have you spoken to the person in charge by telephone?" Maybe Rory could get a warrant to search phone records.

Again she shook her head. "No. I spoke with a secretary to set up the appointment for testing, but that's all. She met our technician in town and escorted him to the site."

I doubted any secretary from WOZ had done that.

"Can you share the specific WOZ email address with us?"

She hesitated. I said, "Murder, arson, and fraud, Ms. Nash."

Her smile was rueful. "I'll have to check with legal. How about if I message it to you if and when they say it's okay?"

"That would be great." Rising, I put out a hand. "Thanks so much for seeing me on short notice."

She rose too. “It was nice to meet you, but if this really is the mess it seems to be, I’d appreciate it if you kept our name out of it. We’ve done nothing except consider a proposal, so it wouldn’t be fair to associate our name with this scheme.”

I said I’d try, knowing I had about as much control over the news media as I had over Retta.

As I drove northward through a veritable storm of falling leaves, I considered what I knew about Stan Wozniak. Was it possible he had plotted with Gail Sherman to sell water to Cold-Clear and then killed her when they disagreed?

As much as I disliked the man, I doubted it. There were practical reasons, such as he wasn’t living in Allport anymore and therefore didn’t have time to run around burning down houses. Of course he could afford to pay someone to do his dirty work, but that would have meant letting others know he was involved in crime. My take on Stan was that if he were willing to commit murder, he wouldn’t have shared that knowledge with anyone.

More importantly, Stan wasn’t the criminal type. Though I believed he would skin a rival on a business deal if he could, he simply didn’t have the subtlety it would take to sneak around buying up the springs. He’d have gone to the owners, bought out those who were willing to sell, and told the rest to go ahead and sue if they didn’t like what he was doing with the water.

Still, Stan was connected somehow. The emails had come from WOZ. On an impulse, I pulled to the side of the road, took out the business card he’d given me, and called his direct line.

“Wozniak.”

“Stan, it’s Barb Evans. Have you got a minute to talk?”

“If it’s about what we discussed last week, I do.”

“It is.” Briefly I told him about the woman from Cold-Clear’s admission they’d been dealing with someone at WOZ.

"Someone here? Who?"

"She's checking with her people to see if she can get permission to tell me."

He paused, and I could almost feel that intelligent brain of his vibrating across the distance between us. "Cold-Clear Water, right? We don't need them to tell us. I'll find out who's been e-mailing them in ten minutes' time."

He called back in seven. "The email came from an account with Landon's name on it," Stan said. "He claims it isn't his, and he showed me the one he uses. One is elandon@woz.com and the other is landone@woz. He says he uses the first one and didn't know there was a second." His voice dropped as he muttered, "I knew the guy was too good to be true."

I'd been thinking as I drove, and I asked, "Could Gail Sherman have accessed Landon's email?"

"Sherman?" There was a long pause before he answered. "Gail, um—she was around for a while last month."

"You were seeing her."

"Not seriously."

I didn't comment. Stan's romantic relationships were neither serious nor lengthy. "Might she have used Landon's email account?"

"I don't see how."

"But she was at your building more than once?"

"Yes. It was convenient for us to leave from my office." His voice changed again. "At least that's what she said at the time." He seemed unsure what to say next. "Gail—Gail was an attractive woman. When I came north to break Landon in, she dropped in a few times with papers for him to sign. We got to talking, and one thing led to another." He cleared his throat. "I soon found her company dull, though. She had no conversation."

I hadn't heard that Stan required scintillating small talk from his women, but age catches up with all of us, I guess.

Unaware of my judgmental thoughts, he went on. "The four of us, Landon and his wife and Gail and I, went out to dinner once." He chuckled. "It was a disaster! Landon has no social skills, and his wife is a looker but as dumb as—Well, she's no ball of fire, either, I can tell you."

Just when I started to like the man a little, he disappointed me again. "Perhaps she saves her fire for her husband."

He didn't get it. "I hope so, because she'd be boring to come home to every night. No wonder En's always willing to work late."

I ended the call, irritated by Stan's double standard where women were concerned. Telling myself there was no way to change men like him, I tried instead to put together the bits of information we'd gathered. There were many possibilities. Using her access to the building, Gail might have invented a second email address for Landon and used it for her own purposes. Stan could have fooled me into believing he wasn't the type to plot with Gail. It was possible Landon was using the second email and lying about it. Or Gail's partner was someone else at WOZ, someone we hadn't yet looked at.

The only clear thing in this case was the water at Sweet Springs.

During one of my rest stops I called Faye, who listened to what I'd learned, asking intelligent questions. Still, I thought she seemed anxious. "What's wrong, Faye?"

Haltingly she told me that Rory was safe from further harassment. Harold Gager had abruptly quit his job at the Ugly Bar and left town, claiming he never wanted to see Allport again. At mid-morning the mayor's office had received a call from a chastened but still anonymous woman who claimed the charges against Chief Neuencamp had been a joke. The state police sergeant assigned to the case had called Rory to report a similar call, saying he was certain things would be cleared up quickly.

Relieved but puzzled I asked, "How did this miracle happen?"

There was a long pause. "I guess it was a group effort: Lars, Gabe, Cramer, and Retta."

Heat rose in my neck. "With Retta as ringleader."

"I was left out, too, Barb." Faye sounded both irritated and defensive. "I was at the farm all afternoon yesterday, and Cramer never said a word about his plans for the evening."

"She wanted to do it without us."

"But it got done. That's a good thing, right?"

I stared out the window, hardly noticing the fallen leaves accumulating on my windshield. It was fair. I had plotted behind Retta's back to get Lars to Michigan, so she'd plotted behind mine to solve Rory's problem. Having spent my career as a lawyer, I knew how to accept defeat *and* recognize when balance had been achieved. We both should have let the other manage her own affairs. Neither of us had been able to do it.

Realizing Faye was waiting for a response, I made a decision. "If this is the end of the interference, I won't give Retta grief about it. When she returns from Wisconsin, we'll just go on."

I felt her relaxing across the miles. "I think that's best."

"I'll talk to you later."

Sliding my phone back into its convenient slot in my purse, I returned to the road. To myself I decided one thing, however. Retta would not win the Battle of the Oxford comma.

CHAPTER FORTY-FOUR

Faye

I'm a sucker for social media, though it sometimes makes me crazy. Despite the drama and comments that reveal a complete lack of understanding of government, society, and religion, there are good things, too, like sites where people share their lives with friends and acquaintances. My oldest son Jimmy lives in North Dakota, and if it weren't for the internet, I might conclude he fell into a sinkhole somewhere. No letters, few phone calls, and on my birthday, an electronic card, usually with dancing animals. That's it—unless he needs money, but that's a whole other story.

I allowed myself ten minutes each morning (which often stretched to twenty) to catch up on which of my sons' friends had married (or divorced), had babies, and got new jobs. In each case I either clicked LIKE or made a brief comment. People want to know their posts are noticed.

As I scrolled, munching on a cinnamon roll I'd taken out of the oven minutes earlier, it occurred to me that Gail Sherman might have had a Facebook page. I typed her name into the search bar, and plenty of Gail Shermans showed up. However, none of them lived in Allport. I tried Gail T. Sherman, Gail Malone Sherman, and Gail Malone, but that didn't help. Another possibility was Instagram, so I went there. Sure enough, there was Gail, who was apparently a big fan of selfies. There were pictures of her in front of an array of houses that would "not be on the market long." I scrolled through, looking for more personal photos. There was a shot of Gail in a group of grinning women. Gail was doing the duck-face, which I've never understood, but there's a lot I don't get about what people consider attractive.

The photo was captioned BIZNESS GIRLZ NITE OUT. I recognized some of the women, owners or managers of local hair salons, gift shops, and the like. I was about to move on when I noticed one of the names in the caption: Diane Landon. By eliminating the people I knew for sure and guessing at some of the others, I identified the person I thought was Enright Landon's wife. As Retta said, she was striking, but where Retta saw glamour, I saw what looked like a spoiled Siamese cat. Diane sat off to one side, above mugging for the camera. The word that came to my mind was *sleek*. I guess that word can be used as a compliment, but you won't hear me using it that way.

The date on the photo was August 8, 2015.

The two women—not together but present in the same group—got me thinking. Diane Landon would know a little about water bottling plants, having worked in one. Retta thought Diane was sweet and a little dumb. I thought Retta liked almost anyone who could converse on hair color and Gucci bags. Checking the time and deciding just slightly after eight was acceptable, I called one of the other women in the picture, Doris Cizninski.

"We go out once a month," Doris explained when I asked about the photo. "It's a chance to socialize and gripe about the economy and men—not necessarily in that order. You girls are welcome to join us."

"Thanks, Doris. You knew Gail Sherman then?"

"Not well." Her tone hinted she could have said more. I guessed she didn't due to the not-speaking-ill-of-the-dead rule.

"How about Diane Landon? I saw her in the picture."

"She only came the one time. All I know about her is that she and her husband moved here recently and he works at WOZ Industries. The wife doesn't have a job, but I guess someone invited her so she could meet people."

"Did she and Gail talk?"

"Yeah. They sat at a table off to one side for a long time." She paused. "I remember thinking somebody should warn the new girl that Gail was likely to—" She stopped herself. "Anyway, they were talking."

"I don't suppose you heard any of it."

Doris chuckled. "Enough to know Gail was bragging, as usual. All about how she was the only heir to some 'perfect water'—whatever that means."

I thought I did. Taking the last delicious bite of my roll, I wadded up the napkin and tossed it into the trash. "Is that the only time you met Mrs. Landon?"

She considered that. "Depends on what you mean by that. I ran into her and her husband at a barbeque on Labor Day, but they didn't see me." She chuckled. "That was a good thing."

"Because?"

"They were fighting."

"About what?"

"I'm not sure. I came along at the end. She was angry about something he'd done, or maybe something he didn't do, and he was apologizing all over the place."

That was intriguing. "You didn't hear what it was about?"

"No. I backed away, like you do when you don't want people to know you've seen their private moment. It's just that it gave me a whole different impression of Mrs. Landon. Not all sweetness and light, you know?"

CHAPTER FORTY-FIVE

Retta

Lars' flight to Albuquerque left just after seven, and mine to Madison was scheduled for nine. We drove separately to the airport, where he turned in his rental car and joined me in the waiting area. Things between us were good, although we were both tired out from a weekend of hiking and foiling crooks.

I wore a navy dress that traveled well, topped with a white, belted coat I'd recently bought online. Hoping I wouldn't see foul weather, I'd worn red heels with a chunky jasper necklace that set the outfit off nicely.

Billie, the airport's everything employee and my former classmate at Allport High, checked us in. When Lars wandered away she asked, "How are things going with your hunky friend?"

"Good," I told her.

"He's just so—everything. You're a lucky girl, Retta."

"Yes," I murmured. "I guess I am."

When I sat down next to him on the bench seat, Lars said for the fourth time that morning, "Rory should be okay now. You did a good thing, Retta." He rubbed the back of my neck fondly.

I nestled closer, liking the feel of it. "When I get back, I'll make sure April made the phone call like she promised."

It was nice sitting there together like an old married couple, chatting about things we'd done and watching the staff ready the clunky little shuttle that would carry Lars to O'Hare to board a much larger plane.

He must have been thinking something similar, because he asked, "Maybe this winter you could fly down to New Mexico for a week or so and get out of the cold for a while."

"That would be nice."

My phone rang, and when I saw the caller ID, I rose and moved away. "Hello, Rick."

"Retta, I tried to reach you all weekend and couldn't."

I paused for a second, making sure I had control of my voice. Fibbing isn't something I like to do, but sometimes it's completely necessary. "My sisters and I went away for the day on Saturday, and I was tied up with business yesterday."

"Did it go well?"

I glanced at Lars, who was gazing out the window. Looking at one handsome man who wanted to be with me and talking to another. It should have felt great, but somehow it didn't.

"Everything went well."

"And you're going to meet Candice today?"

"I'm at the airport now, as a matter of fact."

"You should have called me. I'd have given you a ride."

"That's sweet of you."

Rick cleared his throat, signaling an important message. "I called to say I'll be leaving Allport on Wednesday. Once you get back with the papers, I can close the deal on the property, and I have to go home and catch up on some things." He paused. "I wanted to offer one last chance at the Deluxe Rick Experience."

I glanced again at Lars, who was checking his phone. He looked so sweet with his wide forehead creased in concentration.

"It seems like each time we've gotten together things haven't been quite right for romance," Rick was saying. "I'd like to give it one more try. No business, no bar fights, no other commitments, just you and me and the harvest moon. How about it?"

Lars looked up, caught my eye, and smiled. "I'll get back to you when you're no longer a client," I told him. "I think that will make a world of difference in how we proceed."

"I can't wait."

The scratchy speaker voice called for boarding of Lars' flight, and he stood, stretching to get the kinks out of his back.

"Retta," Rick said in a lower tone, "I want to warn you again about Candice. She's liable to say anything about me. She can't help herself. When you and I get together, we can talk about it. Until then just trust me, okay?"

Lars turned to look at me, and I said, "I trust you, Rick. I'll call as soon as I get back to Allport."

The flight didn't take long, and because of the time difference, I arrived in Wisconsin at about the same time I left Michigan. Searching the crowd for the red blazer Candice Chou had said she'd be wearing, I found her, wearing a tentative smile and all black except for the jacket.

"Ms. Chou?" I put out a hand. "Margaretta Stilson, Smart Detective Agency."

She shook hands, her smile a little nervous. "I took back my maiden name, Edmonds."

"Ms. Edmonds," I corrected. I looked her over, guessing she was doing the same to me. She was pretty, with shiny-black hair, dark eyes, and perfect olive skin.

"There's a coffee shop that way." She pointed down the concourse. "Shall we sit?"

I followed her to the place and bought drinks for both of us, a cappuccino with cinnamon for me and a chocolate latte for her. Cups in hand, we settled at a table with two high stools.

"So Rick needs my signature, huh?"

Though Barbara had explained the situation in the emails, I explained again that Rick was selling their vacation home in Allport. "We need your signature here—" I pointed to a sticky note on the document I'd brought along before turning to the second page. "—and here."

She read every bit of the document, her lips moving when she got to the difficult parts. When she finished, Candice stared at it for a few seconds. "I don't see any way this can hurt me." Looking up at me she asked, "Do you?"

"No, Ms. Edmonds. I honestly don't. My sister, who's a retired attorney, looked it over and says it's simply correcting the mistake that was made at the time of your divorce."

Nodding, she took up the pen and began scratching her name in the places sticky notes indicated. "I was so anxious to get away that I never once thought about the vacation house."

"Tough divorce?" I really didn't expect more than an affirming word, but she seemed to take the question as an invitation.

"The divorce was the easy part. You'd have to know what I went through before that to really understand."

Taking the papers, I slid them into the envelope Faye had provided. Candice didn't seem crazy, but Rick had said she appeared normal at first. "I guess no one else understands what goes on between a husband and wife."

She cocked an eyebrow at me. "Has Rick made a pass at you yet? You're definitely his type."

"Oh, no!" I waved one hand a little too widely, and ended up feeling like one of those animated clowns. "I'm—I'm with someone. A man. He's with the FBI." I was babbling, but I couldn't stop myself. "His name is Lars."

"Then you're lucky." Setting her hands on the table, Candice folded her fingers together and stared at them for a few seconds. "When we started dating, I didn't know Rick was married. When I found out, he swore that his wife was insane. He kept telling me all this crazy stuff she said and did. She sounded horrible."

She sounded like what Rick claimed Candice was.

"After a few months, she found out about us. When she filed for divorce I was relieved. I never wanted to be the Other Woman, but Rick said we couldn't help it. We were in love, and he'd been unhappy for so long."

Though not at all a fan of adultery, I tried to picture it from Rick's side. He'd been caught in a bad marriage. Candice was pretty, and she seemed like the understanding type. "It must have been hard for both of you."

She smiled knowingly. "Maybe you haven't slept with him yet, but you're a member of the Rick Chou Fan Club." When I looked away she went on, "It's okay. That's what he does."

I licked my lips. "Tell me what it is that he does, um, did."

"Okay." Blowing into the foam on her drink, Candice took a sip. "Rick and Marilyn divorced. Somewhere along the line I found out she was dying of some awful disease, kidney cysts or something. Six months after our wedding, she was gone."

She paused again, sipping at her drink without seeming to notice its taste or temperature. "For reasons I don't really understand, I went to the funeral. What I learned there—and heaven knows I didn't tell them who I was—was that Marilyn Chou was the neighborhood saint, funny, intelligent, kind, and hard-working, at least until she got sick."

"Wow."

She held up a hand. "I told myself what you said a few minutes ago. Nobody knows how a spouse acts at home, when it's just the two of them. She might have treated Rick like dirt." She gave her cup a quarter turn on the tabletop. "Then I found out about Doreen."

"Doreen?"

"A woman at Rick's office. I happened to see some emails she sent him, and they were pretty slutty."

"Really?"

Candice smiled grimly and wriggled her brows. "I asked him, 'Rick, what's up with this?' and he says, 'Don't pay any attention to Doreen. She thinks she's funny.'" Her lips tightened. "He acted like it was a big joke."

I was beginning to get it, and after sipping my drink to wet my dry mouth, I said, "That wasn't the end of it."

"Well, I never heard about Doreen again, but a few months later I got a call from Stephanie, who told me I should, 'Let Rick go.'" She made quotation marks in the air with her fingers. "It wasn't fair of me to keep him in a loveless marriage. I should be a big girl and admit he didn't want me anymore."

"Did you confront him?"

The snort she made wasn't really laughter, though it's what she was trying for. "Rick said I must be really paranoid to believe some anonymous woman who made up terrible lies about him." She paused, but I couldn't think of a thing to say. After a moment she went on. "What grinds me is that I believed him—again. It took two more incidents like that to convince me. Heaven knows how many women there were I never learned about."

Candice sipped her drink then wiped a bit of foam from her lip with a bright red fingertip. "The kicker was Marci, who came right to our front door. She said Rick was afraid to leave me for fear I'd slash my wrists. I should get professional help, she said.

A man shouldn't have to live with a wife as crazy as me." She sighed. "I packed my stuff, drove all night, and moved in with my mother until I could find a job and a place of my own again."

"I'm a little confused." I gestured at the airport around us. "You were determined not to let Rick find out where you live. My um—coworkers think he abused you."

"Not the way they're thinking." Pressing her lips together, Candice confessed, "I just can't afford to be tempted again."

"Tempted?"

Her expression turned wistful. "If Rick knew where I live—if he could show up at my door and if for his own twisted reasons he did that, I'm not sure I wouldn't let him in."

"You're kidding."

She gathered our trash and deposited it in a nearby receptacle, leaving the flap swinging. "I know how dumb it is, but don't you feel it? When you're listening to him, and especially when you're looking at him, everything the S.O.B. says sounds like the truth."

What could I say? "Then it's good you're staying strong."

Candice grimaced. "I guess, but how will I ever be able to trust another man?"

"I think you will, in time." Checking my watch, I saw that my flight would be boarding soon. I rose and gave Candice a hug. "It was so nice to meet you."

As I walked away, I told myself I'd have seen through Rick Chou eventually. He wasn't that good, especially when I had a man like Lars to compare him to.

Chapter Forty-six

Barb

After some thought, which I had lots of time for on the long drive home from Bay City, I pulled over at a county park shaded by very tall pines. The day had warmed, so I rolled down the window and took in their fragrance as I called Stan Wozniak a second time. "I'd like to know more about the illegal use of Landon's credit card at the plant in Florida."

"I'll be glad to check into it, but I have to say I've become doubtful that Landon could be a criminal. I've been watching him closely, and he's like a robot. No ambition, no ego. He just wants to do his scientific thing."

"But this all started when he showed up in Allport," I argued. "We have to ask ourselves why. I'd like you to call the bottling plant in Florida and ask one more question."

"What's that?"

"I'd like to know if Landon's wife ever came to visit him at his work place."

Stan was sharp, so I didn't have to explain. After only a brief hesitation he said, "You think she took the company credit card out of his wallet, dressed up like a hoodlum, took as much as she could get out of the ATMs, and then returned the card."

"Landon probably didn't suspect her at the time, but I think his view has changed." I told him about Landon's odd phone call.

"I'll try to reach that plant right away," Wozniak promised."

"Thanks, Stan."

While I waited for his call, I drove on. When I saw a McDonalds I went to the drive-through, got an iced tea, and parked off to one side. Sipping at my drink, I used my iPad to research Diane Landon. From what Retta said, the wedding had taken place in Florida. In the state's marriage records I typed in Enright Landon's name. Sure enough, a certificate had been issued a little over a year earlier for Enright S. Landon to wed Diane S. Mellon. Her maiden name struck a chord in my memory, and I started a new search. She'd listed her place of birth as Toms River, New Jersey, so I switched to that state's records and typed in Diane S. Mellon. When the page loaded, I made a guttural hum of surprise. Diane Sydney Mellon was Sydney Mellon, the contact person for the corporation that had bought the Clausen property on Sweet Springs.

I wanted to tell Faye what I'd learned, but she'd gone to the Meadows. Knowing the doctor visited on Mondays, she was determined to speak with him about Clara, and she'd warned me that her phone would be silenced. I texted her a short message that said simply, DL NOT WHAT SHE SEEMS.

CHAPTER FORTY-SEVEN

Faye

I was almost ready to leave for the Meadows when I heard that gut-wrenching sound so familiar to pet owners. Buddy was throwing up in the hallway. He didn't do it often, but I had to clean it up before Barb got home and gave me that look she gets.

As I put away the bucket and sponge, my phone dinged, and I saw that I'd missed her call. When I read her message, I moved a little faster to get to the nursing home. At the last minute I saw Buddy sitting sadly in a doorway, obviously sorry he'd made a mess. "Want to go for a ride in the car, Bud?" I asked. His thumping tail was all the answer I needed. Buddy seems to feel better when he's on the move.

When I arrived, Glenda gave me an update on Harriet. "She's in a pretty good mood today. Says her breakfast was served just the way she likes it."

"Great. I'll see her later." I headed for Clara's room, but found only her roommate. I asked her where Clara was but she only shrugged. It jarred me to see the alarm from Clara's ankle lying on her bedside stand. I went to find Glenda, who frowned when I asked where she might be.

"I think everyone's out of the dining hall." Leading the way, she peered in to confirm it. "Visiting another patient, maybe."

"It's important that I speak to her." We split up, but when we returned to the nurses' desk, neither of us had located Clara. "Let's ask Sybil," Glenda said.

Sybil's office was next to the outer doors, and she monitored the comings and goings at the Meadows as best she could while answering the phone, directing calls to the correct staff member, and completing general paperwork.

"She left with someone this morning," Sybil told us. "They were going to her niece's visitation."

"Who?" I asked. Sybil flinched, and I realized I sounded like a Nazi interrogator. "I mean, who took Clara to the funeral home?"

Scrabbling through the papers on her desk, Sybil consulted the sign-out sheet and looked up at me. "Signature's illegible."

Which it was.

Her round face took on an expression of concern. "Is something wrong?"

"I hope not."

The description Sybil gave—a stooped, older woman with large sunglasses and a headscarf wearing a slightly worn, blue trench coat—was almost useless. I tried to tell myself it couldn't have been Diane Landon, but when I called Barb, she reinforced my fears. "This time of year it's a pretty easy disguise—coat collar up, hat, scarf, and sensible shoes. It's Diane, all right."

Speaking quickly, she told me Stan Wozniak had learned that Diane Landon had visited her husband each of the times the credit card had been used to take cash from ATMs. "Twice each day," Barb said. "Supposedly to bring him his lunch around eleven, and then later in the afternoon." She sounded disgusted as she added, "The security guards apparently got a kick out of stuffy old Enright having a wife who missed him so much she kept stopping by during work hours."

"She took the credit card out of En's wallet at lunchtime then put it back later in the day."

"It was probably as easy as 'I need shopping money, dear,' and taking his wallet to supposedly get cash. When she came back it would be, 'I didn't spend everything you gave me, so I'll put it back.' If the guy was busy, he probably paid no attention."

"Enright sounds like the perfect man for a scheming woman to hide behind."

"Stan says she often visits him at WOZ, too. She could have contacted Cold-Clear from there to make it look like the company was interested in a water deal. A proposal from an established enterprise would give the project authenticity."

I rubbed a hand across my forehead. "I can't believe this. Retta keeps saying what a nice woman Diane is."

"Retta is easily won over by looks and charm, and Diane has been cultivating a friendship with her to find out what we know." Barb didn't sound judgmental, just tired.

"If Diane is Gail's silent partner, she's a dangerous woman."

Barb made a sound of agreement. "Here's what I found out from a cursory internet search. Diane Landon was a foster child from an early age. She moved from home to home for years but never stayed for long. People took in a pretty girl with a sweet smile but found out later she was prone to stealing, temper tantrums, and sleeping with neighborhood boys who had fast cars or a little spending money. She was released from the system at eighteen, arrested a couple of times for prostitution, and ended up in trouble for taking a john's wallet."

"Let me guess—the judge felt sorry for her and put her into a work program."

"Right. They got her a job at the bottling plant in Zephyrhills, and the rest we know." I heard a slurp as Barb finished whatever she was drinking.

Fear had struck as Barb revealed Diane's background, but I tried not to over-react. "Let me make a call. I'll get back to you."

A few minutes later, I called Barb from outside the Meadows so no one could overhear. She'd resumed driving, and the echo-y sound told me she was using the hands-free feature. "I called the funeral home," I told her. "Clara wasn't at Gail's visitation. If Diane took her, where could they be?"

"She's going to force her to sign over her land."

I made a negative sound. "She can't believe she can still get away with her scheme."

"Why not? No one's found proof of murder in the case of Caleb Marsh or Gail Sherman. Even if there was proof, we can't show that Diane did it."

"But she's going to make a great deal of money."

"Which isn't a crime. She'll pretend to be sad when she hears how aggressive Gail was about acquiring the land, but she'll insist she was simply a silent financial partner."

"How could she force Clara to sell her the land, especially now that she hasn't got Gail to help her?"

"According to Michigan law she could write up a deed herself. If Clara signed it, Diane's claim would be good."

"How does someone write up her own deed?"

"She'd follow the format of the old deed to get the exact property description. She'd simply change the names: Clara would be the Grantor and Diane the Grantee."

"And once Clara signs it, the sale will be legal." I heard fear in my own voice. "Barb, Diane hasn't left anyone alive who could stand in the way of this deal. With Gail dead, there's no one who will question the supposed sale. Diane can tell any story she likes if Clara isn't around to contradict her."

Barb paused, and I pictured her pressing down harder on the accelerator. "We need to find Clara."

I was already trotting toward my car. "Call Rory and the sheriff. Tell them what's happened."

"What are you going to do?"

"Head out to Sweet Springs," I replied. "If Diane needs the original deed, that's where they'll be.

"Faye—"

"Barb, as soon as Diane gets what she wants, Clara's going to have some sort of accident."

"What are you going to do to stop it?"

"I'll slow Diane down until the cops arrive, and they can take it from there."

***

A silver Chevy Tahoe sat in Clara's drive. The plate was from Michigan, but there was a Florida Gators sticker in the back window. I stopped my Escape on the lane, behind some trees so it wasn't visible from the house. Buddy objected with a low growl when I left him behind, but I hissed a command for silence. He obeyed, though his eyes were wary.

On tiptoe, I peered cautiously through a side window. Clara sat at her kitchen table with a box of papers on her lap. She was in profile, and the scene might have looked peaceful except for the taut line of her back and the fact that Diane Landon paced angrily behind her.

"Where is it?" she demanded.

"I don't know." Clara sounded tearful. "My late husband did all the filing. I've had no cause to look at the deed for years." She sounded frightened, and my heart broke for her.

"Stupid old—" Diane stopped beside Clara and slapped her hard across the face. Taking a cast-iron skillet from its hook she threatened, "Five more minutes. If you haven't found it by then,

I'll smack you with this and find the damned thing myself while you bleed out on the floor!"

"I'm trying!" Clara seemed terrified.

My mind buzzed, and I tried to calm the panic that rose in my chest. How could I get Clara away from that woman? If Diane saw me, she might kill strike Clara with the skillet before I could stop her.

"Here it is." Clara took some papers backed with a blue sheet from the box and handed it over.

Diane turned away from me for a moment, scanning the deed. Taking advantage of her distraction, I waved a hand to get Clara's attention. Though she seemed for a moment to glance in my direction, she made no sign she'd seen me. Probably too terrified to notice anything but the threat standing over her.

Turning away from the window, I continued around the house. Could I get in the back door and come up behind Diane?

No. It was locked. The windows in the old house were much too high off the ground for me to climb in, even if one of them happened to be unlatched. I turned, set my back against the rough-sawn siding, and tried to think.

From my new vantage point I faced the chicken coop, and, looking at the small enclosure, an idea formed. It depended on some luck, a little speed, and my dog. I knew I could count on him, and I thought I could be fast enough. That left the luck part.

Staying low, I approached Diane's car and looked inside. At least that much luck was with me. She'd tossed her keys onto the front seat when she got out. Opening the door with painstaking caution, I took the keys and moved away in a crouch. Hurrying back to my own car, I took Buddy out, whispering to him to stay quiet in my arms. He knew something was up, and being a very smart dog, cooperated. We went around the back of Clara's house to the chicken pen, where I opened the gate as wide as possible. I tossed Diane's car keys to the far side, hitting the spot I'd chosen with satisfying accuracy. Setting Buddy on the ground I whispered, "Sic 'em, boy! Go get 'em!"

Short legs pumping, the dog scooted into the pen. I scampered for the back of the house—well, as fast as an overweight fifty-something can scamper.

Buddy didn't understand the danger Clara was in, didn't comprehend my motives, but he got that he was allowed—even encouraged—to chase those chickens. In seconds the area behind me sounded like all twelve birds were being slaughtered at once. I knew my dog well enough to recognize that while he loved chasing the chickens, he had no intention of hurting them. Buddy was providing the distraction I needed to rescue Clara. Since they didn't know our purpose, the hens and their rooster reacted with typical poultry panic.

Crouching behind the woodpile, I waited for Diane to come out to see what the ruckus was about. Sure enough, she stepped out the front door and onto the porch. She couldn't see the pen from there, and the squawks and snarls continued. A large hen ran full-throttle past Diane's feet, turned, and with no common sense whatsoever, ran back the way she'd come.

Diane called to Clara, "You can't outrun me, so don't even try." Descending the three steps, she peered around the corner. Buddy happily chased here and there, and the chickens, not-so-happily, stayed in front of him.

"Stop that, dog!" Diane shouted. "Shoo! Get out of here!"

That must have been when she saw what I'd tossed onto the ground inside. "What the—"

I crawled closer, leaving Dale's neat woodpile for the shelter of Clara's wheelbarrow, overturned on the grass beside the garden. I smelled the remains of the barrow's last load, chicken manure. Ignoring it, I timed my attack carefully. It wouldn't take Diane long to step into the pen and retrieve her keys.

Stopping to look around every few steps, Diane saw only Buddy and his reluctant playmates. With a last look around and a grunt of irritation, she entered the pen, hopping to sidestep piles of manure as best she could. When she stooped to pick up the keys I rushed in, kicked her once in the rear, and retreated. Diane sprawled in the dirt, sputtering a curse. When she turned, I was already closing the gate on her.

She called me things I'd never heard anyone say out loud before. I don't swear myself, but being an avid reader, I do know all the words.

I fastened the gate closed by tying it with twine, putting several knots in and jerking each as tight as I could before adding another.

As I worked, Diane clawed at me through the chicken wire, snarling like an angry bear. "You! Stop that! Let me out of here!"

Not bothering to answer, I left her and hurried to the house, where Clara was coming down the steps. "Good job, Faye!" she called. Her face was red from the blow she'd taken, which made me want to catch the rooster and put him into the cage with Ms. Landon. It would be interesting to see how Diane fared against a creature both willing and able to fight back.

Since that wasn't possible I said, "Clara, my car is out by your mailbox. Get in it and wait for me."

"What are you going to do?"

"I'm going to get you away from here, but I have to get my dog first."

Buddy had tired of his game, and when I called, he turned and ran toward me. "We have to go, Bud, but you were great."

Hearing a snarl, I looked toward the pen. Diane was working on the knots, kicking at the gate every few seconds in frustration. Chicken wire is tough, and I tie pretty good knots. She was going to have to settle down and work to get out of there.

Clara was putting on her seat belt when Buddy and I reached the car. Scooting him into the back seat, I got in, turned the car around, and got us headed in the direction of Allport.

"Are you all right, Clara?"

"I think so. I was so pleased when I saw you in the window."

"I didn't know if you did." Slightly relieved that we were heading in the right direction I said, "I'm sorry I had to upset your chickens. They probably won't lay again for days."

"They're tough girls, like you and me." She frowned. "I just hope that woman doesn't notice there's a little trapdoor next to the coop. In nice weather I open it up and let the girls come and go as they please. She can get out that way, as long as she doesn't mind crawling on her belly."

Certain Diane would do anything to get out of there and get at us, I pressed harder on the accelerator. "My sister called the police. They should be on the way."

"How did you know where to find me?"

"I didn't, really, but when you weren't at the Meadows and you weren't at Gail's memorial, I guessed you were in danger."

"You really are good at your job, and I'm very grateful for that." Clara touched the spot where Diane had hit her. "I stalled as long as I could, playing the dotty old lady."

"You knew where the deed was all along?"

She raised one white brow at me. "Of course, dear. It doesn't pay to be sloppy with important documents."

CHAPTER FORTY-EIGHT

Barb

Driving too fast for US-23, I called Rory and told him where Faye was headed. He was dialing Sheriff Brill on his other line even as he tried to reassure me. "We're on the way, Barb."

"I'm getting close. I'll meet you out there as soon as I can."

When I ended the call, my phone rang almost immediately. The caller ID informed me it was Retta.

"I'm back in Michigan, and wait till I tell you what I heard."

"Later, Retta. Faye's out at Clara's, and she might be in trouble." Quickly I told her what had happened.

"Why did she go off by herself?" she demanded. "Doesn't she know we're dealing with a killer?"

"You know Faye." I bit my lip. "When someone's in trouble, she's got to help."

"Even if it's dangerous," Retta agreed. "The girl doesn't use her head sometimes."

"I know."

"I'm getting into my car now," she told me. "I'll be on the road to Sweet Springs in ten seconds."

"I'll see you out there."

CHAPTER FORTY-NINE

Faye

I drove faster by far than was usual for me, but not recklessly. The road back to Allport was twisty, constructed to skirt farm properties back in the day when farmers had a say in such things. As we traveled I recalled Barb, Dale, Retta, and I stopping along here to admire the view. I hadn't met Clara Knight then, and I'd had no idea she and I would be speeding along this road less than two weeks later, hoping we'd escaped a killer.

We hadn't. Suddenly there was a vehicle behind us—too close. A second after I noticed it, we were rammed. My car lurched to the side, bouncing off the guardrail with a screech of metal. Clara grabbed for the handle above the door. I gripped the steering wheel and pressed the gas pedal hard, pulling away.

It worked for a few seconds, but the bigger vehicle caught up with us and smashed into the back of my car again. I felt my spine react as the wave of the impact traveled up it, whipping my neck. Clara made a soft "Oh!" of protest.

Diane Landon's face showed in my rear-view mirror, and her Tahoe loomed over my car like a hawk chasing down a sparrow. The road curved ahead, tracing the drop-off that overlooked the hay field. If I didn't get around the curve before Diane came alongside, she could force my car over the guardrail and send it tumbling down the hillside.

My smaller engine was no match for the monster she drove, so I couldn't outrace her. I had to outwit her.

Clara's face was white, but she made no sound as I did what I could to foil Diane's attempts to wreck us. When she lunged our way, I hit the brake. When she slowed to correct her steering, I sped up again. I didn't know how long I could keep it up, but we remained on the road—terrified, perhaps doomed, but alive.

After falling behind for a few seconds, Diane pulled out again and came alongside my car. The scenario she would invent flashed through my mind. She and Clara had worked out a property deal. I'd come along and offered to drive Clara back to the Meadows. Somehow on the way we had a terrible accident. All she had to do was get rid of her damaged car somehow, and she was inventive enough to manage that. Who could prove she was lying once Clara and I were dead?

My thoughts were interrupted by another jolt. Diane was beside us, and she turned the steering wheel abruptly, catching my car's front fender. I held on, but there was a terrible grind of metal on metal. When she backed off, I felt something pressing against my left front tire. Steering became difficult, and I had to fight to keep the car going forward. Worse, my speed dropped no matter how hard I pressed on the accelerator. Triumph glowed in Diane's eyes as she kept pace with me. The road ahead split the woods, and though I'd escaped going over the drop-off, the forested area provided her with new opportunities to kill us. One more impact from her vehicle would send us off the road, where we couldn't avoid crashing into a tree—probably many trees.

My hands gripped the steering wheel so tightly it felt like I'd melded to it. Could I hit Diane first and perhaps damage her vehicle? I turned the wheel, but nothing happened except the noise got worse. I tried to brake, but she slowed with me. She was waiting for just the right moment—

"Look!" Clara cried, and I turned from Diane's angry face to the road before us. Someone was coming—in fact, three someones. Lights flashing, two sheriff's patrol cars approached, along with a pickup I recognized. Rory.

Driving in the wrong lane and fully focused on my car, Diane didn't see their vehicles until it was too late. She braked, and I heard the roar of gravel under her wheels, but the big SUV kept going. She steered hard to the left, and her car went off the road and into the trees. She took out the first few, saplings that couldn't withstand the force of the Tahoe, but twenty feet in she met an oak tree that stood its ground. With a horrendous crash, the SUV came to a sudden and complete stop. There was a hiss as something escaped from somewhere, and after a few seconds, Diane let out a loud wail: part anger, part fear, and part pure frustration. Shoving the door open, she struggled against the air-bag for a moment, then almost popped out of the vehicle, where she fell into the arms of an approaching deputy.

CHAPTER FIFTY

Retta

I arrived at the scene of Diane Landon's arrest seconds before Barbara Ann did. Getting out of our cars, we hurried toward Faye and Clara. Sheriff Brill assured us no one was seriously injured, though Diane's eyes were already going black.

Valiantly trying to sound like an outraged citizen, she insisted it was all a mistake. Her voice, strident and angry, was quite different from what I'd heard before. She was definitely not the woman I'd thought she was.

"Save it," Brill told her. "I'm pretty sure we've got a footprint from Caleb Marsh's porch that will match those big old boots you've got stowed in the back of your car, and we have a tire tread imprint that should prove you were out at the Warner place around the time of the fire."

Diane removed the towel she was using to staunch her bloody nose. "*If* I visited those places, it doesn't prove a thing."

"No," Rory agreed, "but now that you've kidnapped Mrs. Knight and tried to kill her and Mrs. Burner, I think a jury will put it all together."

At a nod from the sheriff, a deputy handcuffed Diane and led her to his car. She kept talking, and it was a relief to hear the door slam, cutting off her torrent of lies.

Rory turned to Faye and Clara. "We need to get you two to a hospital and get you checked out."

Though they insisted they were okay, the rest of us outvoted them, and to shut us up, they finally agreed. Tow trucks were called for the Tahoe and Faye's poor Escape, which looked like it had been rolled down a mountain by a fairy tale giant. As Clara was escorted away, her concern was for her chickens. "If they're out all night, the foxes or coyotes will get them."

Faye turned to Barbara Anne and me, and I thought I saw a glint in her eye. "I think my sisters can help with that," she said.

Leaving Barbara's car along the road, we continued to Sweet Springs in mine, mostly silent. I was sure she was mad at me for solving Rory's problem without her. Of course there was the Oxford comma thing, too. The fact that Faye might have died today made both those things seem petty, but I wasn't sure Barbara Ann felt the same way.

We arrived to find most of the chickens scattered around the yard. Three had gone back into the pen, willing to trade freedom for food they didn't have to hunt and peck for. Come night, the others would be easy prey for predators.

"We'd better get this done," I said as we stared across the yard. Barbara was probably doubtful her much-older body would stand up to the task, since it had been decades since she'd chased a chicken. As for me, I was trying to calculate how I'd do this without wrecking my new Michael Kors shoes. In the end I kicked them off near the woodpile and proceeded in my hose, which were much more easily replaced.

I chose a plump hen who'd settled on one of the dock pilings. Seeing me coming, she jumped down and fluttered away, staying just out of my reach.

Barbara went after a bird that was pecking around the woodpile, but as soon as she approached, it hurried around to the other side. When Barbara went around to the back of the pile, the hen reappeared on my side, her head thrusting forward and back like a piston. Barbara cut her off at the end of the woodpile, but the hen merely turned and ran in the opposite direction.

My bird had gone between two of Clara's sheds, so I tiptoed up to the spot, hoping she was looking the wrong way. I almost succeeded, but my shadow fell over her and she sensed danger. Shooting out the opposite end of the space, the hen clucked anxiously and sprinted toward the lakeshore.

Hearing a squawk, I turned. Barbara had actually caught her chicken. Holding it in front of her like a Russian samovar, she turned toward the pen. I hurried forward to open the gate for her, but we hadn't thought ahead. It was tied shut in about six knots. I fiddled with them for a while, but my hands were cold, and the knots were tight. While Barbara looked over my shoulder, the hen sensed her distraction, twisted out of her hands, and bounced away.

Chickenless, Barbara took a stab at the knots on the gate, but she was no more successful than I'd been. "We need to find something to cut the rope with."

As we turned, looking for a tool, I noticed a small, chicken-sized trapdoor near the back corner. "Look," I said, pointing. "If we prop that open, we can shoo them inside one at a time."

"But we're going to have to do it together, so the ones that are in stay in." Barbara got two pieces of firewood and set the trapdoor on them to hold it open.

We chose a hen fairly close to us. Barbara circled and approached from the opposite side. The nervous bird looked first at her, then at me, unsure who was scarier. Barbara moved closer, and the hen jerked toward me, one scaly foot pausing at each step. I stepped into her path so she had to turn left, toward the pen. Barbara took another step and the hen moved forward again. Spreading my hands, I shooed her farther to the left. Without realizing where she was headed, the hen stepped through the trapdoor and back into the pen. Quickly Barbara Ann set a third piece of firewood across the opening at a slant, effectively blocking her inside.

"Only eleven to go," I said.

The next three were fairly easy. The four after that were not. They raced all over the yard, eluding us at every turn. I fell once on the slippery grass, and Barbara cut her arm on a wire when she captured the third hen and pushed her through the opening. While we were catching our breath, two hens actually approached the trapdoor and walked calmly inside, as if returning home from a nature hike.

That left the rooster and one hen. By mutual consent we left the male for last, capturing the female by trapping her against the woodpile. She tried to fly up over it but didn't make a very good attempt, and I caught her by the legs. She made a terrible fuss, flapping her wings and squawking like she was being sent to Guantanamo. Though I didn't like the feel of it one bit, I held on. Hurrying ahead of me, Barbara unblocked the trapdoor, and I tossed her inside.

We stood for a few moments, catching our breath before what we guessed would be our biggest challenge. The rooster had watched our progress from a low tree branch, and I didn't like the look in the eye I could see from below.

Perhaps to prolong the time when we had to challenge him I said to Barbara, "You were right about Rick Chou."

That brow went up, the one that says she's surprised. "He beat his wife?"

"Well, no."

I told her what Candice had said about Rick's philandering. I waited for her to say, 'I told you so,' but she just shook her head. "Mental abuse. I've seen it a lot in my career. Others can't understand why women stay with them, but they do."

On the plane coming back from Wisconsin, I'd considered the status of my relationships. I really liked Lars, and as much as I didn't want to, I had to admit my sister had done me a favor by reminding me the relationship was worth keeping. Stuffy as she is, Barbara Ann has integrity. With Rick turning out to be a big old liar-head, I had to give her credit.

"I guess it was lucky Lars showed up and reminded me what a great guy he is."

"Yes." Her tone was casual. "Did you hear that Ms. Tattletale and her partner gave up trying to get Rory in trouble?"

"That's good, isn't it? Rory doesn't deserve that kind of grief."

Barbara eyed the rooster, who sat on his branch like Yertle the Turtle. "I've done some thinking about the Oxford comma. There's disagreement among scholars about its necessity."

What I said next would be important to Barbara, who hates to be wrong or even *appear* to be wrong.

"I've seen places where it definitely clarifies the meaning of a sentence," I admitted. "It's too bad things like counting spaces and downright carelessness sometimes substitute for clarity."

"You know I hate slipshod grammar and punctuation."

"I know. I read a book last week where the author spelled *all right* as one word, A-L-R-I-G-H-T, all the way through. It irritated me to no end."

"Then it's good that we continue to demonstrate what's correct."

"Yes, I think we have to."

At that moment, the rooster flapped his wings, dropped from his perch in the tree, and strutted over to the trapdoor, where he waited for Barbara to remove the block. When she did, he stepped inside like the man of the house returning from a hard day's work. Barbara removed the wood and I closed the trapdoor as his little harem welcomed him home.

CHAPTER FIFTY-ONE

Faye

I was pleased to be the one to tell Clara she really could go home soon, though her doctor urged her to stay in Allport until someone moved into one of the other properties. That was more than likely, since Gabe and Mindy were ninety percent sure they'd be getting a loan to buy the Marsh place.

"It's kinda old and kinda small," Gabe told Dale and me (looking mostly at Dale). "But Fred Marsh said his family likes the idea that we're a young couple willing to work to fix it up 'stead of tearing it down and putting in a modular or something." Just as I wondered if Mindy's mother was saying prayers for the loan to go through Gabe added, "Mrs. Gains said she'd cosign for us if we need her to." They were sweet kids, but after a year of having them under her roof, Mom would probably throw in cash for the down payment, too.

Gabe also told us about Mindy's dream, and while he wasn't clear on the details, it sounded like a worthwhile idea. "Mindy wants Allport to turn into a place where old people don't have to leave their homes," he said. "If you was to get all the churches and community organizations together with the city and the county and set up a plan, they could make it so there's help available for people on something that slides."

"A sliding scale?"

He pointed at me. "That's it. It means they pay what they can and we figure out the rest. People like me will donate hours of work or bank them for the future, for when our parents are so old they need help. The rest of the money would come from local charities and government programs. Mindy says it's a lot cheaper to keep people in their homes than it is to put them in 24/7 care, 'specially if they can still do some stuff themselves."

"Makes the tax base more stable too," Dale put in. "Not so many empty properties sitting around the county."

"I've heard Barb speak of something like that, but she said it would take someone young and energetic to set it up. You'd have to do a lot of convincing to get people to buy into the idea."

"Well, that's Mindy," Gabe said proudly. "We're gonna start on our own, the two of us, so we can show everybody it's possible. We'll work weekends and maybe some nights too."

"I think that's great, Gabe."

"Thanks, Mrs. Burner. Mindy says Jesus would like it."

"I'm one hundred percent certain she's right, and I'll be glad to introduce Mindy at my church whenever she's ready to start signing people up."

"Do you really think it will work?" Dale asked after Gabe left.

"They'll need support, but Barb might be willing to help. With her practical experience, people can't say it's only the pipe dream of a young, idealistic social worker."

"I'll bet Retta could get support for the project, too. She knows everybody, and she's never been afraid to ask for what she wants."

"True. I'll include her when I get Barb and Mindy together."

***

"It will be nice to have young people out there again," Clara said when I told her. She'd taken Gail's malevolence stoically, glad to have a reason for her own odd behavior. We stressed that Gail hadn't known about the killing of Caleb Marsh or the burning of the Warner's house. In fact, Gail's objections to those things had probably caused Diane Landon to kill her, though she wasn't admitting to anything. Rory assured us she wouldn't get away with her crimes. "Anybody who kidnaps little old ladies is just as likely to commit murder and arson."

Enright Landon was horrified by his wife's behavior, though Rory said he hadn't seemed particularly surprised. "He's probably had plenty of opportunity to see a difference between her public persona and the one he dealt with at home," Rory observed.

"I'll take some cookies over to that young couple as soon as I'm able," Clara said now as we sat opposite each other, working on a jigsaw puzzle. "I know things about that old house they need to hear, like how you fix the furnace when it quits. All it takes is a big needle and a flashlight."

"I bet they'll need all kinds of help from you."

"And you're sure my chickens are all right?"

"Yes. My sisters got them all back in the pen while you and I were at the hospital."

Clara reached over to pat my arm. "I'm glad you weren't hurt. I feel bad about Gail, but—" She stopped. "I recall she had a cat. Will you see if anyone took the poor thing? If not, I always have room for another animal."

"That would be a nice thing for you to do."

"Good. Now go visit your mother-in-law. You shouldn't spend all your time with me."

"Dale's with her," I said. "Besides, when Dale and I came into the room she asked where Rettie was. She likes my sister better than she likes me, even if she never gets her name right."

"Harriet is very proud of you, Faye. She brags about you all over this place, about how you catch criminals and show the police how it's done." She chuckled. "It was a lifesaver for me when I heard there was a private detective who visited regularly."

She smiled ruefully. “I don’t know what I’d have done if you girls hadn’t helped me out.”

“We were glad to.” My mind stuck on what she’d just said. “It’s hard to imagine my mother-in-law praising me or my work.”

Clara waved my disbelief away. “Like other women I’ve known, Harriet resented your taking away her baby boy all those years ago. Now she needs you, which means she has to admit she was wrong—I guess to everyone but you.” Clara’s expression turned sad. “It’s hard for her to acknowledge her own children don’t care enough to act in her best interest, but the woman she’s bad-mouthed for years does.”

“Thank you for telling me.”

“Oh, I can assure you she’s quite obnoxious about it.” Clara’s eyes glinted with humor behind her thick glasses.

Giving her a hug, I promised to see her soon. Dale and I planned to escort her when she was allowed to move back home.

As I entered Harriet’s room, Dale and his mother sat silently, her in the wheelchair and Dale on the bed. A sitcom played on the TV, and they watched without interest. When I sat down beside Dale, Harriet asked, “How is the Knight woman doing?”

“She’s doing well.”

“Word is she’s going home.” Her tone was resentful.

“Yes.” It was odd that Harriet couldn’t remember the last time we’d visited but was able to pick up the gossip at the Meadows and remember it, especially the things we didn’t want her to. I tried to prevent the argument I knew was imminent. “It was a mistake that Clara came here.”

She huffed in disgust. “This whole place is a mistake.” Turning to Dale she demanded, “Why can’t I go home? Did you sell my house?”

“No, Mom, we didn’t sell your house.”

"Then why can't I go home?"

Dale's face flushed, and I stepped in. "How would you get up and down all those steps?"

It was our tried-and-true excuse, because Harriet had to agree. "No. I couldn't do that." Sticking out her jaw, she vowed, "When they're not looking, I'm going to practice walking. When I can get around on my own again, you can take me back home."

"Why don't you ask Derrick to help?" I suggested. "He'll keep you from falling and hurting yourself." It was like a skit we did over and over. Harriet liked Derrick, who was clever enough to promise he'd help her practice walking as soon as he could and then hurry away as if too busy at the moment. It was how we kept her in the wheelchair instead of in a heap on the tile floor.

"That's what I'll do," Harriet said. "I'll ask Derrick."

When we left a few minutes later, Dale squeezed my arm. "You can always handle her."

"Years of experience," I replied, rolling my eyes.

Holding the door for me, he said, "I'm sorry, Faye."

"For what?"

He shrugged. "Your life, I guess. You got stuck with a man who wasn't much to start with then got worse. You have a mother-in-law who's never given you a break." Setting his cap on his head, he finished, "Retta and Barb had their troubles, but they've got nice houses and money to buy what they want."

"Stop right there, Dale Burner!" I followed him to the passenger side of the car and backed him up against the door. "Don't tell me about my life. I married you because I loved you, and I still love you. Your mother can be as ornery as she wants. I don't care. You and I are together, and that's what I want. Not money, not a big house, not an expensive car—though I'll be glad to get mine back and not have to borrow Barb's." I put my arms around his neck. "Whatever life hands us, we're going to handle it—together."

"Get a room!" said a voice behind us, and I turned to see two teenagers passing. They were clearly shocked at the sight of two old people apparently necking.

I looked back at Dale, and the humor of the moment caught up with us. Smiling at each other, we stood in our embrace for a moment longer before I backed away. "Let's go home, Mr. Burner."

"Okay with me, Mrs. Burner."

CHAPTER FIFTY-TWO

Barb

Rory made dinner for us at his place the night after Diane Landon's arrest. As we dined on his version of Chicago-style pizza, which was delicious, we pooled information. "Stan Wozniak didn't seem like a killer to me," I said, "and I checked on Rick Chou, our other suspect. He wasn't in Allport Labor Day weekend, and he has no connections to industry." I smiled. "The guy apparently makes his money as a hand and foot model for commercials."

"Foot model? You mean like for foot fungus ads?"

I shrugged. "Someone has to do it. Anyway, that narrowed it down to one or both of the Landons as Gail's partner."

"And her eventual killer."

Rory supplied details about the crimes. "In the back of Diane's car we found the clothing she wore when she played someone else. Along with the disguise she used to get Clara out of the Meadows, she had several men's outfits, all padded to change her body shape. We found the boots that made the footprint on Marsh's porch, and an assortment of hats, gloves, wigs, and theater makeup. One outfit is probably what she wore in Florida to pose as the gang-banger at the ATMs. Another is like what Retta described as the man who threatened her with a hoe at Clara's place. That one smelled like smoke, so I'm guessing she wore it to set fire to the Warner place—"

I interrupted. "When was Retta threatened with a hoe?"

Rory's eyes widened as he realized I didn't know about that. "Forget I said anything, okay?"

I sighed. Retta was hopeless. If I let on that I knew, she'd blame Rory for tattling, and it wouldn't change any future action she might take. We'd just have to watch her more closely.

"Can you prove Diane killed Gail or Mr. Marsh?"

"Marsh's death will be tough to prove. She covered her tracks pretty well."

"The footprint on his porch?"

"It puts her there, but being on the guy's porch doesn't prove she killed him."

I was disappointed. "How about Gail?"

"There we've been luckier. Diane acted quickly on that one, which meant she made mistakes." Rory settled in closer and put his arm around me. "We think Gail called Diane when she began to suspect crimes were being committed in order to get the properties on Sweet Springs. Sensing Gail was getting cold feet, Diane suggested they meet at the springs."

"Where she killed her."

"Hey, this is my story, let me tell it," he said in mock disgust. "With her fear of water, Diane knew there was no way she'd get Gail out on the dock. She hit her with something—"

"Probably the hoe she chased Retta with," I grumbled.

"They're checking that as we speak. Anyway, she hit her hard enough to daze her, then carried her to the end of the dock, where she bashed Gail's head against a post so it looked like she fell in out there."

"Carrying Gail that far couldn't have been easy."

He shrugged. "You can't say the woman wasn't determined."

"I guess not." I snuggled against him. "But she's certainly evil."

***

When I got home that night, The Brat was waiting, angry but still beautiful. When she smelled that I'd brought some beef home, she let me pet her as she ate, making little growly noises in the back of her throat. When the meat was gone, she stayed, arching her back as I continued stroking her fur.

"Are you full, or should I get a kitty treat for dessert?"

To my amazement, the cat stepped daintily into the room. I dropped into the chair that sat beside the window, and she hopped onto my lap as if it were something we did every night. Holding my breath, I kept petting, and after a few seconds, she curled herself into a circle and lay down. I imagined mentioning casually to Faye in the morning that I'd adopted a cat.

"If we're a couple now," I asked the warm ball of fur on my lap, "are we pet and owner or cat and servant?"

In answer, the cat closed her eyes and began to purr.

If you liked this book, please consider writing a review on Amazon, Goodreads, or anywhere you like.

ABOUT THE AUTHOR

Maggie Pill is also Peg Herring, but Maggie's much younger and cooler.

Visit http://maggiepill.maggiepillmysteries.com and Peg's site http://pegherring.com for more great mysteries.

Have you read Book #1, ***The Sleuth Sisters***, yet?

Learn how the sisters started their detective agency, found a long-lost murder suspect, and almost went from three sisters to two.

How about Book #2, ***3 Sleuths, 2 Dogs, 1 Murder***?

When Retta's "gentleman friend" is arrested for murder, the sisters must brave a winter wilderness, far removed from any chance of rescue. Three determined women, with help from two dogs and a pair of horses, can do anything. Sister Power!

And Book #3, **Murder in the Boonies**

Renters on the family farm disappear without a trace, and the sisters are left to solve the mystery, deal with a menagerie, and stop a plot that would spell disaster for Michigan's famous Mackinac Island.

Books available from Amazon (print, e-book, & audiobook) and Ingram (print only).